Annihilate

Hive Trilogy Book 3

By: Jaymin Eve and Leia Stone

Copyright © 2016 by Leia Stone and Jaymin Eve. All rights reserved.

No part of this publication may be reproduced. Stored in a retrieval system, or transmitted in any form or by any means, electronic, mechanical, photocopying, recording, or otherwise, without written permission of the author.

This is a work of fiction. Names, characters, places, and incidents either are the product of the author's imagination or are used fictitiously. Any resemblance to actual persons, live or dead are purely coincidental.

Stone, Leia
Eve, Jaymin
Annihilate

For information on reproducing sections of this book or sales of this book go to www.leiastone.com or www.Jaymineve.com

leiastonebooks@gmail.com
jaymineve@gmail.com

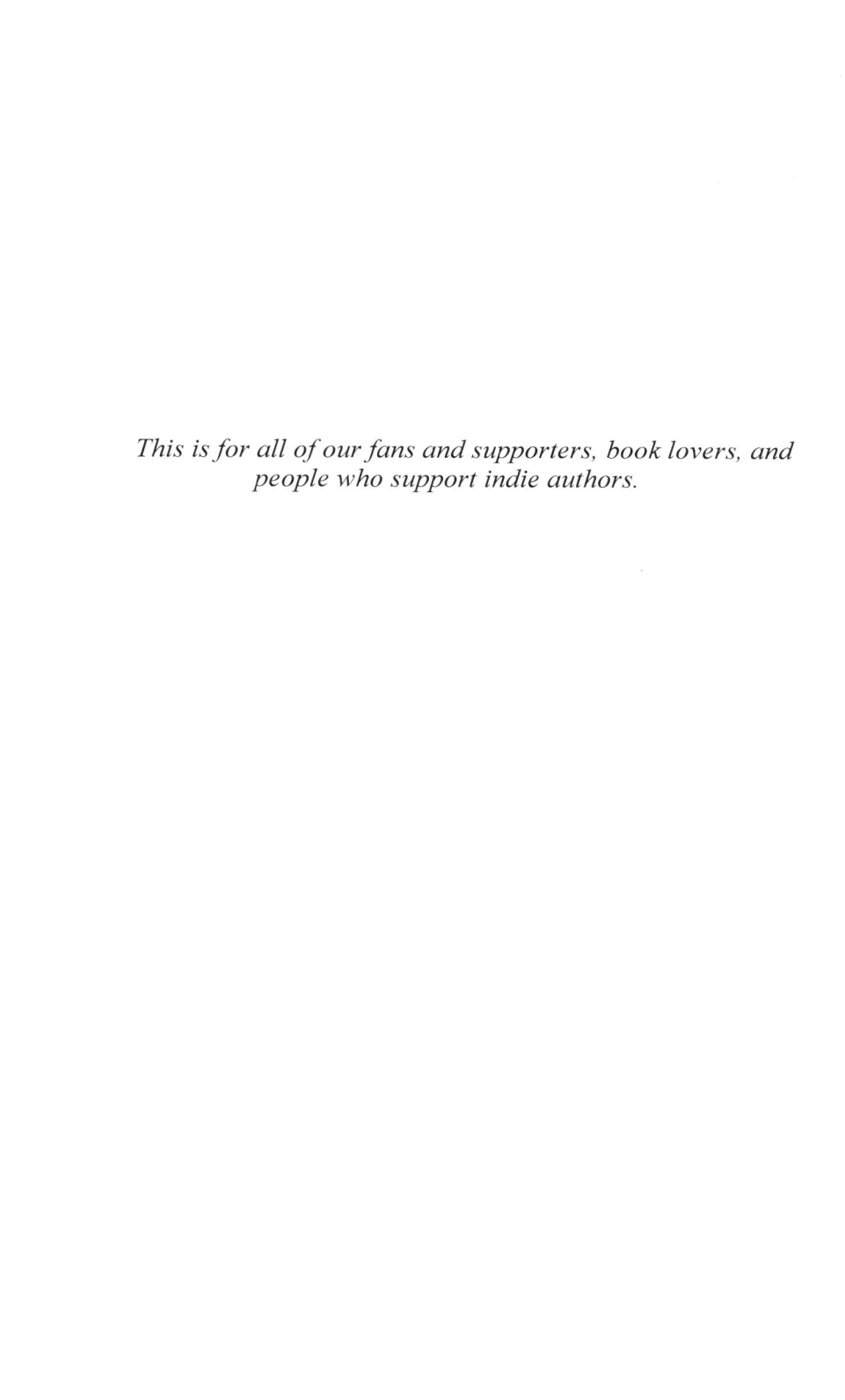

This is for all of our fans and supporters, book lovers, and people who support indie authors.

Contents

Chapter 1 1
Chapter 2 18
Chapter 3 34
Chapter 4 52
Chapter 5 65
Chapter 6 81
Chapter 7 95
Chapter 8 110
Chapter 9 127
Chapter 10 143
Chapter 11 159
Chapter 12 173
Chapter 13 188
Chapter 14 201

Chapter 1

What the actual fuck? I sat inside of the shipping container house that was now our new home and stared at Rebecca … the other unicorn ash. She was gorgeous in that nerdy adorable way and I was pretty sure she didn't know it. Her black and silver eyes were hidden behind dark-framed hipster glasses and her blond hair was in a tight braid with an actual scrunchie holding the end. Yes, a scrunchie. I didn't know they were still being made.

"I'm sorry," I huffed. "I…" What the hell was I supposed to say? My glare turned on Sam; no doubt my eyes were screaming at him "You sneaky mofo. Liar extraordinaire!"

He had the decency to look nervous and I decided that I very much wanted to lash all of my anger out on him. Now.

Standing, fists balled, I let him have it. "I thought I was a freak. It's been a struggle since day one trying to figure out what was so special about my blood before someone decided to kill me over it. You watched me get attacked and bitten by a vampire. And the entire time you knew! Or at least had some answers."

Ryder and the boys were silent. They knew he deserved this.

Sam was now in his quiet, stoic mode, no expression, although his eyes did look a little turbulent.

"Are there more, Sam? Are you hiding an entire fucking army of unicorns? What else are you hiding?" My rage was starting to wane; I was really hoping he'd fight back with me. He was just standing there not saying shit. Just taking it.

Becca stood timidly. "Don't be mad at Sammy. He was trying to protect me, and he tried to get you out of there loads of times, but the timing wasn't right."

The boys and I shared a look. Sammy? I suppressed a grin. Sam was totally riding this unicorn.

Sam turned his unreadable expression on Rebecca and there was a softness there for a split second, but when she looked back at him it was gone. Replaced with his cold hard stare.

Finally, he decided to engage with me, stepping closer and holding both hands out to the side. "I'm sorry, Charlie. But how safe would this place be if it were crawling with vampires? I did what I had to do knowing that in the end both you and Becca would be safe. Hate me if you want, I don't care. At the end of the day I'd never have let anyone hurt you. I always planned to get you out, it just wasn't that easy."

Then he stormed from the room. Dammit!

With a shuddering breath I faced Rebecca. She had taken off her puffy winter coat. The inside of this building was surprisingly well insulated and she was wearing a white lab coat beneath. Okay, so the cool nerd girl thing she had going on was starting to make sense. She was a scientist or something.

Time to cut the bullshit. "I don't want to be lied to any longer. There's some seriously bad shit going on back in our world. Ash are dying every single day, so I think you better explain exactly what this place is, and how you and I even exist."

Her very dark, thick brows rose up and scrunched on her furrowed forehead. Her eyes, which were far less silver than mine, widened. She wasn't used to anyone coming at her so bluntly. Well, get used to it, scientist princess.

She recovered quickly though. "I will tell you everything I know," she said matter-of-factly. "My name is Dr. Rebecca Leander and I hold a PHD in genetics and molecular biology. I have been studying my own blood for many years, trying to work out what it is that created such an anomaly as a female ash. Was it a gene sequence? Was it an immune system response using the pathway—"

"Whoa!" I held up my hand to halt her. She was getting into some smart girl stuff here, which was awesome, but I needed other details first. "Maybe start at the beginning. Your life before being an ash and then how you got to here."

Her expression morphed into something more human then, less robotic. "Oh, right. Of course. I forget sometimes how to talk to people, I'm so used to my computers." She gave a laugh and I was having a hard time being mad at her. She was so damn nerdy and adorable.

I saw some of the enforcer guys exchange smiles. Jayden's eyes were flat-out laughing. Clearly she amused them. But for the most part the males remained silent, letting me lead the questioning. My eyes locked onto Ryder, the only one not smiling. That one look was enough for my heart to clench tightly in my chest. His eyes were blazing silver, his dark gaze stormy. He was angry with Sam, and so much more, but for now he was containing that fury.

I spun back to Rebecca as she moved toward a large sofa. The room we were in was near the front of the strange square shipping container that made up this scientific research center. Or at least that's what the logo on the side of the building said it was.

This particular space was set up as a living area, with a few sofas scattered around, and some other miscellaneous furniture. Everything looked cozy; a heating panel along the far wall was the reason for the warmth in here.

As Rebecca sat, she patted the seat next to her, inviting me to sit also. I cautiously made my way over to the sofa, leaving about a foot between us. The guys straightened and stepped closer. Their protectiveness was a little amusing considering Rebecca looked about as scary as a skittish bunny.

"So, I grew up in a small town in the countryside of England, born in 1964." She had taken me seriously, starting her story right at the start. And considering she should be over fifty now, she didn't look a day above early twenties. Got to love ash genetics. "Life was normal. Both of my parents were academics, and they worked in the local university. I was homeschooled and ended up finishing high school at fifteen, and by the time I was twenty I already had my PHD. I was going to be a leading researcher into genetic anomalies, and the way we are shaping our genome through the viruses which have swept through our world."

"Let me guess," I said. "You were focusing on the *Anima Mortem* virus."

She nodded twice. "Yes, it has been one of the major changes to the human race. It acts fast, killing many, and changing the rest into something which is no longer human. I found the subject utterly fascinating, and I was hoping to be able to present a thesis on it at the end of my research period."

"So what happened?" Ryder's voice was low and controlled, but I could hear the angry currents lacing each word. "There's no record of a female ash before Charlie, so clearly you were able to hide your existence."

Rebecca didn't seem to even notice. "Yes, actually, it was a lucky set of circumstances which allowed for me to be saved. When I was twenty-two I decided to leave the lab for a few hours and visit the zoo. I have always loved animals, the way that their evolution can be as easily mapped as humans. It's where I go to relax."

Holy moly. This chick was the real scientist deal. I was kinda digging her smart talk. I loved to see badass chicks taking on the world with brains as well as brawn.

"I hadn't been feeling that well, or more like I felt strange. For example, two days before I had stayed up forty-eight hours in my lab and never even realized. I was not tired at all. I also had not eaten anything, and every time I tried to drink it tasted bad, so I ended up sucking on a few ice cubes."

Oh yeah, I remembered that all too well. That unquenchable thirst.

"I stayed at the zoo for an hour before my eyes and head started to hurt. I was dizzy and knew my lack of nutrition over the past week was starting to catch up with me. I tried to make it back to the bus stop, but must have collapsed before reaching it."

Sam suddenly appeared. His deep voice washed across the room: "She fell at my feet, literally on top of them. It was almost like fate directed her to me, to make sure I could keep her safe."

The dark-haired enforcer stood propped against the doorframe. I had no idea how long he'd been there, I'd been so focused on Rebecca and her story.

Sam continued: "I don't even know why I went to the zoo that day. I was in England fleeing some trouble in the States. This was about fifteen years before I joined the Portland Hive, and for some reason the zoo drew me."

"Which was lucky for me. Probably saved my life," Rebecca said, a sweet smile lighting up her face. "Sam recognized what was happening to me, and for some reason decided to help me rather than turn me over to the authorities. This was the 80s. England didn't take in ash. They just…"

He growled, low and slightly scary-like. "I couldn't stand by and see them execute a female, or worse, experiment on her. If I brought her to the States, then they would have thrown her in the culling. I could tell right away that Becca wasn't a fighter like Charlie. She's an academic." His eyes blazed. "They would have torn her apart."

Hmmm, I might not have a PHD, but pretty sure Sam just called me stupid. Meh, whatever.

"Okay, so Rebecca's just gone all ash, Sam happened to save her and ferret her off to his secret lair or something…"

Jared's Australian accent was mild as he summed up the story so far. "Then what happened? How did you end up in the ass-end of the icy wilderness?"

Rebecca and Sam exchanged a look, before the blond female started talking in her factual way again. "It was rough for a while there. Sam had to steal us blood, and I was stuck in hiding. My eyes would have immediately given me away, and contacts back then were not designed to hide the silver of our eyes. So even when I learned to control my hunger, I could never go back to my job. But I was determined to continue my research, and I now had the perfect candidate to test on. Myself."

She let out a gust of air, sucking in another deep breath. "I knew of this abandoned research center out here in Alaska. It was used initially to study climate change, but then funding ran out and it got forgotten. So I applied for a permit to use it and was granted twenty years. No one cares what I do here, and no one checks up on me. My parents died several years ago, and basically I was forgotten."

I leaned closer to her, our faces inches apart. "Have you figured out how there are only two female ash?"

Her eyes flicked up for a second to Sam, before they came back to me. "Yes, I figured that out quite early on. Helped in part by my family history."

I nodded at her, waving my hand in a hope that it would hurry her up. I had been waiting for this information for months and she was the first person who seemed to have any answers.

"Well, the truth is there are no female ash. And there never will be. The facts are irrefutable. The X-carrying sperm do not survive the change."

Well, then what the hell were we? This was the third option I kept trying to figure out.

I held my breath as she continued.

"You and I are not ash, we're something different altogether."

Pretty much what Lucas had told me when they first tested my blood. "So ... if we aren't ash and we aren't vampires, then what are we?"

Tell me the damned third option!

"You're what I like to refer to as an ashpire," Sam said with a little twinkle in his eye.

The room got very silent then, and I knew more than one of us was confused.

Rebecca quickly started talking: "Basically, my mother was attacked when she was seven months pregnant with me. Vampires got her and would have torn her to pieces if a crowd of humans hadn't jumped in and managed to pull them off her. It saved my mother's life, but not before the vampires' blood splashed all over her body. Over all the open wounds from the attack."

We all winced then, an open wound around a bleeding vampire was a death sentence. Becca continued: "It was feared that the virus had entered her system. She remained in the hospital under lockdown until they could figure out what this meant for her. Would she turn or die? They were the only two options. But then nothing happened. She had a fever for a day but didn't turn. They tested her blood, and tested it again, over and over almost right up until I was born. She never had any of the virus in her."

"How is that possible?" Markus asked.

Rebecca shook her head. "It isn't possible and yet it happened. They were saying it was a miracle, or that maybe none of her attackers' blood landed on her wounds."

Okay, this story was going to get all weird and sciency now. I just knew it.

"I have studied this virus now for many decades, and I'm starting to see the pattern. It's smart; it develops and learns. It seeks out the strongest and wants to form bonds with that genetic pattern. Shape those cells. So when a pregnant woman receives the virus, it goes to the life it can shape the most, the fetus. But because a fetus is such a fast growing being, I was shaping and changing and fighting the virus every minute, every second. I was pumping out the cure to my mother, which is why she only had a fever for a day. Even being seven months developed in utero, the virus still managed to bond to my genome, and basically start the process of making me a born vampire, which in a way is like a cross of ash and vampire."

Okay then. Ashpire was making much more sense now.

"It still takes a long time for the change to kick into effect, which is where we mimic the ash males, but we're not ash. Our blood is different. Because the virus matures within our body and bloodstream during our early development, we create these antibodies to the virus as a natural part of our system. In a way, it's almost as if we have cured the virus, and what was left was the best version of a vampire, something which mimics the ash."

Holy shit. Hooollly shit. I remembered my mom's story about being attacked when she was very early stages of being pregnant with me. She said that Carter Atwater, Original of the fourth house had saved her, but that he had been injured. Some of his blood must have mixed with hers, which is why I turned into an ashpire. Dammit, that meant the abusive dick of a father who had been in the army was really my biological dad.

I worried at my lip, unhappy about that. My hair color was from him after all. Still … in lots of ways Carter was as much my father. His blood was what changed my genome as I developed in the womb. I had been little more than a single cell when I received his blood. My mom hadn't even known she was pregnant yet.

I needed more information. "So the antibodies we have is why my blood can cure vampires. Does it cure ash as well?" I had been wondering for a long time what would happen if an ash bit me.

Rebecca shook her head. "No, because ash don't have the virus. They're born of a mutated genome and technically never actually received the virus. Therefore, there's nothing to cure."

My brain sort of shorted out then because that shit made no sense to me, but she was super smart and it made sense to her so I just nodded.

"Can you cure vampires as well?" I asked. It would be so great if there were two of us helping to try and deal with the war that was no doubt going to explode in our world.

I was tense as I waited for her answer, and when she shook her head my heart sank a little. "Not really, not permanently. I have some curative properties, which I have been trying to manipulate for many years. Basically, if a vampire drinks from me, they'll partly return to human form. They can walk in the sunlight, and enjoy human food, but unless they continue to drink from me, the virus reasserts itself and they return to vampire."

My eyes found Ryder's and I could see the questions in his as well. "I don't actually know if my blood can long-term cure either, but the vampire we found was definitely human. And had been for a week or more."

Rebecca's eyes lit up. I could see her brain ticking away as she analyzed me and thought about that. "I need to test your blood. We might finally have the secret to this virus. To figuring out how to stop it."

She looked like a kid in a candy shop, ready to drain my blood in the name of science. But curiosity was a dominant trait in my personality too, so hell yeah, let's figure out how to cure these bloodsuckers. I nodded and she bounced up and down on the balls of her feet.

"Come, I'll show you my lab!" Her glasses had fallen on the bridge of her nose and she pushed them up, looking 150% an adorable nerd.

And Sam had noticed.

He was watching her like she was some fascinating creature that he wanted to touch but knew was off limits. Did Becca even realize he felt something for her? Did she feel something for him? Had they hooked up? If not, which one of these idiots was the hold-up, because life was way too short. Even for ash.

Becca walked us back through a narrow hallway that opened up into a huge science lab, all stainless steel benches, fluorescent lighting, massive machines, and shelves filled with beakers, vials, and other science paraphernalia.

"I have all of the latest technology, and I get blood donations from a local blood bank under the guise that I'm researching human diseases. Which I do on the side for fun."

Of course she did. Jayden and I shared a smile.

She continued: "That's how we'll get our food. I have more than enough blood to feed us and continue my human research."

My eyes were roaming over all of the expensive equipment when I saw Sam pick up a white lab coat off the far wall and pull gloves on. Oh hell no. If Sam was mysterious, sexy, a pilot, *and* a smarty pants, I was going to lose it.

"How do you pay for all this? You said your grant was only twenty years? It must have run out by now." I glanced around the room again, chuckling as Kyle touched a heated coil and pulled his hand back, getting burned. Dumbass.

"Sammy funds all of my research now," she said guilelessly.

Of course he does ... probably hacks into crooked politicians' bank accounts to pay for it.

I met Sam's eyes and he winked, confirming my thoughts. He was a bad boy to the core.

"Sam, can you ready the centrifuge?" Becca asked, opening a blood-drawing kit.

Sam nodded and walked over to a big machine and began tinkering with it. Wow, I couldn't imagine these two playing lab partners for decades and not having tumbled between the sheets at least once. I was actually dying to know, and when I looked at Jayden I could see him trying to figure it out too. I knew my BAFF; his gaze was all over these two.

In a smooth, relatively painless move, Becca took a sample of my blood. The moment it exited my veins and entered the tube, the scent of it hit the air. Her nostrils flared, eyes pulsing as she looked at me.

"Incredible! I have the urge to bite you. It's my immune system wanting the cure! It must be worse for full-fledged vampires…"

Okay ... homegirl was cute and totally socially awkward. I was kind of beginning to like her.

"There's something you should know," I said as she pulled the needle from my arm. "My vampire father or sire or whatever is an Original."

I waited for her shock, but she just smiled.

"I know. Sammy told me. That's why I'm so eager to get a look at your blood."

My jaw dropped as I pinned Sam to the wall with my glare. "You told her!"

His expression did turn slightly regretful, but before he could speak, Becca stuck up for him. Again. "Don't be mad. We're best friends, he tells me everything."

What sort of fucking alternate universe was I in? Sam was sitting around some shipping container in Alaska with a hot-ass nerdy doctor, spilling his secrets. I had known him months now and he had said about fifty-six words. Fifty-four of them in the last hour. FML.

Ryder moved then, approaching Sam, who was just placing my blood vials into the centri-whatever thingy.

"Lots of secrets, bro," Ryder said, sounding casual, but we all heard the undertones.

Oliver had Ryder's back. "Not cool."

For the first time in forever I saw Sam look vulnerable, like an orphaned puppy. Eyes wide, bottom lip turned under.

Sam met Ryder's eyes. "You know my story. You know why I keep secrets."

What the hell? I wanted to know his story.

Ryder sighed. "I know, but we're your brothers. You can trust us. Always."

My heart broke a little then. Ryder's voice was filled with emotion. A lot of which felt sad. His best friend had been hiding an ashpire for decades. Hiding information which could have helped me in the early days when we were playing in the dark with my magical blood. A part of him had to be feeling betrayed by this, I knew it.

Sam gritted his jaw. "The less you know, the safer you are."

Kyle came around behind Sam. "Only one way to settle this."

Jared smiled. "I got first round."

Becca looked alarmed. "What's going on? You're not going to hurt him, right?"

Ten minutes later we all stood around the kitchen and dining room. It was a skinny galley kitchen that opened up to a large dining space that could easily fit twenty seats. These shipping containers were super cool, and with the high-quality finishes inside you totally forgot you were in a metal box. My guess was that this lab was built for an entire research team and once fully stocked could house dozens for many months.

A cheer went up then as the male-idiots in the room continued their games. Sam had already beaten Markus and Kyle in arm wrestling. Now it was Oliver's turn. Oliver put his game face on as Jayden gave him a little tap on the butt to cheer him on.

Becca looked confused as she leaned into me and whispered. "I don't understand. What is this solving?"

I smiled. "Sam lied to everyone. Trust has been broken, feelings hurt, so they're hashing it out this way."

Becca's thick eyebrows drew together. "Still makes no sense."

I sighed. Homegirl had some serious social catching up to do. She clearly wasn't used to being around a bunch of burly males.

"Okay, it's like animals in the wild. One of the wolves in the pack does something to piss off the alpha, they need to put him in his place."

A slamming sound had both of us looking up. Oliver was rubbing his arm; it looked rather red around the wrist.

Becca finally nodded, seeming to like my animal analogy. "So Sam's the alpha right? He's winning."

I grinned. Ryder hadn't had a turn yet.

Jared was next. "You're going down, Sammy." He was trying to rile him up by using Becca's term of endearment.

Sam wasn't fazed. He actually chuckled and held his arm up.

"Go!" Ryder called, and Sam slammed Jared's hand down in seconds.

"Wait, wait. I wasn't ready!" Jared pleaded, but Ryder just moved him along.

"Jayden, you want a go?" Ryder asked my BAFF.

Jayden grinned, showcasing all of his beautiful white teeth. "I'll pass, dear. I'm secure with the length of my manhood."

Becca's mouth dropped open.

Oh snap! God I loved that man. Ryder just shoved the comment off and sat in front of Sam. They engaged in an epic staredown. This was the battle of the alphas, and just like wolves, neither looked away.

"You could have trusted me with this," Ryder finally said.

Sam sighed. "It wasn't your burden to bear. You had enough going on."

I knew he was talking about Molly, Ryder's fiancée.

Sam held up his hand and Ryder gripped it tightly.

Sam leaned himself over the table. "You know this isn't a fair fight. You're a descendent from the house of strength."

Ryder grinned his cockiest of grins. "What's wrong? Scared?"

It was on; they both flexed their muscles and Sam's hand started shifting backwards. He grunted and I thought the veins in his face might burst if he kept this up much longer.

With a slam, in the end Ryder won with ease.

Sam looked resigned. "I should have told you."

Ryder nodded and clapped Sam on the shoulder. Just like that, everything was great between the boys again. My animal analogy was really not far from the truth; men had changed very little over the thousands of years of humanity.

Jayden ran forward. "Group hug!"

Oliver laughed as Jayden tackle-hugged a bewildered Sam and Ryder and I decided why the hell not and got in on the pileup. Sam was still sitting in the chair so we ended up just sitting on him or hugging him from the back. Jared reached forward and yanked a hair off Sam's head.

"Ow! Did someone pull my hair!" I heard the silent enforcer yell.

"It was me, mate. Payback."

Gotta love Australians and their payback.

Becca stood there awkwardly and I felt bad for her. She didn't seem to quite fit in with our group yet. But something told me she would, one day.

Sam's muffled voice came out again: "Okay, you've tortured me enough. I'll never lie again. Please, God, just get off of me."

We all laughed and backed away from the Sam love pile. A weight lifted from my chest. Sam was forgiven and we were back to being one big happy family again. I was so relieved to know that I could stop worrying and doubting one of my guys. It was us against the vampire world, and we had to have total trust in each other. Speaking of…

"Okay, now that all of this is worked out, Sam, I need you to find out what's going on back at the Hive. Is Tessa safe?

What happened to Lucas? Has Carter updated with anything about him and my mom?"

Sam smoothed back his mussed hair and nodded. "I have a secure computer here."

Jayden pointed at Becca. "You."

Becca paled. "Me?" she all but squeaked.

Jayden nodded. "You need to take me shopping. I refuse to wear this…" He was at a loss for words to describe his sweatpants and flip-flops. "Any longer."

Becca smiled. "You won't like any of the shops in town, but we get deliveries out here. So you can order anything online."

Jayden's mouth popped open and his eyes almost rolled back in his head. He looked like he was having a mini-orgasm.

Becca handed him a credit card. "Spend however much you need. Sam has us well funded."

Again I raised my eyebrows at Sam and wondered if this wasn't one of the "charities" that had received money from Deliverance.

Jayden's hand shook as he took the card. His eyes were wide and a little crazed. "Unlimited online shopping? Everyone give me your sizes. I'll be in my room for the next three days."

I smiled. Jayden was officially in heaven, but I was hoping they didn't sell nipple pasties online.

Becca held up a hand. "Right. Rooms. We have mostly bunkbed-style shared barracks, but there are two private rooms. One's mine, so … the other…"

Ryder stepped forward. "Charlie and I will take the other one."

Oh my GAWD. Did he just do that? I was trying to decide if it was too forward or the hottest goddamn thing ever. I went with hot. I grinned.

Wait, did Ryder just ask me to move in with him?

Jayden and Oliver gave us glares. I waggled my fingers at them in a half-wave. Sorry, bitches. I earned this.

The room I was officially sharing with Ryder was small but cozy, and most importantly it had a soft bed with a thick down comforter. I had been starting to worry I'd be stuck in a sleeping bag on a cot. I had all of seven worldly possessions at the moment, and so after putting away my cheap plastic toothbrush, plastic package of cotton granny panties, and one extra t-shirt, I went to find the boys.

Turning from the bed, I saw that Ryder was standing in the doorway watching me. His gaze was hard to read, but damn he looked sexy. Even in cheap sweatpants and a t-shirt the guy could be on a billboard.

"Hey," I said.

He stepped in and looked around the small room. Queen bed, bookshelf, and nightstand.

"Hope you don't mind I claimed the room for us." His eyes were saying a lot more than his words.

I closed the distance between us. "Don't mind at all."

He eyed my lips, and a softness trickled across his hard features. It was one of those special little things he did only around me.

Then a small smile quirked the side of his lips. "Should I be worried that Jayden just asked me if I wore boxers, briefs, or a thong?"

I busted out laughing. I loved my BAFF hard; he was exactly what these serious enforcers needed. Ryder's smile went to full throttle, but just for a moment, before it was replaced with a strained expression.

"What's up?" I prodded.

He sighed. "We left them, Charlie. We just left them all to the whims and tempers of the vampires."

Tension skated across my body then and my chest got weirdly tight. Breathing was harder than it had been a minute ago. I knew exactly what Ryder was talking about, and it was something I was trying not to dwell on, but it was slowly eating me up inside.

He was worried about his other enforcers. Being the lead enforcer, he had trained every single one of them, working with many of them for years. And although he was closest with the sexy six, he still cared for all the others. They were his team.

I stepped even closer to him, our warmth wrapping around each other. "We left Tessa, Blake, and Lucas too. If there was another way, I would have taken it."

He pulled me into his arms and I rested my head against his hard chest. "I know," he murmured.

Most of the time I felt like a single, pretty insignificant person. But then there were these moments, like this, where I felt bigger, like I could do something grand, something unthinkable. I was the goddamn cure to our problem.

"Ryder…" I pulled back and he met my eyes. "We have to save them all. The ash. My friends. I want to bring down the Hives. Annihilate the vampires whose power and corruption is polluting our world."

Ryder's face was a mixture of surprise and pride. He nodded once, and I knew that even if we died trying, we would wipe vampires from the face of the Earth. This was the reason I was here.

We remained in our comforting hug for many long moments. I could sense that Ryder was as reluctant as me to part ways and get back to reality, but unfortunately, even in the middle of nowhere, real life was continuing. And we had things to do.

Chapter 2

Ryder and I walked hand in hand through the maze of containers to the boys' room. I was shocked at how large their bunk room was, three shipping containers wide with the middle walls cut out. Each container had a set of bunkbeds with curtains between them that could be pulled for privacy. There were also couches, a pool table, and a TV in a common area. I had a feeling this was going to be the hangout part of this facility.

Becca wasn't in the room. She must be back in the lab geeking out over my blood.

As soon as we entered, Jayden looked up from the computer.

"Charlie, you're a 36C right?" he asked.

My eyes widened as Kyle and Jared cleared their throats. Ryder leveled a look at Jayden; it was a look I'd seen many times. It meant you should stop talking. Now.

Of course that didn't worry my BAFF at all. He was still staring at me, so I nodded to let him know he was right.

Jayden's hands were again flying over the computer keys and I had no doubt that in twenty-four hours there would be four FedEx delivery trucks full of Victoria's Secret, Coach, and other goodies. Jayden was a brand whore, and he had excellent taste in everything.

Ryder was suddenly all business. "Sam. Report." All eyes turned to the dark-haired enforcer in the corner, hunched over a laptop. He took a really long time to finally look up from the screen, and my heart dropped as I lurched toward him. Pure agony was swimming in his eyes.

What the hell had happened?

"You guys need to see this," he said, his voice gruff. It sounded like he was on the verge of tears; his skin was sickly pale.

Everyone crowded around Sam, who was back to staring at his screen, face now void of all emotion.

"Tell us!" Ryder barked, so loud I jumped. Oh shit. This was bad, this was going to be really bad. Don't be my mom or Tessa please.

Sam met Ryder's eyes. "Before we left I made a back door into the CCTV at the Hive so we could watch what they were doing."

Okay, that was creepy and genius. I braced myself for the next thing he was going to say.

Sam actually bit down on his lip. "They killed them … all of them."

Ryder sagged against me. For the first time I saw something like fear and horror cross all of the enforcers' faces.

"Who?" I didn't know what he was talking about, but the boys seemed to understand. They all looked devastated.

Sam's hands were gripped tightly into fists as he fought for control. He had to clear his voice more than once. "The enforcers, ninety-seven of them … all dead."

No! God, no.

Jayden lost it then, cursing, crying, kicking out at things as Oliver wrapped his arms around him to try and calm him down.

Tears welled in my eyes. God dammit! Those asshole bloodsuckers were doing this to hurt us. To punish us for leaving. The enforcers had stopped taking orders once they suspended Ryder and this is what they got. Mass murder.

It took minutes – felt like hours – for Ryder to collect himself. He straightened, and the look on his face sent shivers down my spine and had my knees buckling.

"Show me." His voice was gravelly and pissed the fuck off.

Sam shook his head. "You don't need to see it."

"Show. Me. Now." Ryder ordered again, and I was afraid if Sam didn't do as he asked, Ryder might actually hurt him.

Sam turned the laptop around, defeated, and my hand flew to my mouth. Whether to hold my gasp or stop the vomit, who could tell.

The enforcers' bodies were strewn around the gym, the very gym they made us fight for our lives in. Blood, so much blood. And so many bodies bent at wrong angles. I couldn't look. I'd seen enough. Turning my back, I tried to control myself, counting to ten and thinking happy thoughts. Anything so those images didn't continue to run through my head.

"I want to see this whole thing. Rewind it." Ryder's voice was hollow, murderous.

"Hey, mate, that won't help anything," Jared said, and from the corner of my eye I saw him put a hand on Ryder's shoulder. The lead enforcer shrugged it off.

"I will watch the entire video and every single vampire involved will burn alive." Ryder's voice was low, almost emotionless. Just his eyes displayed the strong emotions churning within him. They were blazing silver.

I knew it wasn't a threat. It was fact. Ryder would go back one day and kill every single one of them. This was different than the culling. These men had served the Quorum for years and this is what they got? Cold blooded murder.

Sam hit a few keys and low sound filtered across to us: screams, curses, and gunfire. My stomach churned, and I swallowed a few times to keep it together. I was shuddering as Jayden crossed to my side, engulfing me in a hug. Eventually he pulled on my hand and I let him guide me away, through the hall, past the kitchen, and into my private room.

He sat on the bed, picking at his cuticles. His face was pale – well, as pale as it could go, eyes sad as he turned to me. "Let's talk about something fun. I need to get that image out of my head."

I nodded. Despite the fact he could go kung-fu warrior, like in the culling, deep down Jayden was a lover not a fighter. Plus I desperately needed to not think about it either.

"You think Sam and Becca are sleeping together?" I blurted out and Jayden squealed.

"I know, right? I wonder … I mean she's nerdy, but hot. Her eyebrows though…" He shuddered. "Girl needs help."

I snort laughed. "They have to be doing it. How could you spend decades out here and not get some action?"

Jayden shrugged. "Vibrator?"

My mouth dropped open and I smacked his arm.

"Ewww, I do not want that mental picture next time I see her."

Jayden grinned. Asshole.

Our conversation died off then, and despite our need to wipe those last few moments from our minds, it was too big to suppress. Our idle chatter was a Band-Aid over a severed arm.

"We're going to fight those bastards, right?" Jayden was now channeling his badass side. He wanted the vampires to go down as much as I did.

I was suddenly on my feet, moving out of the room. "Yes we are," I said, as Jayden caught up to me and we both charged out the door. "We're going to take them down so hard they won't know what hit them, and for that we need Becca."

It took me a few tries to remember the way back to her lab. Jayden was of course no help; his sense of direction might actually be worse than mine.

Finally, though, the bright, overly fake fluorescent lighting came into sight and I knew we were in the right place. Sure enough, as I rounded the corner I zeroed straight in on Becca, who was crouched over a microscope.

She never even looked up as we crossed the cleaned-within-an-inch-of-its-life lab; everything was white, stainless steel, and top of the line. She had tech here which labs across the world would kill for. Which would hopefully mean this was our best chance of creating the perfect weapon to use against the vampires.

"This place gives me the creeps," Jayden whispered as he followed right behind me. "As my BAFF, it's your job to make sure that if I die, no mutha-effer donates my body to science. I will come back and haunt the hell out of you."

I snorted, reaching out and taking his hand. "You're not allowed to die. That's a freaking order." He squeezed my hand tightly then, but any further conversation was cut off as Becca finally lifted her head.

She looked completely stunned to see us there – and we hadn't been quiet – especially for someone with ash senses. Her eyes roamed across our faces, and she must have seen some of the devastation from the Portland Hive video on our features.

"Has something happened?" Her glasses fell forward along her narrow nose as she straightened and automatically reached up to push them back into place. I found it hilarious, and sort of endearing that she continued to hold so tightly to that part of her old life, because she obviously didn't need glasses. Ash had perfect sight, but old habits die hard, and I understood her need. She had lost everything else she loved that day at the zoo.

She was still waiting for us to answer her, so I quickly explained about the enforcers and what we saw. Somehow I got the words out. Jayden and I were both shiny-eyed again as the pain and disbelief hit hard. The images from the computer screen continued to flash across my mind, and I wished I hadn't seen them at all. My heart hurt so hard for Ryder and the other sexy six. But mostly Ryder. He was the leader, and he took his responsibility very seriously. There was no doubt he believed the blood of those ash was on his hands. Which was not the case. The Quorum would have killed us whether we ran or not. And then killed the enforcers. But still, we all knew Ryder was a bad one for holding on to guilt.

Becca was silent then, her eyes darting between me and Jayden. She had not flinched at our news, and something told me that this wasn't the worst thing she'd seen happen in the Hives. She focused all of her attention on me.

"I'm guessing you're here because you want to know if I can turn your blood into a weapon to use against them?" Smart people were the best. No need to explain shit, they already knew.

I nodded and waited for her to continue.

A smile spread across her surprisingly full lips. Girl was actually quite stunning, she just needed a little help with showcasing herself. And judging by the look on Jayden's face, he was already mentally tweezing her brows and changing her lab coats out for an outfit that probably required Spanx and nipple pasties. Poor girl. I should probably warn her, but it was fun to not be his only ash girlie to play designer on.

I forced myself to focus as she started rattling off the science stuff again. "I haven't had much time with your blood yet, Charlie, but I can already tell that it's fascinatingly different to mine. You seem to have a special type of white blood cell, one which is more elongated than any I've ever seen before. It is dominating your blood, and the other cells seem to use it to move rapidly through the body. They're working as a team to fight off any antigens."

So she was saying ... English please.

Instead of acting like I was an idiot, Becca's eyes lit up. I could tell she loved science and teaching. She crossed over to a white board and started to draw and write across it.

"Okay, so in blood you have a whole bunch of components. The red blood cells or platelets binds to oxygen and transports it around the body." She drew a bunch of little concave looking discs and wrote 45% beside it. "This is where vampires and ash need some help. Our cells regenerate far quicker than humans, and our platelets require some help with the level of oxygen needed in our bodies. Therefore, we need to feed. The faster you regenerate, the more blood you require. Which is why vampires need more than us, and are stronger."

Jayden and I exchanged a look, before crossing to take a seat close to her whiteboard. Something told me this was going to be a long lecture, and despite the fact that I wasn't the best at school, this was one subject I wanted to know everything about.

Becca didn't even seem to notice; she was in her element as she continued. "The other 55% of your blood is plasma, and it is here which your blood is unique. Plasma is generally made up of mostly water, proteins, hormones, and antibodies. There are other vitamins and minerals, but we don't need to worry about that right now. The part which is the most fascinating in your blood are the antibodies."

"Yours are unlike any I've ever seen before. I introduced some of the virus to them and they attacked in a way which I could only liken to sharks in a feeding frenzy. They obliterated the foreign vampire blood in seconds."

Becca abandoned her marker and turned to face us fully. "I then introduced another vampire sample, this time from a blood type the same as yours, and again the same response. It seems to be programmed to attack the Anima Mortis virus no matter what form it enters as."

I found myself leaning forward. "Why am I an ashpire then? Surely the cure would be attacking me, like an autoimmune response?"

Becca was almost giddy now. "That's where it's so incredible. You are literally a product of the Anima virus, and yet your antibodies are evolved enough to be able to tell self from non-self, even within the same virus set. There's no evidence it has ever tried to attack your own cells. Which is something human antibodies would not be able to do. They attack foreign antigens, which is how they know something does not belong in the body. The virus is not foreign to you, it formed your very blood and organs and everything else, so there should be no antibodies to it. It should see the virus as self and not attack, and yet ... somehow it knows."

"Would it attack the virus in an ash?" Jayden asked, and I wondered for a second if he would choose to be cured if it were possible.

Becca blinked a few times, thinking before she answered. "I was just starting to experiment with that, introducing Charlie's blood to vampires and ash to see what happens. I expect that in vampire blood her antibodies will destroy the virus, clean the blood, organs, and body from the effects. A full and total cure. Her antibodies hold the components which are missing from my blood. And I have my theories on what will happen with ash blood, but I need to experiment more before I confirm or deny the hypothesis."

Footsteps echoed down the hall then, and I knew the rest of the enforcers were on their way. Becca must have heard them too, because she hurried on. "To answer you from before, Charlie, yes, I think if I have enough time, and some more of your blood, I can manufacture a synthetic version of your cure. Something we could use as a large-scale attack against the vampires."

My body tensed as I jumped to my feet and strode over to her. I thrust my arm forward. "Take as much as you need and get me that cure. I have a plan, and I am going to need an ass-ton of the cure to make it happen."

Becca smiled. "Vampire vaccine, here we come." The determination in her eyes gave me hope.

The boys entered the room then and the look on Ryder's face tore me open. He was trying to hide it but I could see he was in agony. I was one of those people who didn't mind going through hell myself but it killed me to see those I loved in pain. I would rather save them from it all. I wanted to take him in my arms and tell him we would avenge them, every single one. But I wouldn't do that in front of his boys. He needed to be strong for them. They all looked to their leader for guidance in situations like this.

Ryder was all business. "Becca, how safe are we out here? How far are the nearest neighbors? Who knows of you? Have you ever been seen? When do you grocery shop, get mail, water the garden?"

Whoa. My man was channeling his angers into OCD right now. Sam was giving Ryder a bit of a glare, but Becca didn't seem worried. "We're very secluded and safe, in my scientific opinion. The nearest neighbors are two miles south. They're a small impoverished family that own a failing potato farm. They know of me, they think I'm a vampire. They would never turn me in. I saved their daughter's life three years ago. I wear blue contacts when I go into town, and since female ash don't exist and female vampires can't go out in the day, everyone in town thinks I'm a human scientist. Still, I limit town visits to once a month."

Ryder looked skeptical. "You let this farm family know about you? How are you sure they can be trusted?"

Becca squared her shoulders and stared my man down like an alpha. "I trust them with all of our lives."

Holy shit, homegirl went from awkward nerd to possessive mom in two seconds. Jayden and I shared an impressed look. Ryder nodded, letting that line of questioning go.

"Okay, but I still want twenty-four-hour watch. We'll trade days, sleep in shifts, and do four hour watches. It's clear that the vampires will stop at nothing to find and punish us."

The rest of the sexy six nodded.

Jayden raised a hand. "Yeah, that's a problem for me. I need my beauty sleep."

Ryder gave a tense grin, or more like bared teeth as he shook his head. "I didn't include you, Becca, or Charlie in my calculations."

I crossed my arms and glared at him. "Are you saying I need beauty sleep? I'm not sitting on my ass the whole time we're here. I'm still training. I will take a watch too."

Ryder stepped closer to me, lowering his voice, and the boys and Becca busied themselves with inspecting the floor or ceiling as Ryder and I got into it.

"I just lost a lot of people I cared about. I won't lose you too. The answer is no." His jaw was clenched as if he was daring me to fight him on it. And dammit, normally I would, but he was right. He'd just lost a lot of his friends and I didn't want to stress him out now. Instead I stood on my tiptoes and kissed his rough stubbly cheek. "I'm conceding to you right now because of special circumstances. But don't get used to bossing me around. We're a team. Got it?"

He was no doubt feeling out of control and I would give him this one thing. Let him think he could govern my safety.

"Always a team, Charlie. I just need you to be safe," he said, before turning to the boys. "By now the Quorum will know the truth about Charlie. They won't stop at just the Portland Hive."

Kyle frowned. "You think they would take out other ash? Other enforcers? All across the world?"

Ryder shrugged. "I think they see the scales tipping in our favor. We need to start thinking about the bigger picture."

Silence descended on our small group and Becca and I shared a look. This right here, these eight people were my family now. If I couldn't trust them I was fucked. So I cleared my throat and dropped the bomb.

"Becca is going to design a mass-produced-cure with my blood and I'm going to cure every single vampire. Every. Single. One."

"No." Ryder interrupted me, but I stopped him with a hand to the face.

"I believe in destiny, and I think this is why I'm here. My greater purpose. I'm going to cure the world of the Anima Mortem virus and return all these assholes back to their families."

Jayden's eyes were brimming with tears as he looked at me with pride. Holy shit, did I just grow up? Adulting sucked.

Becca nudged her glasses onto the bridge of her nose. "Technically, they can't help being A-holes," she said, her cheeks going slightly red as she stumbled over the last word. OMG, did she not swear? I was pretty sure I couldn't trust someone who didn't swear. This girl needed a lesson in how to speak Charlie.

"What do you mean?" Out with it, woman!

"Well, it's fascinating really, and a little sad. Oxytocin, which is the neuropeptide that has been dubbed 'the love hormone,' is in charge of social bonding, maternal behavior, and trust. And it is completely missing in ninety-nine percent of the vampires. The Anima Mortem virus seems to just gobble it up in the first few months after the change."

Her words flushed fear right into my gut and only one thing came to mind. "Tessa."

Ryder took my hand and looked at Becca. "Her friend was changed recently, but she didn't seem like the other vampires."

Becca gave me the same look I expect doctors give patients right before dropping news of their impending death. Clearly she wanted to say more, I could tell, but she was hiding it.

"Just tell me."

Becca sighed. "Well, they all seem normal in the beginning. It takes a few months. It happens faster in children. That's why not many children mentally survive the change."

Oh fuck. She was saying that Tessa might turn into a creepy asshole like Fugly! No!

Jayden threw his hands up. "Okay, ya'll, this has been an epic shit day! We need to mellow out. Becca, girl, tell me you got some blood wine here."

Becca looked nervously at Sam, who gave her a little wink. Okay, hold up a second. Did silent dude just WINK at her? He never did shit like that. Until this moment I didn't even know he knew how to wink.

"Sam brought some last time, but I was too nervous to try it," she admitted.

We all looked at Sam and he cleared his throat, his eyes fastened to some periodic table poster on the wall.

Jayden saved him from our scrutiny. "Okay, party people, freshen up and meet me in the common room in one hour." He snapped his fingers and took off.

Marcus and Jared shook their heads at my BAFF, but I could see some happiness had seeped back into their faces. Jayden was this beautiful infectious person that you just couldn't stay depressed around. The world needed more Jaydens.

Everyone split up then to go shower and get ready. Becca smiled awkwardly and went back to looking under her microscope.

I lightly pulled her ponytail and she leaned back from the microscope to meet my eyes. "Nope, no more science-geeking out tonight. You're one of us now. If Jayden says meet him in an hour, that means you too."

She broke into a grin and I could see that she desperately wanted friends, but she just wasn't sure how to make it happen.

She pushed at her glasses again, in her very obvious nervous mannerism. "I'm not sure I'll be much fun. I don't know how to ... relax very well."

I felt a real grin rip across my face; she was in trouble now. We were totally making her over. I grabbed her hand and pulled her up. "Do you have clothes, makeup and stuff here?" Jayden had none of his usual supplies, and while he was probably the best ash I knew when it came to transformation, he wasn't a genie. We would still need some stuff to work with.

Becca shrugged. "Uh, maybe. Sam ships me supplies all the time. I only ever deal with the lab stuff. The rest gets stored. There might be something in there."

I felt an unnatural thrill of excitement. God knows why, I wasn't someone who got giddy over makeup and fancy clothes, but something about having everything stripped from me had me wanting to see something familiar. Even if it was only a mascara wand.

I grasped her hand again. "Show me, like now, girlfriend!"

Becca's eyes flicked up and over my shoulder and I swiveled to find Ryder standing there, waiting for me. I turned back to the scientist. "Actually, would it be okay if you go and find Jayden and take him to your storages? He'll figure out what we need. I'll find you soon."

Her beautiful eyes were wide and glassy; the tension in the room had her uneasy, but she also seemed to be liking it. Ryder and I were her very own personal soap opera right now. She managed to nod once at me, before licking her lips and stumbling out of the lab. Which left Ryder and I alone, and let's just say I was facing down one angry mountain of enforcer.

"We didn't finish our conversation from before," he cut in straight away, and I was surprised that he was so forthcoming. Generally, when he got upset, he was a bit like Sam, deadly and brooding. "Your plan to cure vampires ... it's ... what the hell, Charlie? You're only one person, a person I'd like to keep around for a very long time. Yet you keep coming up with these plans that are most likely going to get you dead."

I stepped into him, for many reasons, but mostly because I needed to be closer. The distance between us felt unnatural, like when we first met. I never wanted to go back there. Not with Ryder. "Can you live in a world where vampires are free to kill our friends? Where they can turn innocent children, destroying their minds? Where they control media and politics and the humans?"

As I posed each question, his already grim expression deepened. He knew I was right, but that didn't mean he had to like it. I stepped right into him then; our chests touched, and his arms wrapped tightly around me, like he couldn't help himself. Which had my heart aflutter. But it didn't stop me from finishing my speech.

"I couldn't live with myself if I didn't at least attempt to bring them down. The perfect weapon fell into my lap when I turned ash … or ashpire … whatever. I am the weapon. And now we have Becca, who from what I can tell is an uber-stratospheric-genius that's going to be able to figure out how to give us everything we need for my plan—"

Ryder cut me off in the most delicious way possible, his lips gently skimming against mine. Normally I hated when men used their hotness to halt me mid-conversation, but I could tell Ryder hadn't done it for that reason. His blazing silver eyes were looking all proud of me and stuff; he hadn't been able to stop himself from kissing me. Which just like his arms around me, was the best feeling in the world.

The kiss deepened to the point where we had to stop or find a more private, less lab-type room. As we pulled apart, our breathing rapid, Ryder cupped my face in his hands.

"After tonight we'll get down to business. You'll tell me your plan in full, leaving nothing out. Then with the help of all of our people, we'll figure out if it's possible to pull off with no more casualties. We'll also discuss the best way to warn the other ash and enforcers around the world about what the Quorum did in Portland."

I nodded against his hands. "Thank you for being on my team. I wouldn't want to do any of this without you."

His thumb brushed across my lips, and his first genuine smile in hours emerged. "I love you, Charlie. We're a team. We'll do this together."

My heart stopped beating. It wasn't the first time those words had been uttered between us, but since the last time was when I was about to die via splatting-into-pudding-on-rooftop, this one was so much more potent. There was nothing here forcing it, nothing elevating the natural feelings we'd had since the first time we met, all the way back in the club. Just a guy and a girl. I knew it was fast, and I'd never said those words to any dude before, always shying away from a deeper commitment, but it was different with Ryder.

He was different.

"I love you too," I whispered before raising up on tiptoes.

Ryder's eyes softened and his hands fell from my face to land naturally around my waist. I still wasn't quite tall enough to reach his lips, but he tilted his head down, and as our mouths met for the second time I was pulled tightly against him. Or maybe I jumped him. God only knows. Anyway, something happened and suddenly both of us were hot and heavy, and sex against the closest flat surface was totally in our future.

Panting, I wrenched my mouth from his. "Dammit, we can't do this here. Jayden is going to be looking for me any second, and as much as I love my bestie, if he finds us like this we'll never hear the end of it. And he'll want pictures."

Ryder started to shake against me and I realized he was laughing. He dropped me down to my feet. Uh, when did my legs get around his waist? Meh, the last few minutes were all a delicious, perfect blur of hotness. "Run now, Charlie, before I decide that I'm happy for Jayden to have those pictures."

Ryder flashed me those perfect white teeth, a hint of fang actually visible. My blood called to him the same way his did to me.

With one last look I forced myself to turn and walk away, only risking the final glance back to my silent guy. He was watching me, his expression a mix of so many things. And in that moment I knew something for sure. I would die and kill for Ryder a million times over. The vampires would never stop trying to take us down, and I was going to return the favor.

Chapter 3

"OWWW!" Becca screamed, holding one hand over her eyebrow and the other in front of Jayden's face.

Jayden rolled his eyes. "Girl, it doesn't hurt that bad. You got a zoo up in here. I need a lawnmower to make these things pretty."

We didn't have proper tweezers so we were using the medical tweezers you would use for a splinter from the first-aid kit. And Becca probably wasn't being dramatic, Jayden was a bit of a butcher when he attacked body hair. The look on her face had me busting up laughing before quickly stopping when she glared at me. Not everyone could handle Jayden's special personality.

"It hurts like heck," she said, and Jayden and I shared a look. Nope, this wasn't happening. I refused to live in a small container house with someone who didn't cuss.

"Fuck," I said, and Becca's eyes widened.

"Shit," Jayden followed.

"Ass, bitch, douche—"

She cut me off. "Oh my gosh!" Becca covered her ears and I grinned.

Jayden pulled her hands down and met her eyes. "Come on, one cuss word, that's all we're asking. It's like a test so we know you aren't a cop."

My body was shaking as I tried to control my laughter. He was on fire right now.

"Cussing makes one appear less intelligent," Becca said as she crossed her arms defiantly.

Jayden looked at me. "She's a preschool teacher."

I nodded. "It's kind of cute." This bitch was growing on me.

He smiled. Opening a bag and riffling through some makeup, he inspected a tube of mascara and his jaw dropped. "Oh My God! This shit is like ten years old."

Becca shrugged. "I don't really have use for makeup. I'm usually here alone."

Whoa, that was a mood kill. Aw, crap, my heart hurt for her right now. Jayden and I shared a look. Becca was like an orphaned puppy.

As always, Jayden was the first to break the mood with something inappropriate. "Except when Sam comes in to town, and you guys hang and … stuff." He wiggled his eyebrows.

Becca smiled but said nothing. Dammit! She wasn't going to talk. Didn't she understand girl code? Jayden grabbed the tweezers again and went at her as she tried to protest.

Twenty minutes later I was staring at a blonde bombshell.

"Becca, you're a knockout!" I told her and she blushed, trying to cover her tummy, but Jayden slapped her hands away. We had taken one of her shitty, tight white undershirts and cut it off right under the boobs. Coupled with some kickass vintage 50s rockabilly jeans that were high-waisted and buttoned just above her bellybutton, she looked amazeballs. She had this closet full of vintage clothes – although Jayden said they smelled like ass and prayed they weren't from a thrift store – and they totally fit her personality. Topped off with red lipstick and a pin-up hairdo, this chick was ready to party.

Becca covered her stomach once more. "I feel stupid. There's no occasion for this."

Jayden looked offended. "I'm throwing a party! That's the occasion. Don't be insecure. You look hot. If I wasn't gay, I'd hit that."

I nodded in agreement, but Becca's eyes widened in horror at the casual way we spoke about sex.

Oh man, maybe Sam hadn't tossed in the sheets with this one; she was two seconds away from being a nun. I officially made a pledge right then to take her under my wing. She'd be cussing and screwing Sam's brains out in no time.

As we neared the common room, I could hear dance music blasting out of the speakers. There was laughter and I recognized one of the laughs as my man. It was good to hear him laugh again; this was a good idea. Tomorrow would probably start operation kill or cure every vampire alive, but tonight we would have one last night of lighthearted fun.

When we reached the doorway, Jayden made us pause for dramatic effect. We waited as slowly all of the guys turned in our direction. Ryder gave me a heated stare that made me think of our passionate display in the lab. Jayden's smile was pure happiness when Oliver strode across to him and pulled him into this arms.

And Sam ... oh boy. His eyes were practically bugging out of his head. His breathing was labored and I was pretty sure he was very, very happy to see Becca. Even Markus and Kyle were checking Becca out. Jayden and I exchanged grins. Mission accomplished.

Becca stood there awkwardly while I moved into Ryder's arms, our kiss just short of being indecent. I did notice, though, that Kyle was heading in Becca's direction, but Sam put a hand on his chest to stop him. There it was. In the subtlest of ways, Sam had just claimed Becca as his to all his friends and she didn't even notice. Kyle simply nodded and stepped back, busying himself with setting up the pool table. Guy code. These enforcers never messed with it.

And I was sure of one thing: Sam was totally in love with Becca.

Sam picked up two glasses of blood wine that had been poured and were waiting on the table and brought one over to her.

"Drink with me," he said, and I raised my eyebrow at Ryder. We were totally all listening in and I didn't care, no shame. There wasn't a lot of entertainment out here, so this would be my soap opera.

She took it and looked unsure. "I don't know. Remember that one time in the hot tub?" She smiled and it was a gorgeous white-toothed genuine smile.

Sam actually chuckled out loud and it scared me. I legit just realized I'd never heard Sam laugh. Becca was like the Sam whisperer. She had him acting all out of character.

"I promise you'll not encounter any dead rats tonight," he told her, clinking the rim of her glass. She laughed this time, still looking nervous.

Jayden changed the song to some Britney Spears. Oh hell yeah. Brits was just what we needed to forget for a few hours about all the problems in our lives. Then Jayden flipped his queen switch and transformed into one of Britney Spear's backup dancers. Hands and legs were flying everywhere in perfect rhythm to the song and Oliver was watching him with a sexy grin. Boy had some moves.

Jared put a hand on Ryder's shoulder; his gun was tucked into the back of his pants. "I'll take first watch. You have some fun," the Australian enforcer said.

"You sure, bro? I don't mind joining you," Ryder replied.

Jared looked at me and smiled. "You're one of the few guys here in a relationship. Have some fun. I got this. Sam has all the gear here already, so I'll suit up and see you in a few hours."

I smiled at Jared. "Thank you!" I called out after him and settled into Ryder's arm, wiggling my butt to the music.

Over the next hour we danced and played pool and gave Kyle shit for how bad he was at the game. There were only a couple of bottles of blood wine, so no one really got wasted, just took the edge off. Sam and Becca were in the corner of the room laughing and talking all night. They had barely left that space and I was about to call them over to play pool with us when Jared's voice came over the walkie-talkie. It was muffled and the music was loud. Ryder immediately called for someone to shut off the sound system.

"Repeat?" Ryder said, his voice a harsh whip of command.

"There's a female approaching the facility on skis," was the low reply. "She looks about twelve or thirteen years, ethnic and crying."

Becca jumped to her feet, and by the time I got a good look at her she was as white as a ghost.

"Lupita!" she said as she took off, heading toward the door which led to the outside.

The rest of us followed, only stopping long enough to grab coats before we reached the main exit. I was halfway out the door when Ryder put a hand on my shoulder. "No, Charlie, this could be a trap. You can't be seen."

I literally growled, so close to a dog growl it was kind of impressive. "Ryder…"

No more words were needed, the lead enforcer just clenched his jaw and continued with me out of the house. I'd rather die than be kept prisoner and hide.

We made our way outside, and I could see that in the distance an orange fire was blazing. It looked too big to be a bonfire. Smoke was billowing into the sky.

Becca was up ahead; she'd ran to meet up with the young female, who was crying and out of breath.

By the time we reached her side, I could hear her asking, "What is it? What happened, Lupita?" She had already taken the girl into her arms.

"The barn is on fire! Mama and the others are in town late, cleaning a house. Papa's still in there. He's too heavy for me to lift." She trailed off as her tears overwhelmed her.

That was it. The one sentence was all it took and Ryder and I were sprinting toward the flames. The other enforcers had fanned off around us earlier, checking the perimeter, so I wasn't sure if any of them followed.

How fast could I run two miles? Maybe seven minutes? Ryder was faster than me. He could get there in five.

The snow was kicking up in my face as Ryder booked it in front of me. I tapped into that special place I went when I ran, striving for the most speed, trying not to worry about how I was ass-deep in some snowy wilderness, hoping I wouldn't fall and break my neck, hoping that a little girl's father wasn't possibly burning alive right now.

Shit, it was impossible to navigate this route in near pitch darkness, across these snowy plains. Even with advanced senses, I kept stumbling into large piles of snow. If Ryder hadn't been close enough to yank me free, I'd probably have frozen to death by now.

I tried following his path directly. He seemed to have a sixth sense about where to step. Dammit! This was too slow. I needed a snowmobile or something. My frustration must have ignited some of my energy, and as heat unfurled in my center I remembered a very important point. I was no longer a human who needed a snowmobile. Nope. I was Charlie, the ashpire, and I could tap into my levitation abilities.

Flinging free the burning energy, I jumped. I rose off the ground, and unlike the last few times it was relatively smooth. I was getting better, more comfortable with the power. I was starting to learn how to place my feet, rotate arms to keep balance, and tuck my body up for maximum speed.

"Charlie!" Ryder looked pissed as I passed by him; his speed seemed to increase crazily. I also noticed Jayden was sprinting after us, tapping into his house's power of speed, to make it to the fire. Oliver was close by, the two of them helping each other stay out of the massive snowdrifts.

The view was really great from up here. "See you there," I yelled as my power sent me gliding across the sky toward the huge blaze. It was so large I could already feel the heat. The snow was slush in a hundred-foot radius around the place, the silence of the wilderness broken by the roaring inferno. Fire, in all its deadly glory, was not silent. It was big, and powerful and absolutely mesmerizing. If only there wasn't a man's life at stake, I'd have made Becca find me some marshmallows. Or make some. She could probably whip anything up in her lab.

The distance passed by in a rush, and with a bit of a panic I had to halt myself before I ended up face-planting against the burning barn. Okay, so stopping was harder than starting. Just when I was sure that I wouldn't stop in time, my feet lowered and I came to a running halt about twenty feet from the house.

I didn't stop though, sprinting again, past the small, dome-shaped house, moving toward the large, rundown looking barn. The blaze was thick and heavy as I tried to figure out how to get inside.

"Hello? Can you hear me? Hang on, help is on its way."

I had to shout, offer some reassurance, even though my gut was telling me he was at minimum unconscious. That thick smoke was making it hard for me to breathe, and I'd only just gotten here. I closed in on the front, but it was completely cut off; there was no way to enter there. It looked like this was the thickest part of the flames. Dashing around the corner I found another sliding door, and there were far fewer flames here.

Grabbing a handful of slush, I pressed it against the burning metal latch, trying to cool it enough to touch. I didn't have gloves on, which was a real pain, so this was my best chance.

Luckily it worked, and I was able to nudge the rusted door about three feet across. Black smoke poured out of the opening as soon as it appeared, and I knew that this influx of oxygen was going to give this baby more power. I needed to find him and get him out now.

I ducked my head down low, and pulling my jacket off used it as a shield above me. I wasn't sure how flammable the material was, and it was better to not have it attached to my body if some embers caught. I had to stay very low to the ground; visibility was terrible, and it was almost impossible to breathe. I could see that some beams had fallen down near the front entrance and were fueling the majority of the fire. There was a strange scent in the air, strong and chemical. I wondered what was in this barn, and what the chance of it blowing up was. Moving as fast as was safe to do, I kept scanning the place, hoping to see something.

"Hello! Can … can you hear me?" The smoke was killing my ability to shout, but I continued calling for the girl's father.

A sizzle landed on my arm and I fought back the cry of pain. Yep, that burn hurt like a bitch, but I would heal, the human wouldn't. I needed to find him now. I was halfway through the large barn when I caught sight of a boot and yellow snow pants. Thank the gods this guy liked his gear hi-vis. I scurried over to him, practically on the floor. More of the still form came into view. It looked as if someone had drug him into the corner, away from the worst of the fire. His daughter had done everything she could to save him before coming for us. Poor kid.

Dropping my jacket over the top of his body, I grabbed two handfuls of his thick pants and pulled him out toward me. The fire was blazing harder behind us and I knew time was running out. A cough suddenly seized my lungs; the back of my throat burned. The guy was big and heavy, but not fat. He was someone who worked hard, I could tell.

I would not let him and his family down. He was out far enough now that I could wrap my hands around his shoulders, threading into the top of his clothing, and lift his head up to drag him. It was so hard to breathe, which made the physical stuff almost impossible. Trying to find moisture in my dry mouth, I swallowed a few times, and knowing it was my only choice, tapped into the heat at my center again. Holding on as tightly as I could, my upper body leaning over his body to protect us both, I managed to get us out of the middle and to the side door. I was thanking the gods for my ash genetics, because this man was heavy and my muscles were crying.

My energy gave out then; the man's weight coupled with the smoke inhalation had completely exhausted me. I was unable to breathe as another coughing fit hit me. I was about two seconds from collapsing. Strong hands latched onto me then and someone drug us both out of the barn and into the cool, clean air.

My vision was a little fuzzy, and it took me more than a few moments to cough my guts up and try and bring air into my starving lungs. My throat and chest hurt like hell, and everything tasted like death.

"Charlie, are you okay?" Ryder yelled at me, and in my scattered attention I noticed someone was performing CPR on the guy.

"I got him, but..." Coughing racked me again, and I sighed when Ryder pressed a water bottle to my lips.

The cool liquid was painful and wonderful as it wet the inside of my mouth. He wouldn't let me drink too much. I needed to get the smoke out of my lungs.

"You really need some pure oxygen," Oliver said. "But your healing capabilities should kick in soon." I tried to focus on him, but everything was still blurry and muffled.

"Is the ... dad ... okay?"

Look at me go. Almost a full sentence. I was starting to become aware of this love I had for kids. I would never have kids of my own, but something about those innocent, helpless little bastards spoke to me. First the child they had changed into a vampire, and now Lupita. I would never forgive myself if I allowed her father to die. Every little girl needed her father. I didn't have that chance as a child, and I didn't want her to know what it was like to grow up without a dad.

Ryder and Oliver were monitoring the situation. Just as Ryder was about to speak, the father gasped and a sputtering coughing fit hit him. His body convulsed and he coughed so hard he threw up, but the breath I had been holding left me. He was alive.

Sam, Becca, and Lupita pulled up to us, riding a snowmobile. Lupita jumped off and came after us just as a giant cracking noise sounded behind me and we all hit the deck as the barn roof gave way, sending sparks up into the air.

Ryder and I shared a look. If we hadn't gotten here so quick, he would be dead.

Lupita's father was holding her now. He had a bit more color in his face and Becca approached him with an oxygen tank and mask. Of course she had that shit lying around. Probably standard in any chem lab. But my attention was on Sam; the silent enforcer was circling the blazing building, his face elevated, and he seemed to be sniffing the air. Ryder was watching Sam as well.

"What is it?" Ryder asked his friend.

Sam answered by pulling his gun from inside his jacket. "Arson."

Fear struck into my gut, and apparently into Ryder's, because he closed the space between us and I was hauled up into his arms and shoved on the snowmobile. Oliver sat with us and we drove off, leaving Sam, Becca, Lupita, and her father to figure shit out.

"Ryder..." I said, trying to calm him; he was flooring the snowmobile so fast my head was hitting the bars above us.

"Ryder!" I shouted. He ignored me. Oliver turned, facing the back, gun drawn as if he was waiting for someone to shoot us.

We reached the lab in record time and finally my boyfriend faced me. "This was a trap to get us all outside. I don't know whether it was to see how many of us there are, or to get you!"

Fear sliced through me. "Fuck."

Oliver didn't move from his position, but he called back to Ryder. "Who, though? No one knows we're here!"

That's true. Sam had been so careful. But there was one thing he probably hadn't taken into account. He came to this area all the time, and after decades of coming here someone was bound to notice.

Ryder figured the same thing. "Has to be Sanctum ... one of their scouts. If it was a full team they'd have just ambushed the house. The fire drew us out, and if I know them at all, he's now counted us, identified Charlie, and will be reporting back so a full team can be dispatched. The scouts probably went out to all possible locations Charlie might be."

Oliver let a cuss word fly this time. "What do we do?"

I hadn't even showered since I got here and already with the drama. I was not dressed to take on Sanctum. I was kind of looking forward to Jayden's shipments coming, 36C and all.

My man's face looked menacing. "We go hunting." Exiting the snowmobile, he all but ran into the house.

Holy shit.

I took off after him. After we made it inside, I found him in the main room, pulling forth some duffle bags. They were full of weapons.

I readied myself for a fight. "I'm helping," I told him, crossing my arms.

He stopped what he was doing for a second, but then threw me a bulletproof vest. "I need the extra help; otherwise I would say no."

Whatever ... he said yes, so I wasn't going to argue. In the next few minutes the rest of the enforcers made it back to the research facility. Which was good. If Sanctum was involved, you couldn't have too many people on your side.

Five minutes, that's all it took for the boys and I to suit up and for Sam to ready the helicopter. Ryder was pretty sure there would only be one scout and if we killed him that would buy us about a week before someone came looking for him. So we had to find that scout.

Jayden was going to stay at the house. His job was to pray for our survival. Worship, sacrifice, whatever the gods needed, he assured us he was on it.

Becca was still with Lupita and her father. They were heading for the hospital in town.

The rest of us were geared and ready to go. Sam was in the chopper with Oliver as our eyes in the sky. Ryder and I were on one snowmobile, Jared and Kyle on another. Markus said he was going on foot through the rougher terrain.

We all wore bulletproof vests and had semi-automatic rifles and a handgun. Night vision was limited, so only Markus, Sam, and Ryder got those. The Scottish enforcer had already set out to follow snow tracks. All of us were linked via walkie-talkie.

Time to find us a Sanctum scout.

Ryder and I were following a trail, our snowmobile rumbling along as we moved slowly through the night.

"I doubt the scouts have gotten sloppy enough to leave a trail," Ryder said, his face obscured by the night vision. "But we have to follow all leads."

"Might be a trap, but at least we'll find him quickly."

I was more than happy to find the fire-lovin' bastard.

After following the tracks to a thick forested area that the snowmobile couldn't enter, Ryder cut the engine and jumped off. I trailed behind him, gun held at my side and as blind as fuck because no one took the time to hunt up some more night vision goggles. In their defense, I had never used them, but how hard could it be? Would have to tell Jayden to order some more of those online.

Ryder's walkie lit up then and Markus' brogue came through in a low murmur. "I've got a human form in the trees, by—"

His words were abruptly cut off, and Ryder barely paused before he started rushing through the forest. I stayed right on his heels. If I lost him I'd be completely blind out here.

Sam came over the walkie now. "I see him, Ryder! Your 2 o'clock, one click northeast."

Ryder changed directions slightly, because apparently northeast meant something to him. He smashed through the thick undergrowth which surrounded us, snow and ice flying in all directions. My cheeks were starting to hurt now, that sort of biting cold which was almost unbearable.

My heart pounded wildly as I thought of the way Markus' voice cut off on the walkie-talkie. He had to be okay; my gentle giant could take care of himself. I knew that from all the training sessions where he crushed me into a pile of dust. He was fine.

We were running full force, and with all the heavy gear on; my lungs were still recovering from the barn fire, so I was in shit shape. Not to mention the frigid air and crisp snow biting at my exposed flesh. If Sanctum didn't get us all, the elements would.

A heavy snowdrift cut me off for a moment, and by the time I got through it I had lost sight of Ryder. Luckily he'd left a decent trail of destruction through the woods. I struggled through particularly thick brush and pretty much tumbled into an open clearing. Immediately the sounds of a struggle drew my attention, and I was back on my feet in a flash. I could see figures wrestling, and before I could shout

out, a distinct heavy thud echoed, followed by cracking branches and then a body slamming to the ground.

Ryder, who must have come into this section a few yards away from me, took off toward those two shadows. As he passed me, he ripped off his night-vision goggles and tossed them on the ground, before taking a huge leap and landing on top of a black-clad hulking figure.

Unclicking the safety on my weapon, I stooped down to pick up the goggles and slipped them on. Holy shit! These glasses had thermal imaging as well. I had to blink a few times to let my eyes adjust. My vision was awash in neon green, and before me was a battle of two red glowing figures that the heat sensors were picking up. A large male was unconscious on the ground. Judging by the outline of his face, it was Markus. He'd been the one thudding to the ground.

Moving as close as I could to the fighting duo, I dropped to one knee and steadied myself the way Markus taught me. From this distance it was slightly easier to tell the difference between Ryder and the black-clad male. Both were exchanging heavy blows. Breathing deeply, I centered myself, blocking out all other distractions. I needed to be sure of my shot before taking it. I didn't want to hit the wrong guy.

God damn they were fast. The Sanctum scout was slowing just a bit, as if tiring out already. Markus must have really given it to him.

Just then another red figure jumped into my field of vision. Another one of our boys had arrived. As the figure closed in I could tell it was Oliver. He crunched in the snow, and the snapping of twigs distracted Ryder for about a millisecond. As he shifted to see who was advancing on him, I finally had an opportunity to take a shot. My bullet went right through the scout's neck. I had been aiming for the head, so it wasn't half bad. He dropped like a sack of potatoes, gurgling and sputtering through the blood accumulating in his throat. He kept saying something, but I couldn't understand what it was. Something like "Allie." Was that his girlfriend?

Okay, now I felt terrible. Even if this ash had been here to bring assassins to me and had attacked my men, ending a life was still not something I could ever agree with.

Ryder let out a deep breath, distracting me. "Nice shot, Charlie."

He pulled his weapon then and put a bullet between the scout's eyes. I'll never forget the hot blood meeting the cold snow, and the way it glowed on the night vision goggles.

There was more light in the space now. Oliver had a small lantern. Where the heck had he got that from, and why didn't I have one?

"Charlie, check on Markus for me," Ryder said, before turning to Oliver. "I'm going to need some help hiding the body. The harder it is for them to track him, the more time we'll have." This was the second time in the few months I'd known Ryder that he needed help in hiding a body. The enforcer struggle was real.

Taking off my goggles, I slipped across the torn up area to reach Markus. As I crashed to my knees beside him, he started groaning. I ripped off my gloves, trying my best to feel around for his injuries. The enforcer surprised me by grabbing at his groin and rolling off on his side, panting.

"Little prick kicked me in the goodies!" he growled. "Then when I doubled over, he knocked me out cold." The Scottish accent was strong in his voice. I could barely make out his angry words.

Ryder almost looked like he was holding back a smile. "Sanctum have no rules."

Markus was sitting up now, leaning on my outstretched arm. "It's a code, a universal code between all males. You DO NOT go for the junk."

Ryder's smile came through this time, before disappearing again as he picked up his walkie-talkie, radioing Sam, Jared, and Kyle.

"We've got the enemy down and Markus is okay. Rendezvous at base camp." His cold words cut through the tension now that the immediate danger was over, and I had to admit this military talk was sexy AF.

When we all got back to the house Jayden was waiting, a blubbering nervous wreck. He inspected each of us, including Becca, who arrived back from the hospital at the same time as us, and determined we were all okay.

"Are Lupita and her father okay?" I asked the blond ashpire, hoping there had been no other problems.

She nodded, reaching out and squeezing my hand, which was a lot of emotion for the normally reserved chick. "Thank you, thank you so much. They're my friends, have been for many years. I saved their oldest daughter when she got sick and they have repaid me a million times over in love, friendship, and cake. If they had lost him, well, it would have been devastating for all of them. He's the backbone of the family."

Shit, there must be some debris in my eyes or something, because they were suddenly watering like crazy. Or I was hormonal. Yes, that was it. Stupid ashpire hormones had me leaking and stuff.

I smiled. "I'm really glad I was here to help."

Ryder's voice broke over all of us. "Meeting time. Let's gather in the main room. Hands up for first scout and patrol duty."

Ten minutes later I was settled into the couch and warm again. Finally. Felt like you could literally freeze your butt off up here in seconds. All of us, except for Markus and Jared, who were stationed on the roof watching our backs, were gathered around in the main room again, and the atmosphere was grim.

Ryder, who was still decked out in enforcer gear, had the floor. "We need to run. We can't risk the Sanctum coming back to check on their missing guy, or worse, alerting the vampires to where we are."

"I ... what? I can't leave. I need my lab to create the cure..." Becca's voice was surprisingly strong for someone who'd just had her world turned upside down. She was a little tigress about things she loved. I liked it.

"How can you be sure there was only one scout?" Sam muttered through gritted teeth. The silent enforcer's mind was calculating our next move. I knew it.

Ryder didn't seem surprised by the question, even though his jaw clenched harder, and the corner of his lips thinned out. "Because I used to be one of them, remember? I've done scouting missions. When you aren't sure where a target is, you spread out, five or six guys at different locations where you suspect they may be. Scout and report back. They would have monitored all of us over the time they've been watching Charlie, gathering intel. They know you take these trips away, so it was logical to check out Alaska. My guess is you're usually very circumspect about coming to this particular location though, so he didn't know exactly where you went. That's what the fire was all about, a way to draw us out of wherever we were hiding so he could confirm a sighting. Sanctum wants evidence. They wouldn't send all their people here on a hunch. Probably didn't expect you'd immediately pick up on the scent of the accelerant used in the fire."

Jayden frowned, holding up his hand like he was in kindergarten.

"Jayden," Ryder called on him.

"Okay, I get this whole life or death issue is serious, but I refuse to go on the run until my internet shopping shipments come tomorrow." He crossed his arms defiantly, and despite the heavy mood, we all smiled.

Sam nodded. "I think two or three nights here is safe, but then we need to get on the move."

Becca's mouth was hanging open. "Sam…"

Sam's expression softened as he looked at her. "I'm sorry I brought this to your door. I didn't think they were watching us so closely, or that anyone beside these guys would notice all the years I came out here, but I guess someone did, and they opened their big mouths."

No wonder Sam was always so silent. It was pretty much the only way to ensure a secret remained that way.

Becca shook her head. "I don't care about that, but I want to help Charlie wipe all of the vampires out, and for that I need my lab."

Sam nodded as if he expected this. "Start packing up what you need. I have a safe house about fifteen clicks from here. Nobody knows about it. It's from my human days."

Damn, homeboy always had a plan B.

My eyelids were dropping. I was exhausted.

"Get some sleep. We'll plan our next move in more detail in the morning," Ryder called out, and we all nodded.

I somehow shuffled down the hall, and even though I smelled of barn, smoke, and sweat, and probably a little fear, I collapsed into bed in my t-shirt and granny undies with Ryder right next to me. Then it was lights out. Goodbye, fucked-up day.

CHAPTER 4

The next morning I awoke and saw that I was all alone. As I shifted over, the scent coming from my clothes just about knocked me out. Ugh, I smelled like shit; it was crazy how the smell of a fire could stick to your hair, your clothes, your skin.

Stumbling into the bathroom, I showered and relished in the feeling of the warm water on my skin and the orange shampoo that Becca had in here. The citrus smell was invigorating; those shampoo commercials were really onto something.

After changing into my one spare pair of granny panties, a pair of Ryder's sweats, and a clean tank-top, I began to make my way down the hall when Jayden's shriek tore through the house. Shit! I ran through the connecting containers, cursing myself for not grabbing my gun. Stupid Charlie! We just got attacked last night! I shouldn't go a second without a weapon from now on.

Another scream. Fuck! Blasting through the kitchen, I burst into the common room where Jayden was shrieking … and hand flapping and jumping up and down in excitement at what looked like at least a hundred packages stacked before him.

"You bitch! You scared the shit out of me," I scolded him, and he turned with legit tears in his eyes.

Sam and Ryder, who'd also dashed in from somewhere, were glaring at my bestie.

"Jayden, FOUR delivery trucks! FOUR! You didn't need to order this much stuff, we're supposed to be keeping a low profile," Ryder said with a shake of his head.

Jayden just put one hand on his hip. "You gave a gay man with incredible fashion sense a credit card and told him to do unlimited shopping."

Oliver, who had wandered in late to the party, clearly the only one who had known what his man was shrieking about, shrugged. "It's true, you kind of asked for it."

Sam sighed. "Some of this shit better be useful."

Now Jayden had his game face on. The "I will cut you" face. He rummaged through the packages and threw five huge boxes across the room to land at our feet. They were all identical, about four feet high and two feet wide. Sam raised an eyebrow and produced a pocket knife, cutting open his box. His brows rose as he pulled out a heavy duty, army spec camping backpack, the kind with a metal cage and chest straps and even a sleeping bag tied to the bottom.

"I figured at some point we would need to run. Got us all hooked up," Jayden said, and was glaring at Sam, awaiting his reply.

"Thisisgood," Sam mumbled.

Jayden put a hand to his ear. "What's that, Sammy? I didn't hear you?"

Sam actually smiled then. "This is good. Thank you."

My BAFF looked at all of us and we took turns thanking him. Smug bastard. I loved that guy.

What can I say, after all the shitty events of the past few days, the next two hours were like Christmas. Jayden took turns handing all of us our presents. I got some completely inappropriate lingerie, including some star nipple pasties. But I also got some cute skinny jeans, regular lacy thongs, tight t-shirts – one of which said "coffee before talkie" – and a bunch of other cool camping shit, not to mention an absolute top of the line set of throwing knives.

"Jayden, you're the shit!" I exclaimed.

My smile broadened as I noticed Markus sitting in the corner coloring in his adult-man coloring book. It had different cars and guns in it. I hadn't even known the Scottish enforcer liked art, drawing and stuff, but Jayden did. There was a true friend there under all the flamboyance. Jayden was one of a kind.

I was distracted by Ryder. He got some hot denim jeans and cargo pants, leather combat boots and a sexy-AF black leather jacket. We all got a set of black army fatigues with tons of small pockets for storing cool shit.

Watching Becca open her packages was hilarious. I'd never seen someone turn so red. When she opened the push-up bra, she literally inspected it like a scientist would, squeezing all the padding.

"There must be an inch of padding. That's like … false advertisement." She gawked and we all laughed.

Becca, Jayden, and I all got new makeup kits, and of course Becca got false eyelashes and we both got green contacts. Jayden thought of everything.

"You have a future in personal shopping. I'm just throwing that out there," I told my BAFF.

"I know, right!" He winked, slipping on his Gucci loafers.

We had swapped out those who were on patrol duty a few times so that everyone got to enjoy their gifts, but all too soon it was time to put our shit away and get down to business. And not the fun, sexy kind. Nope, this business was going to be dangerous, scary, and there was a high possibility I was never going to get a chance to use my sexy new lingerie.

Ryder gathered all of us together, even calling the boys in from patrol. Everyone had to be here to chime in on the plan.

We were going to iron it out, make sure it was concrete, and then put it into motion.

"Sam is going to take Becca, all her necessary lab equipment, and everything else needed for a month or more of lockdown, across to his secret house. Becca believes that in using Charlie's blood she can create a synthetic cure or vaccine for the vampire virus, and that we'll be able to use it in a mass amount to take down all the Hives."

We were all hanging on Ryder's words. I don't think anyone was even breathing so as not to miss anything. Because this was it. Finally we were going to be taking action.

He continued: "I was up early this morning, and managed to get a secure, coded call through to Lucas."

Involuntarily I lurched toward him then, my hands lifting of their own accord. Ryder noticed, and answered before I could reach out and grasp onto his shirt. "Tessa's fine, and so is Blake." I relaxed back again, realizing how truly afraid I'd been for her. "From what I could infer, they're playing their part, acting as if we have all betrayed the Hive, and that they hate ash. Lucas said there's not much he can do right now. They put him in the pit for a few days and now have him under strict surveillance. It's only his money and power stopping them from killing him. He did have some ideas of how we could get the cure into each of the Hives at the same time."

I was excited to hear Lucas' ideas.

"Every three months, all of the Hives receive a shipment from the blood banks, and at the same time there's a turnover of human feeders. The government requires all volunteer feeders be changed quarterly to keep them healthy. The new feeders all have to report to a few select hospitals across America. There they have their blood checked, catalogued, and then they are shipped out to Hives across the country."

Damn, I knew so little about this world. Why did I not pay attention in these classes? I hated when I wasn't as informed as I needed to be. "So the humans who we and the vamps feed from could be from anywhere?" I asked. "How is it that Tessa managed to get into Portland Hive? She never said anything about her blood being tested."

Jayden answered me, and I realized that we actually had a very good source of information sitting right here in this room, the very ash who'd been front line in the feeding center. He did the paperwork, he would know all about this stuff. "Tessa had all the paperwork. It was correctly filed and everything. I think maybe someone in the Quorum, Fugly perhaps, forged it and rushed her through so she was always there to be used as a weapon against you. Right from the start it was all in play, even before they knew what you were."

Fuck! Made sense, but still…

Oliver posed the next important question. "How many of these hospitals are there across the world? Because this sort of plan needs to go down on the same day. Otherwise the Hives will lock down and we'll never get to the vamps again. Our timing must be perfect."

Jayden answered: "Two in America: Texas and California. They transport blood and humans out to North and South America. There are three in the UK and Europe: London, Belgium, and Sweden. And finally there is one in Indonesia, which only deals in bottled blood, not humans. It's massive though, shipping out to Australia, Japan, and China. These are the only other countries with Hives, and each only has one. Their human governments are not as lenient as the American one, and vamps were mostly killed off there, allowing only a small percent of the vampire population to live."

Jared nodded. "Yep, my old Hive in Brisbane does not allow any more cullings or new vampires. All ash and newly changed vamps are killed upon turning, unless you can convince another Hive to take you. The vampires stay holed up in their massive compound, and only use bottled blood. So we don't have to worry about humans going there for feedings."

"So these shipments happen every three months," I said. "Do we know when the next date is?"

Jayden grinned, and I took that as a good sign. "We're in luck. The Christmas shipment is due to be processed in about three weeks. Which means if we can somehow get the cure into their blood supply and into the humans before then … well, we might be vampireless by Christmas."

Ryder straightened. "If Becca is done by then, getting the cure into the blood won't be too difficult. But how will it work with the humans? We'll need to make sure it not only enters their blood but stays in there long enough for them to make it to their many destinations."

All eyes went to the science geek in the room. If anyone was going to know about blood and stuff, it was Becca. She blinked a few times, pushing her glasses up in a nervous, awkward manner. "Uh, well, I can definitely give the cure the ability to stay in the blood, but those cells do not last indefinitely. Red blood cells last about four months and white a little longer. It'll all depends how the cure bonds to the human cells. I need to do some experimenting once I create it. I'm going to need a vampire or two to test on."

No one blinked or looked horrified by her suggestion for vamp testing. I for one thought it was a much better idea than testing on an innocent animal. I wasn't planning on getting consent from a vamp.

Jared even chuckled. "That can easily be arranged. I know more than a few vamps who could stand to be poked and prodded a little."

Nods all around. None of us were fans of our sires.

Jayden, who must have been mulling over Ryder's previous words, piped up then. "All of the humans are required to undergo blood tests, and to receive a vaccine that covers them for the flu and some other illnesses. The vamps don't like their subjects to get sick while they're working for them. If we could get the cure into the flu shot, or whatever it is, then we could make sure the humans and bottled blood are covered all in one go. And I think the easiest way with the cure is to somehow infiltrate the Cellway warehouse. That's the company who makes the special UV resistant bottles for the blood. Get the cure into the bottom of those bottles, pose as delivery drivers, then drop cure-laced bottles off. The blood will then be added to the cure without them knowing."

He turned to Becca. "Will the cure be only a tiny amount of liquid in the bottom of the bottle, like virtually undetectable?"

She took a second to think before nodding. "Yes, it'll be very small in quantity per bottle, and clear."

I could feel the excitement through the room. This was all coming together, a plan we could actually work with. OMFG. My body was practically vibrating as more of our plan started to come together. It wasn't going to be easy, and we would have to be so careful because one word of this getting back to the vampires and we'd all be screwed. But this could really work.

I could actually end this, all of this. No more vampires with no oxytocin, no more forcing ash into cullings. No more new ash at all. Life as we knew it would completely change.

"So what's the actual plan for us while Becca is working on the cure and before we take over the Cellway bottle shipments?" I said. No way were we just sitting around here playing cards.

Ryder's eyes were light silver, so he was dealing okay with the plan so far, even with the inherent danger to me and his men. I think the loss of all the Portland enforcers did something to him. Hardened his resolve. He was now right there with me. The vampires needed to be ended.

"We need to get a warning out to all the ash across the Hives. There's this network which is underground and exclusive for ash. A place for information exchange. Was initiated years ago when an infamous ash tried to rise up and rebel against the cullings. He's dead now, but the underground lived on and it's online now. A way to share messages with other Hives and ensure that only the ash will see it. The only problem is that a single ash controls it all, and no information gets up there without his input."

My head swung around and I nailed Sam with a look. "Are you telling me that you're not in charge of the underground computer ash program or whatever it is?"

The silent enforcer actually chuckled, and Becca's eyes were all a swirl of silver. "I was offered it once, but it requires you to basically drop off the radar. The informant for the underground is a heavily protected secret, a single ash who holds the key to all information. He'll have to move around freely, and have no liabilities. I had Becca and the guys to worry about, so I passed on the position."

"Where does this ash live?"

Ryder and Sam exchanged a glance. Sam answered me. "No one knows. Rumors circulate, but nothing concrete. Last I heard he had a brother holed up in the California Hive. The only way we're going to be able to find out is if we go down there and draw out their enforcers. Someone will hopefully have the information. Find the brother, find the leader of the network."

"Are we all going?" I had to ask, because knowing Ryder, he'd already decided to stash me in an igloo at the top of a mountain somewhere.

Instead, the lead enforcer surprised me by nodding. "Yes, I don't trust anyone else but us to watch your back, and I need all the boys there in case shit goes down. We'll travel in two groups and meet up when we're all there."

I nodded, okay holy shit. It was scary going back to a city with a Hive. Everyone was gunning for me. This was going to be like real life on the run.

Becca stood abruptly. "Well, I've been working on something for Sammy, a surprise. I only have four of them so you'll have to share, but it'll be perfect for your trip." She dashed out of the room.

Upon return she had four camelbacks in her hand. They were water pouches with straws that you could hook on your backpack, but the tops had some metallic tape or panel. I'd seen hikers use these often in Portland.

Becca looked ready to bubble over in excitement. "Taste it," she told Ryder.

He looked skeptical for a moment but put his lips to the straw and sucked. What looked like blood come up through the straw and into his mouth. He raised his eyebrows, looking impressed.

"It's cold!" he said.

Becca smiled. "Yes, I built solar panel fabric into the top. As you hike or walk around, the panel gets charged and runs current down to the cooling element inside the fabric. Cold fresh blood no matter where you are. It holds quite a bit because I have expanded the inner lining. This should get you to California and back."

Sam's eyes hadn't left her. "Thank you, Becca." His voice was gruff.

She gave him a shy smile and handed him the pouch. When their fingers touched I saw her eyes blaze silver.

Then she got nervous and dropped her hand, mumbling, "I'll go pack the lab." Turning, she ran off again and the rest of the guys dispersed to begin packing their things. Sam was just staring at the door, chest heaving a bit.

"You know … some girls expect the guy to make the first move." I patted his hard right pec, winking and walking away before he could reply.

One glance over my shoulder told me that he was both intrigued and confused. Hopefully I'd just stoked the fire burning in Sam's chest. I wanted to see him happy, and with no more need to keep secrets.

An hour later I had completely filled my camping pack. It was stuffed to the brim with all my necessities. A camping meal kit with pan, fork and knife. A bag of dry beans, rice and spices, water packets, clean clothes, and a toiletry kit, including my new make-up. Because a girl's gotta still try to look pretty even when sleeping in dodgy places. I was assuming we were going to be full-on camping or staying in broken down cabins.

A sound at the doorway drew my attention. Jayden, in all his Gucci glory.

I smiled. "Hey."

He came and sat at the edge of the bed. "Hey."

We were silent a moment and it felt weird. Things were happening fast and even though it would be for the better in the end, it was shitty now.

Jayden put a hand on mine and turned to me. "I'm going to stay back at the cabin with Becca. She's going to need my bubbly personality to keep her company."

I smiled. What he hadn't said was that although Jayden could channel badass, like in the culling, he really wasn't suited for camping and killing. Plus, he made a good point, Becca would need the company.

"I'll keep an eye on Oliver," I said, and all of a sudden Jayden's eyes were leaking. He turned quickly and pulled me into a bone crushing hug.

"I love you, Charlie Bennett. You're the best thing that happened to me."

Now my damn eyes were leaking! I didn't like that he was saying goodbye; it was like we were back in the culling all over again. "Jayden, there are no words for what you mean to me."

He pulled away then and wiped his eyes.

"Now for some good news," he told me, and I raised one eyebrow.

My BAFF was bubbling over with excitement now and it had to be something good to change his mood so quickly.

He squealed. "Oliver just asked me to marry him, so after all this shit goes down … will you be my best man?"

My jaw dropped and laughter erupted out of me, along with pure joy. My eyes were filling again. "Of course I will!" We hugged for the second time and the moment was perfect. It gave us all something to look forward to, a happy event on the horizon. I would make a damn good best man.

The rest of the day passed rather quickly. The boys were planning every detail of how to get us to California and get word into the Hive to draw this guy's brother out. Sam and Becca were taking runs of equipment up to the secluded cabin. She was relieved that Lupita's family promised to keep an eye on the main lab, although she made them promise to lay low and avoid all strangers. She was going to be hard at work on the cure; we all decided that we'd bring her vamp test subjects back with us from the California Hive. Should give her enough time to have something to test.

I was sitting in the kitchen watching Jayden. He was busy cooking banana nut muffins to see us off with.

When the true darkness of night washed away the twilight it was time to say goodbye to Jayden and Becca. They were heading to the secluded cabin now; the sexy six and I would sleep one more night here and then take the chopper to Canada at the break of day tomorrow. Or whatever sprinkle of low light was masquerading as daybreak in this part of the world. Alaska was not only freezing, it was perpetually dark. Jayden was all packed up, his bags taking up the majority of the space in their snowmobile.

I was really just grateful that they would be safe there and that Becca would have the company of my best friend.

Jared, Markus, and Kyle said goodbye and then set out to patrol with the night vision goggles – scout around to make sure Becca and Jayden weren't followed. Sam, Ryder, and I helped with their final bags, and Oliver and Jayden shared a sweet kiss in the corner of the outbuilding, saying goodbye.

Becca entered the room then, dragging a cooler behind her, and Sam met my eyes. *Kiss her, you fucking idiot*! I wanted to shout at him. But he just pursed his lips and then stalked over to take the cooler off her hands, barely making eye contact with her. Ryder was fiddling with his walkie-talkie as I crossed the large area and stood next to him.

"What's Sam's deal?" I whispered.

Ryder glanced over his shoulder at Sam, who was strapping down the water cooler, Becca watching him with sad eyes.

Ryder looked back at me, wrapping his arms around my waist. "He was a prisoner of war. They tortured him within an inch of his life, trying to ferret out secrets. Sam's always been good at keeping secrets. He never broke, not even once."

Oh fuck. I knew Sam had issues but I didn't know it was that bad. Jesus.

Ryder looked proud of his friend. "He held out through the worst torture you can imagine. They were just about to kill him when the war ended and he was rescued. But it was already too late. He was a changed man and soon after turned ash. Now, even more so, he keeps secrets and is afraid to care too deeply. He would die if someone took Becca or targeted her just because of their relationship. The thing with Lupita's family was a huge reminder of that."

Shit. Knowing how loyal and honorable Sam was, he was never going to act on his feelings for Becca. He would protect her forever, when it was clear all she really wanted was his love.

Jayden was strapping himself into the driver's seat of the snowmobile, so we walked over to say final goodbyes.

Sam awkwardly held up his hand in a fist bump. "Later, Becks."

Becca's whole face lit up at the nickname. "Bye, Samuel."

They had hundreds of inside jokes after a lifetime of memories together. I suddenly felt it was my moral duty to crash their two heads together and force them to recognize the blazing love and adoration they had for each other, because we all saw it. Ah, but as always, the timing wasn't right. So I walked over and gave Jayden a long hug. "I love you, bitch," I told him.

Becca's mouth quirked a little, but I could see she was getting immune to our cussing.

"Love you too, bitch," he replied, and Becca just shook her head.

"You should try it sometime. It's freeing," I said to her.

She just smiled and waved goodbye as they drove out of the outbuilding and into the snowy grounds. Twenty feet from us the snowmobile ground to a halt. Sam stepped forward, pausing when Becca's head popped up and she turned, facing us.

"Bye, bitches!" she shouted, and held on to the roof bar as Jayden peeled out. I could hear his laughter echoing through the night.

Sam's mouth was gaping open. "Jayden is a bad influence on her."

I busted out laughing. "Jayden will make her fabulous. One month locked in a cabin with him and she'll be wearing push-up bras and giving you lap dances."

Well, hello. Was that a little interest I saw there on Sam's face? Not to mention the slight grin.

Ryder laced our hands together then and started leading me toward the house. "I'm tired. I think we should go to bed." His voice was low, like a caress. Heat curled through my belly. Bed was definitely code for sex.

There was no more leading after that. Ryder had to haul butt to keep up with me. This was our last night in this snowy wilderness and I was going to take full advantage.

CHAPTER 5

The sun was killing me right now. Why was everything so bright in this state? Seriously, it was amazing there was even a Hive in California; the vamps would be prisoners for the vast majority of the day in summer, and even right now, on the cusp of the Christmas season, it was still warm. Well, especially compared to Alaska.

"Don't rub at your eyes, Charlie."

The sun and hours of travel had left Markus cranky too. But he had a point. I kept dislodging my sunglasses by lifting them to rub my tired eyes. And of course that was really ruining my "not an ashpire" disguise. Me, Ryder, Kyle, and Markus were all perched against the railing of Santa Monica Muscle Beach. This was our rendezvous point with the other guys, who had taken a slightly different route down here.

"What time is it?" I asked. "Are they late? Should we be worried?"

There were a lot of people around, and despite the intense sun it was starting to lower in the perfect blue sky. So it was late afternoon or something. I had sort of gotten used to not having a cell phone attached to me at all times, but it still frustrated me when I wanted to know the time. Or check my horoscope.

"They're not late yet. No need to worry, they'll be here," Ryder said, drawing a comforting arm down my side and pulling me into him. He was trying to keep me from stomping around. But all he did was make me worry more. Seriously though, I did need to chill out, because my agitated eye rubbing and pacing was surely going to draw attention. And that was the last thing we needed.

"What if they figured out the ID's were fake?" My voice was muffled against Ryder's side.

Kyle laughed then, his deep tones booming out across the beach. "Charlie, girl, you're worrying for nothing. We made it here and the boys will too. If they knew our ID's were fake, we would have been detained at the airport. Relax."

As I pulled myself out of the very comfortable embrace of my enforcer, I noticed that people were starting to stare at our group. A lot of them were women. Scantily clad women. Didn't they know it was winter? Damn. Still, it wasn't a huge surprise. These three men commanded attention; they were tall, handsome, and had that extra something which my mom always called charisma.

"We should move," Ryder said. "We've been standing in this spot for too long. Time to start blending in with the locals."

Blending. Sure. We could do that. It wasn't that long ago I was a human. So why did it feel as if it was years ago and they were suddenly this weird, alien species I couldn't understand?

#ashpireproblems

The beach was calling us, so we left the path and made our way onto the golden sands. I loved the feel of the salty air and the rush of waves breaking against the shoreline. My leather boots were calf high and kept the majority of sand out, but I felt an urge to rip them off and sink barefoot into the white grains.

"Ryder!" The shout came when we were halfway to the water, and as a group we spun around to find Sam, Jared, and Oliver speed-walking our way. Thank God!

As I started stumbling across the sand toward them, I noted they were dressed the same as us. Glasses clad, and looking quite sophisticated. Jayden had outfitted us before we left, insisting that if we all wore our favorite black enforcer gear, we would stand out in Cali. So now we were in a mix of jeans, army-style pants and neutral-colored cotton shirts. Jared even sported a button-up Hawaiian number, which suited his surfer boy looks.

When I reached their side I threw myself at them. "Where the hell have you guys been? I've been worried sick!"

Arms wrapped around me as each of them gave me a hug.

"Sorry, Mum," Jared said. "We got a little delayed at one of the airports. Apparently Sam forgot you can't carry a pocket knife on a commercial flight."

The silent enforcer grimaced. "It was one tiny little knife set. The way they freaked out you'd think I was trying to haul an AK-47 on board."

Ryder pulled me out of Jared's arms and deposited me at his side.

"Getting too used to traveling by private plane, Mr. Money Bags," I teased Sam.

He surprised me by reaching out and ruffling my hair. Hmmm, someone had loosened up just in the short time we'd been in Alaska. Sharing that secret part of his world with us had fortified the bonds of our group. The trust was strong. No more secrets.

As the boys gathered closer, I knew it was time for part two of the plan to go into action. Sam pulled out a cell phone; he was the only one allowed to touch this high-tech, completely untraceable piece of technology. Sliding the screen, he pressed out a few numbers and lifted it to his ear.

Unable to pace when I was smack bang in the center of the sexy six, I started to bounce from foot to foot, my nervous energy needing an outlet.

Sam's voice jolted me. "Hello, I need to report an ash causing havoc on Santa Monica Pier. You need to get your enforcers down here immediately. He's feeding on humans."

My jaw dropped. Okay, way to stroll into Cali under the radar. But it was kind of genius, and since it was still daylight no vampires would be accompanying the enforcers. Now let's just hope these enforcers were friendly.

Within five minutes, two lifted black SUV's peeled around the corner to the pier.

"Let's split up. If for some reason they aren't friendly…" Sam didn't need to finish.

Ryder tucked me close to him and started walking fast toward the vehicles, while Kyle and Sam took off after us. The other three boys disappeared, but I knew they were watching our backs from afar.

When we were ten feet from the SUV's the doors opened and out stepped about eight hottie Californian enforcers. As they spilled out of the vehicles, every girl on the beach turned to stare. The enforcers paid no attention to the humans though, and I was both surprised and intrigued to see that they were almost as well trained and disciplined as my boys. They looked around with hard rapid glances, trying to identify the commotion that had prompted the call. Ryder whistled loud and the men looked at us. Then Ryder removed his glasses and one of the leaders stepped forward, gun drawn.

He was over six feet tall and had the stereotypical blond shaggy hair and surfer look, but in his eyes was a lethal predatory gaze. He was the alpha of this little posse. As he approached Ryder, I also took off my glasses. That's when the leader sprang into action like I'd lit his ass on fire. Holstering his gun, he rushed forward.

"Put your glasses back on and follow me. They watch everything we do now."

He calmly walked onto the sidewalk and hung a right; we followed with a few of his men trailing behind us. There was a cute mom and pop coffee shop and the enforcer slipped inside. Ryder waited, unsure, but I yanked his hand. If we couldn't trust our own people, we were fucked. Sam, Ryder, and I entered the coffee shop just in time to hear the pretty blonde, wearing next to nothing, behind the coffee bar.

"Hey, Zack, your usual?" she called out to the enforcer, giving him bedroom eyes.

"Not this time, Angela. I need to use your office." She looked past him at us for a second and then nodded.

We followed him back to the surprisingly large office, and as I looked at the green velvet couch in the corner I tried not to think about what this guy and Angela did on there.

He turned to face us. "I'm Zack."

Ryder, Kyle, Sam and I were all in the office, with two of his men guarding the door. He was outnumbered if we wanted him dead. I liked having the upper hand in these situations, so I gave him a nod and pulled off my glasses.

"Charlie." I shook his outstretched hand.

He grinned broadly. "Well, I'll be damned. You're real. The female ash. The cure."

Hope sprang in my chest. If he knew, that meant the rumor mill had begun to spread. I nodded.

Ryder shook his hand next. "Ryder."

This time Zack looked absolutely gobsmacked. "Ryder Angelson? As in the very ash who was instrumental in setting up the enforcer program?"

Ryder nodded. Zack's impressed expression deepened. Kyle was next for the introductions. Sam didn't bother with his name; that wasn't my silent enforcer's style. He said: "I need to find the Controller. We need access to the network."

Zack's friendliness disappeared and suspicion darkened his features.

I growled, "Come on, man. We came all the way out of hiding because we know his brother is in your Hive."

He swallowed hard. "Why do you need to see him?"

I didn't like his mannerisms; he was acting sketchy as fuck. Ryder noticed it too. I stepped closer, giving him my baddest staredown. "Because I'm going to cure all the vampire douchebags and I'm going to need help. Not to mention that all ash and enforcers across the Hives need to be warned. Shit is about to get real, and if you're not prepared you're going to end up dead."

His mouth popped open and then something settled in his eyes as he gave a wry grin. "Well, since you put it that way ... hi, I'm the Controller."

Sam eyes narrowed, like he thought Zack was full of it. "I thought he was on the run and his brother was here?"

He shrugged. "I like to start rumors to keep people off my trail. This way I get a real home, and ash can still find me if needed."

"We need to organize a major undertaking," Sam told him.

He nodded and eyed the doorway. "I'll do everything in my power to help you, I promise, but not here and not now. The Hives have gone into complete lockdown except for emergency calls. If we don't get back soon they'll suspect something. I'll have to tell them it was a crank call."

"Who is your tech guy?" he asked me, and I nodded to Sam.

Zach pulled out his phone and handed it to Sam. "The picture of the pug in my photos is the back door into the network. I don't have time right now to get the full story, so you're going to have to figure out how to access the network and get your message into the world."

Sam nodded staring at the phone like it was made of twenty-four carat gold.

Zack eyed the door and then spoke softer: "Some Hives are taking away all electronics, going back to the Dark Ages, and there's talk about cutting the enforcer program altogether, in which case we'll never be allowed outside again."

Ryder groaned next to me. Shit.

"We need to get word to every Hive in record time," I told him.

He nodded. "Put it on the network, but I'm telling you, nothing spreads faster than word of mouth. I was just in Seattle escorting my Quorum to a meeting when I heard about what happened to your enforcers. I'm sorry." He directed that last comment at Ryder.

Ryder nodded solemnly.

"Use the phone. I'll meet you here tomorrow at noon. If I don't show, leave the phone in the top desk drawer. Angela can be trusted."

We all nodded and he took another second to glance at me. "The cure…" He shook his head in disbelief and then left the room, leaving us all to stare at each other.

Ten minutes later we were all walking down a side road that paralleled the 3rd Street promenade.

"We need somewhere to lay low while I figure out this phone," Sam said, still clutching it like it was the most precious thing in the world.

Jared spoke up: "I have an old surf buddy who used to live a few blocks over. He'd be in his sixties now if he's still around. Total chill dude who'd never rat a brother out."

Ryder didn't look like he was immediately jumping on board with this plan. "You still trust a guy you haven't spoken to in decades?"

Jared gave Ryder a bit of a glare. Unusual for the normally happy Aussie. The stress was getting to all of us. "Me and this guy went through a lot, okay. I trust him.

Ryder nodded; that was enough to placate him for the moment. We followed Jared down a side street. After a bit of getting lost, he finally recognized the small blue beach shack five blocks from the ocean. There were Tibetan peace flags hanging over the front door and a marijuana leaf sticker in the window. I raised an eyebrow at Jared, but he just chuckled.

"He's still here. I knew he would never leave the beach." Jared walked right up to the door like he owned the place and banged on it.

Sam, Oliver, and Markus hung back on the lawn while Ryder, Kyle, and I stood behind Jared. I heard some shuffling and then the door opened. Standing before us was a buff, graying old guy with surprising good looks for his sixty-plus years. He wore tan cutoff shorts and a tank-top, his skin leathery and dark from all the hours under the sun. He looked confused for a second, and then Jared dropped his shades. "Hey, mate."

The guy broke into a grin and actually began tearing up. "Oh my God! Jared. Buddy." He jumped out the front doorway and took Jared into a hug. Now that he was in the sunlight I saw that he was missing one of his legs but wore a cool, carbon-fiber prosthetic.

He pulled back. "I haven't seen you in ages. I heard you were an ash and that was it. How you been?"

Jared smiled. "Good, man. I'm good. My buddies and I are kind of having a hard time. We need a place to crash…"

The man immediately stepped aside. "*Mi Casa es su casa.*"

Jared looked on the lawn. "There's seven of us total…"

"The more the merrier, brother. I've got plenty of beer and I was just about to make some pasta. You guys eat, right?"

We all chuckled as he led us into the house. Ryder waved for the boys to come in off the lawn. I was glad to finally unclick these heavy camping backpacks and release the weight from my shoulders. I was grateful we would have a roof over our heads tonight.

After handing out water and beer, the old timer introduced himself: "I'm Brian, but my buddies call me Shark Bait." He smiled and Jared shook his head, chuckling.

"How do you guys know each other?" I asked, trying to make small talk.

Brian gave the Aussie enforcer a somber look. "Jared saved my life when a shark in Australia took my leg clean off."

Okay, so "sexy surfer hero" was totally my new nickname for Jared. Always knew he was a brave one.

Brian nodded. "I heard Queensland had some killer waves, so I sold my VW van and bought a one-way ticket to Gold Coast in the '80s. Met Jared and his mates on the water. Barely knew him six hours, and when the shark pulled me under Jared swam after me like he had known me all his life."

Jared raised his beer. "Surfer code, bro."

Brian clinked his beer. I had a feeling we were going to be hearing lots of bros over the next twenty-four hours.

"What happened?"

Brian shrugged. "The second I got dragged under and felt that crunch, I passed out. Woke up with Jared hovering over me, tying off my leg."

Jared looked haunted at the memory. "You still surf?"

Brian smirked. "What do you think? I'm the best damn one-legged surfer in the Pacific. No shark's going to take surfing from me."

It hit me then, how you had these moments with people, these bonding moments that could literally tie you to someone for a whole lifetime. Jared and Brian had one. And I'd had more than one with each of these enforcers. I'd known them only a few months and would die for each one of them, no questions asked.

Over the next few hours I helped Brian cook, and except for the silver gray hair, forgot about his age. He had this contagious personality, always happy and chill – probably the marijuana. I learned that he'd had a live-in girlfriend of thirty years, but she'd died a few years ago of breast cancer. Now it was just him and the waves and he was more than happy to help Jared out in any way.

After buttering the garlic bread and popping it in the oven, I went in search of the boys to see if they needed a beer refill. I heard their voices outside. Stepping into the back yard for the first time, I was completely struck by the scene. Ryder was on the hammock napping, Oliver and Sam hunched over the phone, Markus coloring in his book, and Kyle and Jared sitting on the grass having a nice chat. Just like a normal family, no evidence that we were about to rain hell on the vampires.

I inhaled the salty air and decided then that if we survived this whole thing, I wanted this life. A small blue beach house with white picket fence and a hammock, preferably with Ryder inside. When I had first heard I was an ash, it'd dashed all of my domestic dreams. But we had a chance to change all of that. We didn't have to be slaves to the Hive. We could live among humans again. At least I hoped.

Long after dinner was done and Brian had retired for the night, Sam finally cracked the code into the underground network. I was impressed. It had only taken him a few hours to maneuver through what he referred to as one of the most insanely encrypted paths he'd ever encountered. He, of course, was annoyed it had taken him that long. Think it gave him an entirely new level of respect for Zack though.

All of us waited, tense and silent, as he started to shift his way through the information. After some time I couldn't stand the waiting.

"So anyone can access the network to receive information, but how do other ash or enforcers normally put information on there?" I asked.

Sam was busy, so it was Markus who answered me. "Either they do what we did and track the Controller down via the clues to his whereabouts. Or the other option is to send a letter. Snail mail is pretty much untraceable. There's a mailbox which is monitored by someone. Then that letter is posted again to someone else, who then posts it to a final, secret, destination. It's slow as hell. But everything else was always being interrupted by the vamps. Then the Controller is supposed to assess the importance of your information and post it up on the forum."

Well, that explained why we needed to come out here in person. We did not have time for that weird runabout way of getting information out to everyone.

"What about the network that Sam was using to figure out the Quorum hired Sanctum to kidnap me? Looked like anyone could post on it."

"They can." Sam said tense. "But it's not a network for ash, it's one for all the Hives and it's the dark web. You don't want to know what other stuff is on there. It's not a place we can post this sort of information. The vamps would have it in seconds and they would rain blood down on the world. Zack's network is for ash only, very separate, very secure. This is what I'm accessing right now."

I liked that. Always have a backup plan. Except we didn't really have one for our "annihilate vampires from the face of the Earth" plan. Oh well, if it failed I'd think of a plan B. I always did.

"Sam will be the first ash, beside the Controller, to be allowed a backdoor access into the network," Ryder said. "Zack gave us much more than we expected. I thought we'd have to try and get the message to him and hope he would load some of the information. Instead—"

"He's allowing us to post our own message and information," Sam said, cutting him off. "He's giving us full access."

Sam's fingers were flying over the phone's keypad then, and I knew he was posting now. "I'm warning all Hives that the vampires are killing ash. Locking them down. I've told them that we are planning to wage war on the vamps, that we will infect their blood and donors with the cure, and that war will probably ensue after this and to be ready to fight."

All of us knew we wouldn't get every vamp. It just wasn't feasible. Some would have old blood. Some might be out of the Hive for the delivery, and by the time they made it back others would be cured, and no one would touch any blood then.

"Tell them we're relying on them to help us finish this job, to remain with the Hives and take down any vamps who are not cured. Because they will seek out humans," Ryder added to Sam's post.

"Shit!" I exclaimed. "We need to let the humans know too. The government or something."

Ryder nodded. "Yes, I've already considered this. Do you remember Lincoln, the SWAT boys who took on Deliverance with us?"

Oh yeah, I remembered Blue Eyes. Bastard told me to stand down.

Ryder gave me that sexy, half-grin. Guess my thoughts were clear across my face again. He continued: "I can easily get word to him, and he has plenty of contacts in the higher levels of the US government. Secretary of state, etc. At this stage I'm trying to figure out how to do this but keep the information secret. I'm ninety percent sure the humans will be on board with a vampire-free world."

Jared gave a dry laugh, not really sounding amused. "The humans have been looking for a way to get rid of vampires for a long time. This will appeal to them, because firstly the plan is to cure them, not kill, so it won't look like a mass slaughter. This is something which has always hindered governments trying to take down vampires before, the fact that they were once human. They're people's family members, and the humans would revolt against a mass slaughter."

Oliver leaned up from where he was slouched against the step. He missed Jayden terribly when they were apart, leaving him quiet and introspective. "There's no doubt the leaders will jump at this. They're sick of being stuck under the control of vamps. I have a few contacts in Washington and they keep me updated."

I shifted closer to him. "When should we tell the humans?"

Kyle, who had been half-asleep in another hammock, rolled over then and landed flat on his butt. His "oomph" broke the tension and all of us had a good laugh at the confused enforcer. "Dammit, how do people sleep in those things? Roll over to swat a fly and fall on my ass."

Ryder leaned over and punched his best friend on the arm. "Man, you should be awake. We're only planning the end of the world as we know it."

Kyle returned the punch before swiping a hand across his eyes. "Shit, I know. I've been so tired lately. Think I need a good dose of blood from the source."

That reminded me that all of us were going to need some blood soon. I could now go a day with no worries, and the boys even longer, but we had to make sure this was all finalized before I started to lose my mind. Luckily, we had those devices from Becca, but even that supply was limited.

Sam got to his feet then, the small phone clutched tightly in his right hand. "Okay, it's all live on the network. There's no way for ash to post replies, but there is a button for them to acknowledge they've received the information, and I'm already getting positive acknowledgements across the country."

"Are we sure that none of these enforcers are in the pocket of the Quorum?" I asked, suddenly nervous that our plan could be easily derailed by simple betrayal.

None of the boys looked worried. "Never," Kyle said. "Ash are oppressed and murdered daily by vampires. There's not a single one who wouldn't jump at the chance to take them down. They don't even pay us well."

Oliver agreed. "Yep, and not to mention that anyone who brought this information to the Quorum would not only get themselves killed, but all ash. The vamps would start systematically wiping out all of us in a bid to maintain power."

True. So very true. And the ash knew it. Vampires had treated us like expendable possessions for long enough. We were taking our freedom back.

"To answer your question from before, the human government is going to be a bit more difficult," Ryder said. "Plenty of them are in the pocket of vampires. I trust Lincoln. Maybe he'll have a thought about how to do this."

It didn't sit right with me that we might bring this war down on humans and never give them a heads up. I had human friends and family. I wasn't close to any of them, but they didn't deserve to die at the hands of a vampire.

"Maybe we wait until all the blood is done and delivered," I said. "That way this information only has a small window of chance to be spread. The bad humans won't have enough time to tip off their vampire allies, but the good ones can help us and warn their law enforcement agencies around the world."

All of the boys exchanged a glance, and I didn't love the look of it. Despite Ryder's earlier thought of sharing with Lincoln, it now looked like he had mentally axed that idea.

"I think we play it by ear," Markus finally said. "The ash will help us, and with some luck the humans will not be affected. I'm not sure it's a great idea to even tell them at all."

The other boys' hard expressions did not change and I realized all of them felt the same way.

I stood up. "Have you forgotten who feeds you? Have you forgotten who will be looking at us once the smoke settles? The humans are everything in this plan. We need them to know that we acted with them in mind so after the vampires are gone or cured, we can settle into an easy alliance and pray that they still donate blood to feed all the ash."

Ryder was nodding now. "She has a point. It's good PR to let them in. We'll always need them."

Sam was looking at me in a calculated way.

"What?" I growled at him.

"The crooked government officials would spill our plan and ruin it…"

I began to protest but he shut me up.

"BUT … you have a point. We need to get the humans on our side. So, I have a plan…"

Sam with the plan. Always. He stared at the grass for a minute and I could see the wheels turning in his head. Then he grinned.

"Out with it!" I prodded him.

"We get a hold of the blackmail files and start making the crooked politicians work for us. Just until this battle is over. Then we send it all to the press."

My mouth hung open. "You want to blackmail people?"

Oliver and Markus were nodding. Sam even smiled. "I do. It's the only way to ensure their silence."

Shit, those photos of that guy with the gag ball in his mouth, that stuff was awful. I didn't want the bad karma of dealing with that. But … we needed all the help we could get.

"How do we get the files?" I asked. Last time I checked they were in the basement of Portland Hive.

"Lucas," Ryder said. Our man on the inside.

My sweet vampire that had a major ashpire crush would do anything to help us.

Sam busted out his secure laptop. "I'll get word to him. If he can scan the files and upload them to my secret server, then burn the originals, we would be in business."

That was a lot to ask my vampire ally. We had already asked enough of him, but this could really seal the deal with the humans. If we could cut off all outside help and control the Hives fully, we had a shot at taking them all out.

"Okay let's do it."

We barely slept, Sam was up all night counting responses from the Hives on the network and communicating back and forth with Lucas on a secure server. Lucas had agreed to do it. He was going to have a trusted ash infiltrate the filing room so that it couldn't be traced back to him. He said things were getting rough in the Hive and that Fugly was getting closer to Tessa. I didn't like that shit. At all. I wanted to drive down there and get her ass out of the Hive, but obviously that wouldn't work.

Jared's buddy had already left to catch the morning waves, and as much as the golden-haired enforcer wanted to join him, he stayed with us so we could plan our next move.

"I think we should split up," Ryder said. "A few of us will meet with Zack, give him back the phone and make sure their Hive is up to date with the plan. Meanwhile, Charlie and some of the guys pack up our stuff here so we're ready to move out."

I glared, hoping he didn't think I was too stupid to realize what he was doing. Making sure he kept me safe in the beach house. Whatever.

"Move out where?" I asked. What was our next move?

Ryder's expression was calm, but his eyes were swirling. "While we wait for Lucas to get the files to us, we need to get a vampire or two to Becca so she can test the cure serum. We have to be ready to distribute it through the hospital systems before the Christmas shipments go out."

Sam nodded. "Becca tells me she has a few batches ready to go. But she does need some test subjects."

Well, that should be easy. Just kidnap a vamp or two and hope for the best.

When did this become my life?

Chapter 6

Ryder, Kyle, and Sam took off for the little café again. They had the secure device with them, and they hoped Zack would be there so they could figure out a way for us to communicate directly with him. That way he could keep the ash around the world updated as the plan progressed. Sam said the phone had locked him out again. Zack had allowed us our one chance to post and now he was back in control. I knew the silent enforcer was impressed with that. "Always have a backup plan" was his motto.

After they left, the rest of us sat around, waiting. Markus, Oliver, and Jared were better at it than I was. They were soldiers, and knew when to burst into action and when to conserve their energy. Meanwhile, I was a mess of worry. Tessa, Lucas, Becca. Every single one of them occupied a huge part of my mind as I tried to figure out how this was all going to play out.

Bouncing on the couch, I turned to them. "What's the plan to kidnap vampires? How the hell are we going to get them back to Alaska? I mean, the airlines might notice if we drag gagged, cuffed, and unconscious vamps onto the plane."

Markus flashed me a broad grin, before chuckles escaped from him. "Ah, lass, you're good for this old ash's heart. I think Sam plans on chartering a private plane and flying us all out again. There's a settlement of vampires in Canada which we'll target."

Okay, that made sense.

"So vampires to Becca first, then files from Lucas, then get the cure to the blood banks, then we alert the humans and shit." My words were fast and jumbled together, but for some reason I felt calmer when we had a timeline, when I could focus on the next task and know where it was all heading.

The boys exchanged grins. "Sounds about r—" Jared was cut off by an explosion ripping through the side of the house.

Everything moved in slow motion then as I ducked, hands flying up to protect my ears. Something heavy hit me from the side. Pain shattered through me as I was slammed into the floor, someone over the top of me in a protective pose.

A tinny, high-pitched noise was reverberating through my head, and after a few moments I realized it was muffled screams. I was deaf from the explosion. The heavy weight lifted off me for a second, and then another blast rocked through the house. More heavy objects hit me hard, and on instinct I covered my head and squished myself into a small ball.

I was completely deaf now, so didn't hear anything as a grip like a steel band wrapped around my middle. I was yanked up and thrown across a shoulder. Whomever had me was huge, I could tell that much, but there was so much smoke and debris that I didn't know which one of my boys it was.

As we stepped out of the destroyed house, I winced as the sunlight cut into me. My gritty and burning eyes slammed shut for a few moments, but worry that someone might be hurt had them flying open again. It was then that I saw the clothes. The dude who had me was not Jared, Markus, or Oliver. They had all been in California casual. This one wore all black, and I recognized the ninja style garb.

Fuck. Sanctum. A fucking Sanctum ninja was kidnapping me!

Despite the agonizing pain which was making itself at home in my body, I swung into action. My legs and arms moved at the same time as I slammed them both hard into my kidnapper. I didn't exactly take him by surprise; he seemed to be expecting something, because he barely flinched, but his grip did loosen for a second and I used that to elevate my upper body and slam my elbow down into the back of his neck.

Noises were still muffled; only the occasional high-pitched sound was making it through, but I felt him groan beneath me. His body started to lift and we were running. I sensed there were others around us, but I couldn't see anything from where he had me pressed down. Fighting and screaming as hard as I could, I found a gap in his ninja outfit and gouged at the skin. Biting and clawing was chick fighting, but I wasn't in the best position for anything else right now.

Or was I?

Markus had shown me a few self-defense moves for situations like these, but it was so hard to remember with the cloudiness of my head and the adrenalin coursing through my veins. I knew my life depended on it though. Once Sanctum were through delivering me to whomever hired them this time, I'd be dead. I had to fight now while I still had a chance.

Giving myself a second, I let my body relax, almost as if I'd passed out. The grip on my body did not ease; these guys were professional through and through. Dropping my hands, I grabbed a hold of the material below, hoping like hell this wasn't a one-piece outfit. A sob of relief left me when I felt the give as the material rose. I kicked out again, utilizing the small movement I had in my legs. My hope was that he'd focus on my kicks and not realize what else I was doing. Kicking again, I pulled up the back of his shirt as hard as I could. When I had it near his neck, I snaked my arm along the front of his throat, and grabbed onto the shirt on the other side, effectively freeing my upper body so I could lock my arms and start to choke him, using his own shirt as leverage.

He ground to a halt and we struggled for a few moments. I kept my grip as tight as possible around his throat, and at the same time kicked off hard from his shoulder and surprisingly enough he released me. I slammed into the ground. Scrambling on the road, I looked about, hoping like hell someone was around to save me. But there was nobody but the five ninja dudes now circling me. Shit.

Yep, five. Because I had a chance to even take down one of these highly trained mercenaries.

The one I'd choked out was straightening his clothes, glaring at me. He had a mix of Western and Asian features, and I would classify him as beautiful but deadly. He opened his mouth, saying something, but my ears still weren't working properly. All I could think was escape, get away.

I didn't scream again, no point really; the explosion would have been heard for miles and any help was heading in that direction. Instead, I got to my feet, as steadily as I could. None of the mercenaries moved closer, and the beautiful one was still trying to talk to me.

Screw this. "I can't hear you because you decided to blow up a house that I was inside."

No idea if I'd shouted that or just spoke. I did know that anger had my chest heaving, and fear had the blood in my veins running icy cold. Were the other guys okay? The enforcers. No one had followed us, which gave me a very bad feeling. Shit. I really hoped Ryder and the others got back soon; there was every chance that if they could get medical attention and blood to the boys, they'd be okay. They had to be okay.

After my shouted statement, and flipping him off, the Sanctum guy stepped forward. I raised my hands up and prepared for a fight. Of course, I should have known he was nothing more than a distraction, as a small prick hit the side of my neck. I brushed at the jabbed area, and knocked off whatever little dart had hit me.

Oh crap. Crap, crap, crap. This was going to kill Ryder. My heart stilled then, and as the sedative pumped through my veins, I let the enforcer's image enter my mind. I couldn't leave Ryder; we had such a short time together and I wanted more. So much more. I wanted forever.

I held on to his image as long as I could. Tendrils of foggy darkness closed in around it and I fought with all my will. But there was nothing I could do, and as I slumped forward, a single tear trickled from my eye as the blackness took me.

My first thought upon waking was, "I'm not dead!" Then a raging headache slammed into me and I groaned, fighting through the fog like a thick blanket. Wait ... I'd heard that groan. My hearing must have healed in the time I'd been unconscious. How long had it been? Damn, I hoped my boys were okay. I wondered what the odds were that I'd see any of them again.

Ready to bust out of wherever I was being held, I struggled to open my eyes and finally managed to do so, sitting up.

Okay ... what the eff? I was in a super fancy hotel room suite. Weird place to bring someone to kill them. Death in style, what a way to go.

The door was open a crack and I heard the TV on in the other room. My eyes darted all around as I tried to plan my escape. The idiots hadn't tied me to the bed! I wasn't even cuffed. I assumed the window to the left of the bed would be sealed shut. All hotels were. Probably for this very reason ... they didn't want me jumping out of it. The bathroom to my right was windowless. Crap.

Should I rush whomever was outside the room, hoping to take them by surprise? Or pretend to still be passed out, and when they checked on me rise from the dead and take out as many as I could?

"Princess is up."

Eyes appeared through the crack in the door and I groaned. Element of surprise gone already.

Popping to my feet, I stood on the bed, fists raised. No one took down Charlie without a fight. One of them kicked the door open, and upon seeing me on the bed he smiled. They all shuffled in one by one, dressed in black, and I realized I was still with Sanctum. Were they retrieving me for someone or was this my last stop?

A figure stepped forward and I recognized Laz, the creepy shithead who had kept Jayden captive in my apartment. That POS was on my list. And my list was not a place anyone wanted to find themselves.

Black eyes with a sliver of silver flashed at me. He threw both hands up in front of him. "Calm down, Princess, we're here to talk about a truce," Laz said.

I wasn't falling for that shit. I didn't lower my hands. "Yeah right. You want the millions the vampires put on my head."

He nodded. "I won't deny that in the past that was true. We're mercenaries. We work for whomever can pay us the most money. It's what we've had to do to survive in a world where vampires dominate. But now … well, now we know you're the cure."

Shit. My tongue was stuck to the roof of my mouth. I don't know how long I was passed out for but I needed blood soon.

"I'm the cure … so what? If you wanted a truce you wouldn't have blown up our house. You could have done something civil like … I don't know, knock on the damn door!"

For the first time frustration crinkled his face, and with a sigh he ran his hand through his hair. "We tried that in Alaska and you killed our scout."

I saw red again, anger bursting from me in a torrent of curses. "You set fire to our friend's barn! Stop destroying shit and we might stop killing you."

One of the other guys stepped forward. "So if Toby had knocked on the door you would have welcomed him inside for a chat?"

Well, shit, he had a point. I didn't reply, just groaned. We had such bad beef with these guys that anytime we saw them we just killed on sight. My head was pounding way too hard for this conversation, and I was really worried about the sexy six. If these morons had hurt any of them, they could forget a truce. We'd have a damned war.

Laz opened his hands. "Here's the deal. We've heard about your plan on the network and we want in."

Fucking Sanctum was on the network? FAIL. Zack needed to rethink his security measures. I knew it was supposed to be for ash, but these guys were not the sort of ash you wanted to share secrets with.

"Why should I trust your bullshit? Last time I saw you, you had a gun to my best friend's head."

He shrugged. "Last time you saw me it was in my best interest to capture you for millions of dollars. Now it's in my best interest to help you take out the vampire race."

"Why?"

Everyone had a motive. I wanted to know his.

He gestured to his buddies. "It's clear that the ash are the superior race. Vampires can't go out in the sun, can't eat food, and need too much human blood to survive. I want to be on top of the food chain, where I belong."

Okay, I didn't exactly agree with that motive, but we could use all the help we could get.

"You're going to have to prove your loyalty then." I crossed my arms, tilting my chin in defiance. I wanted these ninja bitches to work for it.

He nodded. "We are up for any task you assign."

Okay, now that's the kind of talk I liked to hear. Was this really happening? Was I partnering with the Sanctum? I searched my brain for what we really needed help with. "We need to infiltrate Cellway, lace the bottles with cure, and then be able to deliver them to the Hive-approved blood-distributing hospitals. The Californian and Texan ones, plus all the international. Can you help us with any of that?" With the Sanctum's help, we might be able to do all this with minimum human casualties, and much more smoothly.

He nodded. "We already have a man in management of Cellway. He will start the paperwork for the enforcers as warehouse workers and delivery drivers. That part is easy." Apparently Sanctum was both evil and resourceful. "It will take us about a week to get our men into the Hive-certified blood banks and hospitals around the world. But it won't be a problem."

As easy as that, apparently. We'll see.

He reached in his pocket and pulled out a cell phone and tossed it up toward me. I caught it. "It's untraceable. We'll be in touch," he told me, and they parted, making room for me to step down.

"One more thing," I said. "If any of my boys are hurt, you're dead."

Laz suppressed a grin as if he thought I wasn't capable of killing him. "None of your pretty boys are dead."

Relief exploded in my chest. This whole thing was really unnecessary. Couldn't they have, like, taped a note to the door or something?

He stuck out his hand. "On my honor, I call a truce on behalf of the entire Sanctum. Don't try to kill us if you see us around."

I reached out and shook his hand, not sure how much honor he had. "I accept your truce and I expect you to pay for rebuilding my friend's house." I kept his hand in a firm grip.

"He's just a human. A bottom feeder."

Oh hell no. This guy was a mini-Hitler in the making and I had just aligned with him. Fuck.

"Leave the bottom feeders alone," I stressed.

Our eyes remained locked for many moments; he was sizing me up, but I would not break. Eventually he just nodded and we broke apart.

Why did I have the feeling this might come back to bite me on the ass in a couple years? Oh well, I'd worry about it then.

"Where am I? I need to get back to my boys," I said as they started to head for the exit.

Laz turned back to me. "You're at a hotel about five miles from the surfer's house. Your *boys* are in room 514."

My eyes widened. "We're in the same hotel as them? Do they know?"

He just grinned. "Nope."

Shit. These guys really were a force to be reckoned with. They freaking kidnapped me, followed the enforcers to the hotel, and then set up shop right next to them while I slept off my dart hangover. If anyone was going to have the skills and resources to infiltrate the hospital, it was Sanctum. I did not like or trust them, but we had a common goal, so we would tolerate each other. Despite everything that had happened, this might actually be our lucky day.

"We'll be in touch," he said, tapping the phone in my hand.

I just nodded, mentally urging them to GTFO. I needed to see Ryder and everyone. Make sure they were all okay. As soon as they were gone, leaving behind no trace that they'd even been there, I left the room. In the hall I saw that I was currently on the sixth floor, room 614. I chuckled. These smooth-ass fuckers had even got the room right above Ryder and the boys. Probably spying through the vents or some shit.

I started jogging down the hallway, sluggish and thirsty as hell, trying to keep my eyes down in case I encountered a human. Finding the exit door I plowed through it and pretty much threw myself down the stairs, emerging onto the fifth floor. It took me no time to find room 514.

I banged on the door like a cop about to do a raid. "It's me!" I shouted, and one second I was banging and the next Ryder was filling the doorway, assaulting me with all of his hotness.

I drank in the sight of him, his rugged features, sexy tousled hair and blazing silver eyes. For a few moments today I'd been sure I'd never see him again, and standing there, both of our gazes locked, I drank in every inch of him. My heart swelled, and it almost felt like it wasn't large enough to contain all of the emotions exploding through me.

Ryder reached out a hand then; his eyes were wide. He looked speechless. His thumb brushed down my cheek and his lashes fluttered, as if he couldn't believe I was standing right in front of him. I almost couldn't believe it. Without a sound his arm lowered and his hand cupped around my shoulder as he pulled me into his body. His palms began running over my back like he was inspecting my body, making sure I was all in one piece.

I tried to reassure him: "I'm fine. Sanctum didn't hurt me. They want a truce," I said.

He still hadn't said anything and something told me he was too pissed to speak. He just pulled me tighter into him and squeezed me within an inch of my life, burying his face into the side of my neck. I was pretty sure he was smelling my hair.

Finally, after we stood like that for many moments, he said, "I'll kill them all."

I heard murmurs from behind him, and knew the other boys were back there and in full agreement.

I sighed and he released me. "You can't. We need them."

Another voice broke through the tension between us: "What happened? Tell us everything." It was Sam. The enforcer seemed to be thinking a little more clearly, and with one last brush of my hand along Ryder's arm, I stepped into the room. My eyes alighted on five faces. Each and every one of my family was unharmed.

"They blew a hole in the side of the house and kidnapped me. Tranq-darted me with what I can only assume was that AT20 stuff you guys were talking about."

Ryder was pacing now, fists clenched.

"And then I woke up—"

"Where? Where are they?" Ryder was seeing red, his anger too large to be contained. I had to find a way to get through to him.

Before I could say anything else I finally noticed the room beyond the enforcers. The far wall, which must have been where the television and chairs were originally situated, was now completely stripped and had been turned into a board of Charlie. Surveillance shots of my face were seriously everywhere, along with lots of maps, papers, and other paraphernalia. There were these long strings connecting things across the place, and large red dots which were clearly checkpoints.

Seriously, I could have only been gone a few hours and already they had the mother of all police boards going on there. I took a few steps closer.

Markus' brogue washed over me: "Sam was hacking into all the security footage around the streets where we were. We had narrowed it down to this area, which is why we checked into this hotel. We were regrouping before tracking them down."

I couldn't stop myself from crossing to the burly enforcer and throwing my arms around him. My voice started in a hurry, words spilling over each other: "I'm so glad you're all okay. I was so worried. You guys were definitely tracking them in the right direction – they had me one floor above you." I barely stopped to breathe, it was so important to get it all out.

"They knew I was the cure. Probably before half the vampire world did. They sent that guy out to Alaska to draw us out, to discuss a truce. He was supposed to get us out in the open so we didn't go nuts and attack him before he could talk to us. Of course that didn't exactly work out when we totally freaked about the barn and hunted him down." Releasing Markus, I turned and sank tiredly onto the couch. It had been a long day. "Then they saw our message on the network. They want to help take down the vamps." I pulled the cell phone from my pocket and gently laid it on the small table off to my right. "This is the phone we'll use to communicate with them."

Markus groaned. "That Sanctum spy in Alaska, he kept saying 'ally' to me." I did remember the spy murmuring something. "So that's what he was talking about. I thought he was faking, that it was a trap."

Ryder seemed to relax a little. "I did wonder why they left Markus alive. That wasn't their normal MO, and the scout could have easily taken him out. Still, why would we truce with the devil? Sanctum should never be trusted."

Okay, it was clear Ryder didn't think too highly of them. And since he was the one who knew them the best, I felt we needed to heed his warnings.

Kyle crossed the room to crash in next to me, his long arm slung around me. "This isn't the worst thing that could have happened," he said. "We're wanted criminals within the Hives. Sanctum have stealth and the numbers to get around easily. They also have many more connections than we do. But why are they helping us?"

Ryder was the one to answer: "They're elitists. They have always seen the humans as the bottom of the food chain and the ash on top."

I nodded. "That's pretty much what Laz said. He believes ash are superior even to vampires, and he hates the way they control us." Ryder locked eyes with mine, and even from across the room the air practically sizzled between us. He was still furious about what happened, and only time was going to allow him to release the fury. "Sanctum has a man in

Cellway. They're going to get us in as workers and delivery drivers. So that part of the plan should go smoothly. Laz also assured me that his people can infiltrate the hospitals. They have the skills and numbers, and that was always the biggest risk in our plan, the part where failure was a true worry. Someone noticing the cure in the bottles and informing someone."

Jared was uncharacteristically somber, standing near the board which detailed the last few hours of my life. "Can we trust something like this to mercenaries who can be bought off?"

I shook my head. "We trust no one, but it's the best plan we have right now. And that's also why I want us to be the ones to get the cure into the bottles and transport them to the blood banks. We can at least keep an eye on some aspects of the plan. Hopefully Sanctum can just be used to make it that much easier."

"What's your gut saying, Charlie?" This was from Oliver, the more intuitive and gentle of the enforcers. "You spent time with them. Heard them speak of a truce directly. Do you believe they are double-crossing us?"

I worried at my lip for a moment, wondering if my next words might be the downfall of us all. "I believe they're legit. We have a common goal, and they have a multitude of very large reasons to want the same thing as us. Of course we'll also be wiping out their largest predator from the food chain, so I think they're going to be a problem for us in the future, but right now I think they're honestly going to help us."

Ryder finally crossed to me and I could tell he'd held out as long as he could. I was hauled up off the couch, Kyle's arm falling as I found myself in Ryder's lap. His warmth enveloped me, and on instinct I relaxed into him, our bodies fusing together in something that was both sexual and comforting.

His chest lifted beneath me as his low voice filled the room. "Charlie has good instincts on this, so for now we trust her. It's time for us to get back to Alaska, pick up some vampires for testing, and get this cure ready to roll. This is the last time I want to worry about any one of you. It's time to end it."

Here's hoping Becca was ready for us to deliver her an early Christmas present. Trussed up vampire was the perfect gift under the tree, right?

Chapter 7

"Uh, guys, I really don't need this many test subjects."

Becca stood out the front of her hidey-hole cabin. She looked thin and tired; her eyes had dark circles that would have been driving my BAFF insane. There was two things Jayden detested, and that was unkempt eyebrows and uneven skin tone. Poor Becca had probably lost her mind listening to him fuss over her for the past few days.

Sam's eyes were locked on the ragged ashpire as he untethered the five vampires he had strapped to the roof of his snowmobile. As I jumped out of the buggy I'd shared with Ryder, I stretched my legs and back. We'd been traveling for at least a billion hours. Flights out of Cali, then a private plane, then vampire hunting – which I was annoyingly excluded from – and then finally the huge ass trip to this tiny speck of civilization.

Sam had not been kidding when he said his bugout place was isolated. We'd driven for a long time in our snowmobiles. Would have been quite the sight with five vampires strapped to the roof, but luckily there was nobody out here to see us.

"Better to have too many than too little," Ryder said to her.

It was nearing midnight and the sauce that Jared and Sam had concocted to make the vamps groggy would be wearing off soon. Turns out AT20 could be home brewed. It involved blood wine, sinus decongestant, and some other weird shit I didn't recognize. My hand went to my neck where the Sanctum had darted me and I shivered, thinking of that drugged feeling.

After helping the boys load the creepy vamps into the basement of the charming 1920s hunting cabin, I collapsed onto the couch.

"I could sleep for a week," I moaned to Jayden.

All of the boys were downstairs securing the vamps with bolts and chains. Becca was in her makeshift lab making tiny final corrections to her formula.

Jayden was grinning and giving me this crazy look.

I groaned. "What? I'm too tired for your games."

Jayden leaned forward, positively bubbling with excitement. "Becca and Sam hooked up one dark snowy night two years ago."

I sat up quickly, almost cracking him in the face. "Shut up!" I whisper screamed. "You got that out of her?"

Jayden nodded. "Best sex of her life. Only sex really, and then she wakes up and realizes it was all a mistake."

My mouth dropped open. I was totally in love with Ryder, but damn, I didn't think sleeping with Sam would be a mistake. Boy had it going on.

"What? She's loony."

Jayden nodded, picking at his cuticles. "She realized he was her very best friend in the whole world and didn't want to ruin that."

"Ughhh." Those two were the worst. One of them afraid of ruining the friendship and the other one afraid to have any liabilities to be used against him.

Whatever. Totally not my business. I could stay out of it … maybe. Okay, probably not.

Becca came out of her lab then and I threw myself backward on the couch.

"Hey, what are you guys—"

"Nothing!" I blurted, and Jayden snort laughed. Becca looked confused. Shit, I was such a bad liar.

She let out a few uncomfortable chuckles. "Okay, well, if you're doing nothing, do you want to help me prepare the samples? I need an assistant or two."

I jumped up. "Yep. Sure."

I really wished Jayden hadn't told me about the hot sex. Now I couldn't stop thinking about it. Taking a few deep breaths, I made a concerted effort to put it to the back of my mind.

"So..." Becca said as we entered her makeshift lab. "I have three candidates for the cure that I'm ninety percent sure will work, and two that are fifty-fifty."

I could see a bunch of beakers and empty syringes lying around. "Okay, tell us what we should do."

She nodded, and over the next hour Jayden and I helped her label the cures one-five and put them into the syringes. Only at the last minute did she add some type of stabilizing compound I didn't understand.

After we were done she stared at the five syringes and chewed a fingernail. The liquid inside was clear and it amazed me that with one bag of my blood she was able to extract the cure and turn it into this vaccine of sorts.

"Okay," she said.

"Okay," Jayden and I echoed.

I realized then how much pressure we had put on her. Here we were making this entire plan for curing the vampires and setting up the network and spreading the word and she hadn't even figured out the cure yet.

She grabbed the labeled syringes and slipped them into her pocket, and as we turned to leave she picked up a tiny handheld camcorder with tripod and handed it to Jayden.

Crossing through the hallway, we made our way down a dim and narrow set of stairs and into the dark, creepy, freezing basement. The walls were cement and the fluorescent lighting cast eerie shadows on the tied-up vampires before us.

The vampires were chained to various things. Two were on the steel drain pipe, two on the water heater, and the other one chained to a large stabilizing column.

"They're all yours, Becks," Sam told her, and my heart pinched at the endearing tone in his voice. She pulled out the syringes and motioned to Jayden to turn on the camera. He set it up and began filming her.

"I'm Dr. Rebecca Leander and this is trial one of the vampire cure," she told the camera.

Whoa, it didn't hit me until now how monumental it was that we were curing an entire race.

Becca walked to the first vampire, a scraggly male who was moaning softly. "Subject one will receive cure number one."

She pulled out the syringe with a one on it and inserted it into the man's vein at the elbow. His eyes flew open and his mouth widened as he bared his fangs at her. Before anyone could act, Sam was there blindingly fast, ripping Becca out of harm's way.

The two shared an intense look for a moment, and finally Sam spoke: "How about I inject them?"

Becca gave a slight smile and nodded. Sam proceeded to inject the other vampires with the other cures.

Before we had tied them up, Becca had taken blood from each one of the subjects and written their subject number on their arm in black permanent marker. She was meticulous in documenting everything that was happening, every step of the way.

Now she stared at all of the subjects, lost deep in thought.

"What now?" I asked eagerly.

"Now we wait."

Jared, Sam, and Markus stayed downstairs while the rest of us went upstairs to wait it out. Becca headed back to her lab to test the subjects' blood for God knows what, and I was staring at the lines of worry crossing Ryder's face. Sleep was going to take me soon; I hadn't had a good night's sleep since we left on the trip to California, and here, safe in this cabin on this old comfy couch, I felt my eyelids drooping. But I was worried about my boyfriend.

"What is it?" I asked him softly.

He seemed to consider my words before turning to me. "The enforcers that the vampires killed back in the Hive... I recruited every single one of them. I brought them to their deaths."

By mutual agreement, none of us spoke of those who'd been killed. We couldn't deal with that and with everything else that was happening. But it was never far from my thoughts. Clearly Ryder's either.

My heart aching, I grabbed his hand. "Ryder, you can't do that to yourself. It's not your fault. Ash don't have many choices in the Hive. It's enforcer or some other dead end job, which could also get them killed by a vampire. That's why we're doing all this. To give ash a chance at a real life."

He didn't seem to buy my words but he did attempt to give me a reassuring smile. One which did not even come close to reaching his hardened eyes. "I need retribution for them. The thought that they were slaughtered like that ..."

Shit. He was right, and there was nothing I could say to make this easier. I squeezed his hand and snuggled myself closer, trying to offer him comfort. Eventually, I lost the battle with my eyelids, and surrounded by Ryder's warmth, I fell asleep. My dreams were filled with blood and loss.

I awoke to screams. Heart pounding in my chest, I was up and off the couch in seconds, completely disoriented and looking around to get my bearings. On the floor close by were Markus and Oliver curled in their sleeping bags, dead to the world.

The screams came again and I grabbed my gun, taking the stairs to the basement three at a time. When I turned the corner and the scene came into view, I cringed.

One of the vampires – number two – was thrashing and screaming, surrounded by a pool of bloody looking vomit. The other vampires were watching with calculated looks. Sam and Ryder had guns drawn, and Becca was frazzled trying to put something together with Jayden.

"It's a reaction. His version of the cure was too potent and his immune system is going haywire, attacking itself."

"What did you do to me, you bitch?" the vampire screamed, and his eyes were bloodshot; lines of broken capillaries filled the whites and even some of the silver. Sam took two paces forward and the butt of his gun came down on the back of the vampire's neck. Lights out. One of the other vampires was watching with a look of unease. He was frowning and ... was that fear in his eyes? I peered closer and I could see his eyes were less silver. Subject three was written on his arm.

"Becca, he's healing," I blurted out and pointed to number three. Becca looked up from her tray and with her laser-like focus started doing her science observation thing. The silver-black irises beneath her fake glasses were practically glowing. She handed Sam a syringe. "Give this to him," and motioned to the guy he'd just knocked out.

Subject three backed up as Becca walked closer. "What's going on?" he asked.

Becca smiled. "We're going to cure you."

His mouth popped open and I saw the shock register. "I heard rumors but…"

Becca shifted the camera around so that it focused on test subject three. "How do you feel?"

He rolled his neck. "Achy. Hot. Tired. Hungry…"

Becca and I shared a look. Holy shit, he said hungry not thirsty. I looked at Ryder, hoping to share the excitement, but all I saw was an emotionless face, dark circles under his eyes and nobody home. What was happening to him? I knew he was struggling with the death of his enforcers, but this was really taking a toll. Had he slept at all when I passed out on him? In fact, I couldn't remember the last time I'd seen Ryder even go to sleep. I always seemed to crash before him, and he was up before I got up too.

I was distracted for a moment as Becca crouched next to number three. "I'm going to take a blood sample, okay?" Her voice was low and calm. A few of the other vampires were pulling against their chains, fighting whatever was going on in their bodies, but he just nodded.

Jayden stepped up. "I'll get blood bottles for the assholes and a sandwich and water for the nice one."

Hilarious. Jayden had impeccable timing. Becca just dismissed his comment with a nod of her head, and he turned to run upstairs.

I slipped in beside Ryder. "You look tired. Get some rest. I'll take over now." We had at least three enforcers down here at all times with guns and a Taser. Electricity was a good way to take out a vampire for a short time. We also had some more of that homebrewed AT20. Worst case, we could always break their necks.

Wow, never thought I would say that.

Ryder just shrugged. "I'm fine. I can't sleep."

Dammit, I didn't like that tone. We had been so busy trying to get to the Californian Hive and steal these vampires, I had neglected to see the signs that were wearing Ryder down. His entire enforcer team had been slaughtered and we didn't even have a funeral for them. Their bodies were probably unceremoniously burned.

Becca was done now and she met subject three's gaze. "If you're feeling better by tonight, we can untie you."

He nodded.

"Untie me too," one of the vampires said, his voice growly. "I like my blood warm."

His gaze was making me uncomfortable, and he wasn't even looking at me.

"That's not happening," Jayden said, coming into the room holding the tray of blood bottles and food. "You will drink this cold and bland, just like the rest of us."

Becca looked at subject one, who had just spoken. "He can't help it. His oxytocin was practically nonexistent." That was her way of calling him an asshole. So damn polite. We really needed to do something about that.

Shuffling back so Jayden could get to the vampires, a waft of stale clothes from a zillion hours traveling hit me. Since it looked like they were okay down here for now, I needed to get changed. "I'm going to go shower," I said to Ryder, and he just nodded.

My heart was clenching in my chest as I walked up the stairs. I couldn't shake the awful feeling that this thing with Ryder was getting worse. He was pulling away from me and I had no idea how to stop him.

By the time full darkness had fallen, everyone was exhausted. Becca had been in her lab all day. Every three hours she was taking samples from subject three and reporting that his oxytocin was rising and the virus was virtually disappearing from his system.

Ryder was basically ignoring me. He went from outside perimeter watch, to a few hours' nap time, and then back to vampire test subject watch. I couldn't get a moment alone to pull him aside. Finally, just after dinner, Becca came charging out of the lab, grinning broadly.

"It's the cure!" she said, waving some papers in the air.

I was playing cards with Markus. We both threw them down and stood.

"Number three?" I asked.

She nodded. "It was one of the ones I put fifty-fifty odds on. I expected that this cure wouldn't bind properly to the white cell, or not long enough to enact a full body response. But it did! Subject three is permanently cured in less than twenty-four hours."

Holy shit. I let her news sink in. We had a cure for the Anima Mortem virus.

"Can we mass produce this here?"

She seemed to consider. "I'll need some of my bigger machinery down at the main lab."

Ryder's voice came out of nowhere. "I'll take her."

I turned, frowning. "I can come too."

Ryder waved it off. "I'll take her and load up the snowmobile and we'll be right back. Nightfall is the perfect cover."

Markus shared a look with me but didn't push it.

"Fine." I shrugged, pissed off and worried. Mostly worried. Yeah, the snowmobiles were small, and if she was lugging big equipment up here, there wasn't really room for me too, but I didn't like this feeling that Ryder was deliberately avoiding me. Felt like we'd jumped back to those early days when he was messed up about his fiancée. Ryder internalized too much, and carried too much guilt. I needed to find time to talk with him properly, but it clearly wasn't going to be now.

Becca gave Jayden some instructions. He had officially become her lab bitch – his words, not mine. Sam was still downstairs on vamp duty.

Ryder crossed the space and kissed me quickly on the cheek. "I love you, Charlie."

He dashed off then before I could say anything. I took a step after him, but he was already in the snowmobile with Becca, and then they were gone. I stood outside in the cold as everyone else trudged back inside. Jayden was on his way to release number three.

As snowy winds whipped around me, I crossed my arms over my chest, as if I could halt all of the fear and worry from tearing out of my heart. I couldn't stop thinking about Ryder's last words. The way he'd said it ... had my heart aching and my stomach tied up in knots. Initially I thought it was just because I hated that we would be so far apart, especially with the mental distance already between us. But as I stood there forever, the cold chilling me to the bone, I realized that the reason for the potent fear filling me was that his *I love you* had sounded a lot like *goodbye*.

Three hours after Becca left, she returned ... alone. The second she walked in with a note in her shaking hand, I knew.

"I couldn't stop him," Becca said, and tears lined her eyes. "He loaded the equipment and then drove me to the safety of the thick trees and then he—"

"Noooo!" The word ripped from my throat as I ran for the door. Becca's hand came out quickly. I paused long enough to see that the note she was holding was in Ryder's handwriting.

"For you," she said.

I could barely see through the tears overflowing down my cheeks. I knew that last "I love you" had been different. Fuck. This couldn't be happening. Why would he just leave us like that? We could have helped him.

Clutching the note, I forced myself to read it.

Charlie,

I'm not the man you fell in love with. The genocide of the enforcers has broken me. I can't sleep without seeing their blood spilling. We should have known that our anarchy would bring about more consequences than just for us. We never warned them and they paid the ultimate price. I can't live with my mistake one second longer. Leave no man behind. I failed them and I need to make up for it. Justice will be had.

I love you and I'm going to make it right.
I'll be back for you.
Ryder

I collapsed into a sobbing mess, and of all the people to close his arms around me it was Sam who held me tight and rocked my body.

"Shhhh, it's okay. We'll figure this out," he whispered in my ear as I clutched onto his shirt.

The pain settled over me, weighing my limbs down so that I could barely stand. That motherfucker. The love of my life just went off on a suicide mission. He was a badass, but one man couldn't take on the Hive, could he?

Heavy footsteps caused me to pull away from Sam and meet Kyle's wide eyes as he ran up the stairs.

"What's wrong? I heard you scream." Kyle was scanning me for wounds. He wouldn't see them; my wounds were internal. I couldn't even find the words, so I just thrust out the note.

The enforcer observed mine and Becca's drawn features as he took the note. As his eyes hit the paper, his face fell. When he was done he crumpled it up and threw it against the wall. His face was an agonized mesh of emotions, his eyes screaming. I knew Kyle would share my pain. All of these guys were close with Ryder, but Kyle and Ryder had a special bond. A lifetime of friendship.

Breaking away from Sam I stepped into Kyle's space. Our eyes met and something passed between us; no words were needed. Like the time we'd waited for hours in the hospital room, not knowing if Ryder would live or die, this was another moment for us, and I knew without any words that Kyle and I would get Ryder back.

Sam never missed a thing. "You can't go running off after him like idiots. We already risked ourselves once. Let's think this through."

I turned on Sam and I knew my eyes would be blazing silver. The fury and fear was filling me, washing away the tears and leaving pure bitch in its wake. "Ryder is not thinking clearly. If he was he'd know that storming into the Hive out of anger will only get him killed."

Sam put his hands out. "I know, and that goes for you too. Let's take tonight and think up a proper plan. Ryder is long gone, you won't catch up with him. I'd bet my life that he took the chopper. I showed him how to fly. He knows I have contacts that could get us another one if we needed it."

I felt sick. Ryder, alone in a chopper, hell bent on taking down the Portland Hive? FML. What was he thinking? Boys were stupid.

"In the morning we're leaving." I gestured to Kyle and myself. We all knew the others would have to stay. Becca and Jayden couldn't handle all those vampires alone.

Sam shook his head and I walked to the door. "I need some fresh air. When I get back, we figure out a plan."

I brushed past Becca and burst out the front door of our little remote cabin, taking off into the snow-drenched forest. I missed my running, the days when I could jog without a care in the world. Jumping over fallen logs, the anger subsided slightly, and with that there was a sliver of space for the pain to hit again. Crap. Tears started to flow.

As a girl with daddy issues, Ryder leaving me felt like total abandonment. I know he didn't think of it or mean it like that, but it tore a hole inside of me. It felt like the lives of his men trumped our future together, because even he must have realized the odds of making it out alive were slim. And why? We were so close to curing them all and ending this forever. But no, that wouldn't have been enough for Ryder. He had to make the Quorum pay. His men deserved this from him, and he would not rest easy until he fulfilled his vengeance. I just wished it didn't come at such a steep price.

Footsteps behind me caused me to slow my pace and turn. Kyle was barely winded, standing before me with blazing silver eyes. Neither of us were wearing a jacket and neither cared. The pain was keeping me warm for now.

"I've known Ryder since before I could walk. You're his soulmate and he would never hurt you on purpose. He isn't thinking clearly. He thinks he's protecting you."

His words just made me cry harder, because most of me knew he was right. I nodded as the tears fell down my cheeks and onto the forest floor. My wet lashes were starting to freeze on my eyelids.

"We'll get to him before he does anything stupid," Kyle promised, but I didn't see how that could be possible. I wanted to run out right now and be hot on his trail, but Sam was right. If my lead enforcer was hell bent on enacting revenge, than he couldn't do it alone and we needed a solid plan.

Kyle's arm came around me and we walked back to the cabin slowly. Every step I took away from Ryder made my gut tighten in anxiety.

Back in the cabin I began to load up my backpack for the trip to Portland. The second the twilight of day hit I was out of here. Going through my personal stuff my stomach dropped when I realized one very important thing was missing. I charged into the lab, where Becca was doing her science nerd thing and Sam was hunched over his laptop.

"Sam, please tell me you took the Sanctum phone from my bag?" My heart was pounding in my chest.

The look Sam gave me told me all I needed to know. That little fucker!

"So that's his plan. Get Sanctum to help him." I couldn't believe Ryder had stolen the phone from me!

Sam thought about it for a second, his head tilting to the side. "It's actually brilliant. We're days out from the plan going into place. Paperwork arrived this morning from Cellway. Our covers are assured. But Ryder is still worried about their loyalty. He's going to make them jump through a few hoops before the plan."

I growled, despite Sam making a lot of sense. I didn't want to see logic right now. Ryder took that phone and left me, that's all I saw. Although a part of me felt slightly better. Involving Sanctum meant this wasn't a complete suicide mission. Ryder really did plan on returning to me alive. Of course, I might kill him when I got my hands on him, so that would be redundant.

Sam's computer buzzed and he read something for a second and then grinned.

"Ryder is using the secure phone to contact us. This definitely wasn't as irrational as we thought. He seems to actually have a solid plan."

Becca stopped what she was doing now and I strode across the room, avoiding the wires and machines. "What does it say?"

Sam smiled. "He says: *I bet our little unicorn is fuming mad. It's safer this way, she's everything to me, tie her up if you have to but don't let her come after me. I'm not alone here, the plan is already in place.*"

My mouth opened at that last part and I found myself flexing my muscles, readying myself for his attack. Sam's eyes locked on me, and I could tell he was actually considering it. Ryder was still their leader, and they were used to his orders. I straightened, and started thinking of every self-defense technique Markus had taught me. I was going after Ryder, and none of these assholes were stopping me.

That's when Becca said, "Samuel! You can't be serious. What if I had run off on my own and said you shouldn't follow me?" She put one hand on her hip.

Sam's face was frozen in hard angry lines, as if the mere thought of Becca disappearing without him had his insides turning to ice.

"I'd kill anyone who got in my way of going after you, Becca. You know that. I'll always come for you."

Becca swallowed hard, clearly not prepared for the emotional depth of his answer. The fact that they had had sex once and never again continued to astonish me. The feels were real between them. I could practically see the attraction and emotion spiraling through the air.

Since it seemed Sam was not about to attack me, I left them to their eye-screwing and slowly crept out of the room. I needed to find Kyle. We were leaving, stat; Ryder was stubborn as hell but so was I. There was another ding from Sam's computer just as I was crossing the threshold.

Pausing, I turned around. "Tell him unicorn and BFF are inbound and I'll be the one tying him up later. And not in the fun way."

Sam smiled, and with a shake of his head turned back to his computer to read the note. His face fell. "Oh shit. Tessa."

Those three words were enough to bring my whole world crashing down.

Chapter 8

It was 5AM and I had barely slept. Every time I closed my eyes I saw Tessa in the pit being starved to death by Fugly, and Ryder being killed the second he stepped into the Hive. Lucas had written to tell us that Tessa was caught doing something suspicious against the Quorum and they threw her in the pit for a month. That was two weeks ago. He could only now get word. He said the entire Portland Hive had been turned into a military regime where Fugly's word ruled all. Any rebellion was met with the pit or death. Sounded like Tessa was lucky to get the pit, but something told me they still had plans for her. Plans which involved me.

Sam had called in a favor and got us new identification and a chartered private plane. Being rich really was awesome. Thank you, Deliverance.

I was itching to go. When Sam and Kyle entered the room, a burst of excitement flooded me. We might be finally ready to go.

Sam looked at Kyle and they seemed to be considering something, then I saw the scissors in Sam's hands. Both ash faced me.

"Hey, Charlie … how attached to your hair are you?" Sam asked.

Oh hell no. "How attached to your penis are you?" I countered, hands on hips and eyes narrowed.

Kyle tried to hide his laugh but couldn't.

Sam groaned. "It won't be long before the humans know there's a cure. My gut says that your picture could be plastered all over the news by sundown. I've got you new passports, but a new look would really give you guys a fighting chance."

Shit. Was he serious? I loved my long hair. I wasn't overly vain in that type of way, but it took me forever to grow it out from this horrendous bowl cut I had in middle school. Not to mention my jaw was wide and short cuts didn't look good on me. But dammit, Sam had a point. I couldn't go walking around like this much longer and expect not to be noticed.

I just nodded. "Fine. Just do it."

My hair was in a low ponytail at the base of my neck. It hung down my back past where my bra clipped. Sam gave me a sympathetic look and took a firm grip on my pony tail. I closed my eyes, telling myself to grow the fuck up and put my big girl pants on.

"PUT THE SCISSORS DOWN!" Jayden's voice boomed down the hallway and my eyes snapped open. My BAFF was looking at Sam in shock and clutching his chest.

"How dare you try to cut her hair so barbarically! Sam, for future reference, when a gay man is available, you always ask him to do these things."

My face lit up with a smile. Jayden would make sure I didn't have another "middle school bowl cut." Sam handed him the scissors and Jayden wasted no time in pulling out a dining room chair and placing a plastic bag over my shoulders.

"Okay, honey, do you want the Jennifer Aniston from *Friends* bob or short chunky like Charlize Theron?"

"Ohhh, Charlize, definitely," I said.

Jayden was in his element as he brushed out my hair and started to slice away. I nearly cried when I saw twelve inch strands falling to the floor, but ten minutes later I had a super cute short chunky hairstyle that actually looked good. Somehow he'd managed to accent my nicer facial features and hide those which were not so attractive. Like the fat chin ... it was looking positively slender.

Jumping to my feet, Jayden dusted me off, and when I was finally clear of my departed hair, I pulled my BAFF in for a hug. "Thank you for everything," I whispered. "I love you, and I'll do my damn best to return to you and to bring all of our boys back."

His grip was tight on me; his chest heaved a few times but he didn't speak. Something told me he couldn't. With a breathless "Love you," he took off into the house, and I fought the urge to follow him. His pain was my pain. But right now there was no time for either of our agony. We had a job to do.

Squaring my shoulders, I grabbed my pack and Kyle and I left. As we crossed those front porch steps, part of me knew I would never see this place again. I threw my pack into the back of the buggy, and Kyle was just about to jump into the driver's seat when I stopped him.

"My turn to drive," I said.

He gave me a lopsided grin before leaving the door open and crossing to the passenger side. The enforcers tended to be a little old school, thinking the dude drove while the lady emulated Ms. Daisy. Time to remind them that Charlie Bennett was no lady. She was a BAMF, and she was getting her guy back.

As the engine roared to life, the front door to the house smashed open. I turned to find the entire crew descending on us. Markus, Sam, Jared, Oliver, Becca, and even number three, who I was yet to officially meet.

They all spread out across the porch and each of their faces was somber. I lifted myself up out of my seat and through the open roof. I took a moment to examine all of them. My family. My team. The best damn people I'd ever have the luck to know.

"I love you guys!" I shouted. "Except for you, number three. You, I don't know." There was laughter all around as I blew them kisses and all of them returned the favor. Even number three, who at least seemed to have a sense of humor.

"Be careful, wee lassie," Marcus bellowed. "We'll see you very soon. We're heading off to Cellway as soon as Becca has the cure done. We'll meet you three once we have the trucks locked and loaded." His Scottish brogue was always stronger when his emotions were strong. Right now all of us were on emotional overload. But I liked that we were getting very close to the blood and cure being united as one.

With one final salute, I dropped back next to Kyle, and shifting the buggy into drive we took off. Snow shot out around us, and the air was freezing, but I barely felt anything. We were on our way to Ryder, and there wasn't a damn other thing that mattered.

It took most of the day to travel to the private airfield. Losing the chopper was a huge blow, but at least this chartered plane would take us straight into Portland. No more screwing around. Kyle and I carried our bags on board, and I was surprised to find this was the fanciest plane we'd been on to date. Wide-cushioned leather, captain-style chairs, plush carpets, huge screen television that was showing an action flick. If only I could enjoy it. I was in panic, lockdown mode.

"Charlie, calm down," Kyle said, his warm hand wrapping around mine to stop my fingers from drumming right through the arm of the chair. "We're close now. We know it's going to take Ryder and Sanctum time to get everything into place. I think we'll make it before they hit. Everything will work out. The other guys will meet us as soon as Becca has the mass cure."

I nodded a few times, my head bobbing rapid and jerky. "Yes, I know. But we're cutting our timing so short. The cure needs to be in that blood within a week, and right now it doesn't seem as if Sanctum is in position or anything yet."

Kyle's thumb rubbed across the back of my hand, over and over, the motion soothing. "Ryder would not jeopardize the plan. I know him, and there's no way he hasn't thought through every single facet of what he's doing. Trust in him, Charlie. Trust that he does the right thing no matter what. That's the guy you fell in love with. The one who cares. Too much. He has one of the best strategic minds I've ever encountered. That's why Sanctum wanted him originally. That's why he's such a good leader. He's got this."

My heartbeat calmed as Kyle's reassurance invoked a clarity which had been missing from me for days. Panic had eaten away at my common sense. The fact that Ryder had been so cold and distant, so emotionally wrecked before he left me, had caused me to forget the fundamental personality traits of the man I fell in love with.

"I trust him," I said. "He always does the right thing." My head drooped at little. "I shouldn't have lost faith in him."

Kyle chuckled. "Yeah, and he shouldn't have left without explaining that plan to us. He still needs an ass kicking, but you can keep your faith."

I snorted at that. "Oh, he's getting a butt kicking, don't you worry about that. Fugly has nothing on me when I'm pissed."

We settled back into the plush chairs then, the engines roaring around us as the plane began to taxi down the runway. Finally, we were on our way.

Portland was cold, but compared to Alaska I felt like I could walk around in a tank and shorts. The flight had been uneventful; our new identifications passed at the airport and car rental place without question. Kyle and I both wore sunglasses and contacts to hide our eyes. I even convinced Kyle to wear a little blush with me to look more human. The chill would be reddening the humans' cheeks and I wanted to blend in as much as possible. We needed to make sure no reports of ash traveling to Portland reached the Hive. They had their little spies everywhere. As we walked out into the cloudy parking lot, I pulled my hoodie up. I knew with that and my short hair, I was pretty incognito.

"Did Sam send coordinates for us?" I asked. He was using some sort of satellite frequency to track Ryder and the Sanctum. He hoped anyway.

Kyle powered up his phone, a special one from Sam. Then he frowned. "Nothing yet."

I sighed. "Alright, I know a place close to the Hive where we can camp out until we get word…"

Kyle nodded and we made our way into our rental car.

An hour later Kyle and I were sitting along the Willamette River. It was about 3 P.M. The Hive would be coming alive shortly, the vampires soon to be waking up to start their day. If Ryder was going to make a move, it would be in the next two or three hours. My leg bounced nervously on the grass as Kyle finished off his hot dog. I was trying not to think of Tessa. My sweet Tessa locked away in the pit enduring God knows what. Just before I was about to lose my mind, the phone in my hand buzzed. I unlocked it and read the text from Sam.

GPS shows Ryder at a house near you on Maple Grove. The address was at the bottom with a map.

"We got him," I told Kyle, jumping up as nerves and excitement thrummed through me. Ignoring the fact that Sam knew that the house was near me – I was tempted to look in the sky for cameras or drones – I clicked the map to open it. Ryder was only half a mile from where we were.

"We should drive," Kyle said, glancing over my shoulder at the map. Good point, we might need our car. I literally had no idea what we were about to get into.

It took us only a few minutes and then we were parking in front of a small Craftsman style house on Maple Grove

Street. Before I could say anything to him, Kyle jumped out of the car and began stalking up the front steps. Oh shit. I'd been assuming we would go in through the back and unobtrusively see what was going on. Or maybe have Sam tell Ryder we were here.

Nope. Apparently we were going in brazen as hell.

Kyle didn't look back once as I scurried after him, and I realized then how much he was hurting too. Ryder was his best friend and those enforcers had been his men too. All of the boys were suffering, and each of them had been doing it silently and alone. This was one area we'd fallen apart as a team. The moment we saw that video surveillance of the slaughter, we should have dealt with it. Together.

Anger was bubbling inside of me again. Ryder shouldn't have done this without us. He'd majorly fucked up and I was putting him on my naughty list this Christmas.

But first I needed to see he was okay.

Kyle banged on the door hard. "Ryder!" he shouted.

Since he was more than a little occupied in his pissed-offness, I kept an eye on our surroundings. There were no humans around; the neighborhood was almost too quiet for this time in the afternoon.

Unease filtered through me, and I took a step close to Kyle. This could be a trap; we didn't know Ryder was here, just that his phone was. There were footsteps and then the door opened.

It was Ryder, standing there wide-eyed in black fatigues, looking hot as fuck and pissed as hell.

He was pissed? Oh no, buddy, not happening. I stepped right up into his personal space.

"That's right. Operation Tie Charlie Up in the Basement With the Vampires failed!" Moving even closer, he backed into the doorway and I poked him in the chest. "We're a team, dude! You don't leave me behind EVER again or the only ass you'll be sleeping next to will be Kyle's."

His lips quirked the tiniest bit. "You cut your hair," he said softly.

Oh … yeah. I had forgotten about that.

Looking behind Ryder, I noticed we had an audience. A mishmash of a dozen Sanctum and a few of what looked like a human SWAT team. I recognized Lincoln immediately. Old Blue Eyes was in his element, surrounded by a wall filled with pin-ups of dozens of maps and pictures.

"Welcome to my home, come right in," Lincoln said with heavy sarcasm. We stepped into the house and closed the door.

Ryder met Kyle's eyes and it was a total staredown. Finally, Kyle spoke under his breath: "I understand leaving Charlie, but why me?"

Ryder looked vulnerable, his eyes shuttering as he fought for composure. "No one else gets hurt."

Kyle chuckled. "Aren't you a fucking hero."

Ryder clenched his jaw. "I didn't—"

Lincoln groaned, cutting Ryder off. "We don't have time for this! Either get in on the op or get out of my house."

Kyle brushed past Ryder and took his place with the rest of the men. Ouch. I was beginning to feel bad for Ryder now. Maybe we were being a bit hard on him; it was clear he only wanted to make sure none of us got hurt. But dammit I didn't want him hurt either. He'd put me through hell over the past twenty-four hours, and all because he thought he was the hero and could do this all alone.

Before I could decide what to do, Ryder's hand slipped in mine and he pulled me over to join the group. After scanning the faces of the newcomers, my eyes stopped on a tall redhead chick with huge amber eyes. She was completely sleeved with tats, gave off a don't mess with me vibe, and if I was being honest she was hot AF. She was a human, so she must have been with Lincoln's crew. Kyle had noticed her too and his eyes were definitely lingering on her.

Lincoln cleared his throat and we all looked up. "Ryder gave us intel late last night. I've been in briefings ever since and have had about zero hours of sleep, so don't fuck with me." A few of the Sanctum douches shifted in their seat, but strangely enough no one questioned Lincoln taking the lead. The SWAT leader continued: "Our orders are to help Ryder release one human girl, a Tessa Grace McNair from a place known as the pit, where she is being held in captivity." He held up a photo of her from about two years ago, which I was pretty sure I took. How the hell did Ryder get his hands on that?

And ... did Lincoln just say Tessa was human? I shifted on the spot, and Ryder squeezed my hand. Meeting his eyes, he gave the smallest shake of his head.

Holy hot damn. He'd lied. He lied to save my best friend and get him in the door so he could kill Fugly. It was brilliant and stupid all at the same time.

Lincoln was still in the midst of his update. The looks on the SWAT team's faces were menacing. "It's a direct federal violation to keep a human feeder against their will." Then Blue Eyes gestured to the Sanctum and Ryder: "These ash enforcers have agreed to go in on the job with us, since they know the inner terrain better than anyone."

My eyes cut across to Ryder again. My my, he'd been a busy guy, lying all over the place. Lincoln was going to kill him when he found out. I also found it quite offensive to have the Sanctum linked with my enforcers. They were nothing like the enforcers and never would be. But for now I'd play along.

Lincoln walked over to some high-powered rifles. "We've got some AT20, but that doesn't last long in a full-fledged vampire. If they're hostile, our orders are shoot to kill."

Ryder cleared his throat. "And by shoot to kill he means cut their heads off, burn them alive, or completely pulverize them."

I grimaced. Jesus. In the back of my mind I knew Ryder was doing this now because once Becca got the cure in everyone, they'd all return to cuddly oxytocin teddy bears and it would be hard to hate them. Ryder wanted Fugly to have his reckoning and I agreed. Even with oxytocin, something told me Fugly would always be evil.

Kyle remained stony-faced, even as the others in the room got to their feet and started to gear up. Kyle and I hadn't come with much. I was already wearing my black fatigues, so I wasted no more time in strapping on a few knives and finding myself a rifle.

"If I asked you to stay behind, would you?" Ryder's voice was soft and made my heart clench. He'd done absolutely everything he could to keep me out of this and we'd showed up anyway. But he couldn't bubble wrap me, that wasn't the girl he fell in love with. If I had to accept Ryder as he was, then I deserved the same. Plus, I would never leave my best friend in there.

I shook my head. "No."

Ryder made me look into his eyes. "What if I begged?" His hands went through my freshly chopped locks.

I tried my best to harden my resolve. He was doing that thing where he completely disarmed me. "Becca has the cure now, so if I die it won't matter."

Ryder's mouth thinned; his eyes went blazingly silver. He opened his mouth, but I interrupted before he could speak. "Hurts doesn't it? When someone you love has no regard for their own life."

He looked down at his boots and nodded. "Shit. I'm sorry, Charlie. Okay!"

I sighed, and then nodded. That would have to be enough, because the boys were suiting up big-time. Ryder realized it too. He switched straight into hardcore enforcer mode.

"Have you used one of these before?" he asked me, gesturing to the rifle.

I hadn't seen Ryder grab any weapons earlier, but I wasn't worried. Half the time he went to bed more armed than a drug lord fearing for his life. Just because I couldn't see them didn't mean they weren't there.

Gripping the heavy weapon, I shook my head. This model was not one I was familiar with, but it looked semi-automatic and hugely powerful.

Ryder then spent the next few minutes running me through the mechanics of the gun and how to reload it. I had refills of the sleek canister darts filled with the AT20, and some extra rounds of bullets. My handgun was bullets only.

The rifle was definitely heavier than I was used to. Ryder made sure I was able to sight my target properly, and how to adjust for the pull. I forced myself to pay attention because this gun was my chance to make it out of the Hive alive. Everyone in the vampire world was after me, and I was just going to bust right in and say "Here I am." But it was Tessa. And it was Ryder. I would do anything for those two. They already had the cure, so I was less important in the grand scheme of this plan.

Once everyone was ready to roll, Lincoln led the large group through the house and out into the back yard. We crossed the yard to stand before a dilapidated old shed. Luckily for me I was an ashpire, because the place looked like a tetanus epidemic waiting to happen.

The SWAT leader reached to the side of the door and flicked a cover off a panel of numbers. Quick as a flash – I was standing right behind him and couldn't follow along – he keyed in a bunch of digits. The door slid across with a whoosh. As we followed him inside, lights flickered on across a large warehouse space. Okay, seriously? This was like James Bond shit or something. The old tetanus shed was actually a state of the art hanger filled with cars, quads and a bunch of other military style machinery. No wonder the house was so tiny; this shed must have taken up the rest of the house block, plus the one behind. What a nicely hidden gem in the middle of suburbia. It must be linked to the industrial building I'd spotted next door.

We made our way right to the back, where a long line of SUV's waited. Each looked a little different, definitely reinforced, and I had no idea of their various makes, but they were all black. Black seemed to be the color of choice in this business.

"With this sort of mission, we hit them hard and fast so they have no time to regroup or prepare," Lincoln said. "Fill the cars. We'll take as few as we can."

There had to be forty soldiers in this room. Testosterone was high, especially since there were only two chicks, me and hottie tat girl. Although, she was not letting our sex down at all. With a rifle over her shoulder, and handguns on both thighs, not to mention the mini sword strapped to her right forearm, she was female badass goals.

I ended up in one of the middle cars, squished between Ryder and Kyle. I could tell the boys were going to stick close to me as much as they could. We all had our mission, sure, but we three were a team. Protect our own. Even if Kyle and Ryder were on the outs, they were always brothers. In the end, only six cars were needed to get everyone out of the garage and on the way to the Hive.

The ride was silent. Lincoln wasn't in our car, and none of the Sanctum were ones I knew – aka the assholes who had tranqued and kidnapped me. I shifted a little. Ryder's gun was jammed into my side, and unfortunately that wasn't a sexy euphemism.

Familiar landmarks flashed past me, and the tension within the SUV increased as we crossed the invisible boundaries of the town, which signaled we were heading for vamp territory. Shit. I really never thought I'd come back here, especially not before the cure was working its way through the Hive. As the large gated compound came into view, I straightened, and breathing deeply, prepared myself for the next few moments.

"Stay close to me, Charlie," Ryder murmured in my ear, his lips brushing against my skin. Tingles rocked through me and I swallowed hard, hoping this wasn't the last moment we had together.

"I love you," I said, my voice barely audible. "Even if you are on my shit list and sleeping in the doghouse for the next six months."

Ryder's grin was brief, but the sight was beautiful. "Love you too."

Our lips briefly touched. The front SUV smashed into the gates and with a huge crash we were through. Ryder had already spun to his window, which was now down. Every window was down in our car and I knew our assault was to start immediately.

Ash sprinted in all directions; it was too early for vamps to be on guard duty yet. There were so many, at least twenty. The numbers assigned around the perimeter had been seriously upped in our absence. Someone in the second car hung out the window and took out a few of those running toward us. The ash were getting tranqs, not bullets. They were going to be given a chance to survive, per Ryder's orders. Any vamps we passed definitely wouldn't get that same choice.

Ryder had his gun up now and was firing steadily. At least four or five went down in moments.

"They're warned now, and will be locking down the upper level vampires," Ryder said, yanking himself and his gun back in. "We have to take out the soldiers first to reach those who make the most impact. Do not hesitate. They're going to come at us hard."

Hard was actually an understatement. By the time the Sanctum guy driving our vehicle screeched to a halt beside the others, ash were pouring out of the front of the Hive. Inside, the vamps were hopefully still in their beds. The element of surprise was our best hope to get in and out cleanly.

Sirens blared to life then, and with that whooping sound we lost our element of surprise.

The ash before us weren't enforcers and weren't properly trained. The stupid vampires had taken out their best line of defense. But I did recognize Jose with a gun in his shaking hand. When his eyes met mine he lowered his weapon in confusion.

"Stop!" he screamed, holding up a fist.

Ryder jumped out of the SUV, with me hot on his heels.

"Ryder?" His name was being murmured around. A few ash had recognized us, and hope sprang in my chest as I saw them lowering their weapons, relief crashing over their faces.

"If you surrender, none of you will be hurt!" Ryder projected his words loud enough for all of them to hear. I could sense the bodies stepping into formation behind us as we prepared to charge the front door.

One of the ash close to us didn't seem too sure; he still held his weapon. "You left us to die. Why are you back?"

Ryder swallowed hard and I knew that tore him open. "Revenge."

I was hoping Blue Eyes wasn't in earshot, because getting Tessa out of here was supposed to be our cover.

"Is it true about the cure?" Jose – who was very close to me now – asked softly. Our eyes locked.

I nodded. "By next week, vampires won't exist."

Jose must have seen the intel on the network, because he accepted my assertion with no more explanation needed. He nodded and turned to the rest of the ash.

"Let them through!" he yelled, and just like that the ash parted and allowed us to walk through the front doors of the Hive.

Our easy run was short-lived, though, because the second we entered the foyer and headed into the dark stairwell, all hell broke loose. Vampires were raining down on us like a goddamn dog pile. They weren't retreating to their safe upper floors, they were fighting. They didn't trust the ash to guard them anymore, which was smart, but sucked for us.

"Ooofff." The wind got knocked out of me as a vampire dropped from above, landing half on me and slamming me to the ground so fast my chin cracked on the pavement.

Shots were fired, and in the close quarters it made my ears ring. Suddenly the weight on me lifted and a strong but feminine tatted-up arm was pulling me up. #lifegoals again. Chick was badass to the core.

"Thanks," I said, pulling my blade from the thigh sheath I wore.

She nodded, sticking close to me as she too pulled her blade. Together we cut our way through the mess of bodies to get to the door that led to the floor which had the elevator down to the pit. I was going for Tessa. She was my sole focus.

"Hit the deck!" Lincoln yelled, and without question I hit the ground as a small but powerful blast rocked the floor above us, slowing the onslaught of vampires.

When we were able to gain our feet again we tried the closest door. It was locked. Of course. Dammit, where was Sam when you needed him? Tattooed chick busted out some device and stuck it in the lock. She tinkered with it and I heard a beep and an airlock sigh. Well, how about that. Looks like we had our female version of Sam. Rocking the silent thing too. Looking over my shoulder I saw Ryder on the front lines fighting back to back with Kyle.

Go or stay? Go or stay? Ryder or Tessa? As if reading my mind, Ryder looked up for a fraction of a second and yelled. "Go! We'll hold them off you."

That's all I needed. I was barreling down the hallway with this chick and a few Sanctum and SWAT on my ass. *I'm coming, Tessa.* There was only one way in and out of the pit, and luckily it was on a separate grid to the rest of the Hive power. So they couldn't easily shut the elevator down. Here's hoping they hadn't figured out a way.

Using the hand signals Ryder taught me, I communicated with the others behind me about the potential for trouble as we passed the regular elevator and continued on to the gold-colored door. There seemed to be no vamps on this level. Either they hadn't expected us to try and gain access to the pit ... or it was a trap. Probably the second one knowing Fugly. He'd be expecting me to come for Tessa.

Power was still on at the elevator, but that also meant the security was too. Lucky for us, tattoo chick was not only a lethal weapon and lock picker, but she could hack too. Slipping some sort of electronic device from her pocket, she hovered it near the security keypad and within seconds we had access.

The elevator doors opened easily and I stepped inside with the six others. Which actually included Blue Eyes. I hadn't noticed him until right now. Go observation skills. Our eyes met, and I was struck with the sudden suspicion that Ryder had sent Lincoln along to keep me out of trouble. I inclined my head slightly and he returned the gesture. We were allies in this moment. Badass chick remained close to my side and I was finding her presence as comforting as that of my enforcers. Once we were zooming down, I turned to the others.

"This elevator leads into the Hive prison system. It's filled with hundreds of cells, so it's going to be hard to find Tessa. Be on guard, there'll probably be vampires down here waiting for us. I don't like that they left this elevator unguarded."

My plan was to kill any vamps protecting this place and then run through the cells as fast as I could, searching for my bestie. Worst case scenario, I'd scream Tessa's name at the top of my lungs and hope she responded. I just hoped seven of us were enough to take on whomever was waiting in ambush.

As the doors chimed at the pit floor I fell into formation with the others. I sheathed my knife again and grabbed for the semi-automatic slung across my back. The doors slid open silently and my eyes flicked around the place, trying to determine where the vamps were hidden.

There was nothing.

"Clear," Lincoln said, before flashing those blue eyes at me to confirm. He knew my senses were much stronger than his. I nodded to assure him it was clear.

Guns still at the ready, we stepped out two abreast. Taking no chances but also not wasting time, we rapidly crossed the stone area, past the front desk which was empty, and into the damp cell area. The smell of this place never left you; it was rank and depressing as fuck. The mumbling and moans coming from the cells as we passed gave me the chills. So far there was no sign of Tessa, and I was for sure thinking they had her stashed right at the back, the hardest place to retrieve her. Of course. With my recent luck I should have expected that.

Chapter 9

We crept along, no one speaking, all on high alert.

I slowed as we passed the third path that veered off the main. A rustle caught my attention a second before someone jumped out of a dim alcove. Without thinking, my arm struck out, slamming the person with an uppercut to the jaw. Around me were the sounds of weapons locked and loaded. It took me a split second to recognize the groan and familiar white coat. Okay, not so white at the moment; it was thoroughly streaked with blood and grime, but still the signature outerwear of the only vampire I trusted.

I threw myself forward in front of the male, holding my arms out as I shouted, "Don't shoot. It's Lucas!"

I didn't relax until all of the team had lowered their weapons. Turning, I found Lucas still rubbing his jaw. His eyes roamed over my new haircut and then a smile graced his lips.

"Hello, Charlie."

I couldn't stop my own smile as I gave him a quick hug. It was so good to see him. I had feared that when I left him on the roof all that time ago, I'd never seen him alive again. He was one tough bastard to survive the Hive as an enemy for this long.

Lincoln shifted on the spot. His expression was hard and I could tell that good and bad vampires meant nothing to him. All vamps were the enemy. But for now they were following my lead and not attacking.

"Where's Tessa?" I asked Lucas. There was no time for pleasantries.

He didn't seem surprised at all, and with a nod he took off running. Okay, that worked for me. Please let her be alive and not mentally fucked up from being tortured. I was feeling good about this plan. It was going really well; there seemed to be no vampires down here. They must all be busy fighting Ryder and the rest of our crew. I was seconds from seeing my best friend. That's when my thoughts jinxed me, because the moment we turned the corner a flashbang grenade went off right in front of my face. Cue deafness for the second fucking time.

I really needed to quit this job and work on a farm or some shit.

I hit the ground, grabbing my ringing ears and trying to orient myself. The fucking sound bomb had worked too damn well in disabling my backup soldiers; we were all on the ground, wincing in agony. The humans in our group would take longer to recover, which put us at a decided disadvantage. Of course, I should have known Wonder Woman wasn't going to let a little sound grenade keep her down. She was up before everyone and was already spraying bullets at the onslaught of undead coming at us.

Lucas and I were close behind her. Blue Eyes and the Sanctum males recovered quickly too. The humans had actually fared better than I'd expected. One or two were still on the ground, so right now it was five versus at least thirty. My instincts had been right. This was a secondary trap, primarily for me. I wondered how long Fugly had been planning this. These vamps had probably been down here for days.

Vampires weren't big on weapons usually. They considered themselves to be enough of a weapon, but some of them were shooting at us, so we had to use one of the little alcoves for protection. I wasn't able to get out of the way fast enough and a bullet grazed my left arm, opening a four-inch gash that was now bleeding freely. Just a flesh wound, so I didn't bother to give it more than a glance. Blue eyes dragged his other men in, while tatted chick and I started blasting away at vamps.

They were coming straight for us, clearly not caring that we were easily taking down their front line. I think they expected to have enough numbers to reach us before we could kill them all. And it looked like they were right.

I dodged to the left, avoiding a rain of bullets that clinked into the stone right where my head had been.

"They're too close now," I said to the badass while I reloaded my gun. The tranqs were not going to work on these assholes – bullets all the way.

She nodded, and before I could say anything else she did a dive roll out, a gun in each hand, firing away like a crazy person. And from what I could tell, every shot was a headshot. This chick was not human, I don't care what anyone said.

Lincoln and I followed her. Lucas, who didn't have a weapon, remained protectively crouched close to my side. While firing my semi-automatic, I handed him a handgun, and it turned out that he wasn't just a pretty face. Dude had game. He was slicing through the charging mass, each hit a headshot too.

The vampires were down to about twelve when the front line finally reached us. A body toppled next to me, and I glanced down long enough to see one of the humans dead on the ground, bullet to the head. Shit. We were all wearing tactical gear with bulletproof vests, but a bullet to the head couldn't be avoided. Turning swiftly, I used my gun to both shoot at the assholes and also smack a few of them around. I cracked a vampire in the face with the butt, knocking him back a few paces, before swinging the weapon around and shooting the male in the temple.

Lucas growled at my side, and by the time I glanced to the left he'd completely torn a female's head off.

"They're not used to combat," he said with a grin. "Too many years of getting ash to do their dirty work."

I didn't have time to answer, I was being double-teamed by two beefy vamps. I'd never seen them before, but that wasn't unusual; vamps and ash did not mingle much. They came at me at the same time. I hit the ground, sweeping out with my feet, knocking down the one to my right and yanking my knife out to slice the other's femoral artery. It dug deep into his thigh, but I hit the spot. It wouldn't kill a vampire, but it would slow them down long enough that I'd find killing them much easier.

On my feet again, the one who'd hit the ground first was already rising. I dived and slammed into his chest. The impact radiated up my arms, but thankfully I didn't drop the knife. In these close quarters my ashpire blood was working in full effect; the vampire growled and struggled to get at me. A few drops of my blood had dripped on his face. He stilled before his fangs extended full force and his eyes went crazy. He leaned up as if to bite me, and I used the distraction to shove the knife straight into his eye socket. Had to hit the brain to kill them.

My stomach roiled as I forced the blade in, up to the hilt. Holy hell. When had this become my life? I could now casually stab people in the eye. 'Cause that's not fucked up. Shivering, I finished the job and he fell to the ground, limp. Lucas was going around to all of the vampires we had dropped and was snapping their necks. He did this with such ease and precision it was clear he had done it many times before.

He noticed me watching and explained: "When you snap a vampire's neck hard enough, it severs the spinal cord. This type of injury takes hours to heal and renders the vampire unconscious for that time."

I wasn't sure it was a good idea to leave them alive, but time was important too. And we needed to get moving.

Blue eyes was watching Lucas' movements with interest, but said nothing. We were six now, and I felt awful that he had lost one of his men, especially because he was about to see that Tessa wasn't human and they'd risked their lives for a vampire. Fuck me. He would probably kill me.

Making our way over the piles of unconscious or dead vampires, we continued down the hall and followed Lucas to a door. Cell 213. Lucas stopped in front of it and turned to hand me keys. By this time we were only a foot apart and his eyes had started pulsing, fangs distended. I was covered in blood, and a lot of it was mine. Damn unicorn blood.

"Lucas!" I forced as much authority as I could into that one word. For a second I thought he wasn't going to snap out of it, but thankfully with a shake of his head he dropped the keys into my hand and stepped back.

"Sorry, they have restricted my feedings as punishment," he murmured, his voice low and hoarse.

Shit. Well, hopefully the plan went off in the next few days, with no problems of course. Then we would cure all the vampires and end their sadistic rule. A moan from inside the cell drew my attention.

"Tessa!" I shouted, and began fumbling with the keys. "I'm coming for you, girl!"

"Char…" Her weak reply was cut off. Finally getting the key into the lock, I threw back the rusty handle and opened the door.

The first thing that hit me was the scent of urine and blood. The second thing was the sight of Fugly standing over my best friend. Fuck. Fuck. Fuck. He had a lit torch in one hand, inches from Tessa's bleach-blond hair. I knew her obsession with curling products. She would go up in flames in a moment.

Everyone froze. Lincoln was on my left, tattooed chick on my right. We just stood in the doorway staring into the tiny cell, helpless to do anything.

"Charlie, Charlie, Charlie," Fugly said. "Still stupid I see. I knew you would eventually come for her."

Tessa was hunched over, skinny and pale. She was staring at the floor. When she finally looked up at me, my breath caught in my throat. My best friend was broken. Not an ounce of the fun-loving girl that I grew up with looked back at me through those dim silver eyes.

Lincoln stiffened next to me.

"She's a vampire," he growled.

Double fuck. "They must have changed her," I said. Not a total lie, just a stretching of the truth. Right?

Oh, God, please don't let them leave me.

Fugly cranked the side of the torch, making the flame dance higher. "Charlie have you been lying to the humans?" His voice was so calm and even, like this was just a regular ol' day for him.

Lincoln was giving me a side glare as I internally panicked. Would he really light her on fire? Alive? I felt my last meal threaten to come up at the thought. Where the fuck was Blake? He'd better be dead, otherwise I was killing him for not helping.

"Let her go and I'll give you anything you want," I said, using every ounce of acting skills I had to keep my voice and face calm.

He grinned. "I was hoping you would say that."

We all waited in silence for a beat.

"Charlie, I'll let Tessa go right now if you take that gun and shoot yourself in the head." That sent a shock through me. He wanted me to kill myself?

Of course he did.

Lincoln shifted slightly beside me, finally turning his glare onto someone else. "Why would you want that?" he asked the maniac, who was holding that damn flame way too close to my bestie's product-fried hair.

Fugly looked delighted. "She hasn't told you? She's the cure for vampirism. She could end all of this." He waved his hands around. "But instead she ran away, leaving her friend in my care."

"Is that true?" Lincoln turned to me. I'd never seen him so enraged.

Uh … shit. "Yes, but—"

Before I could finish, Lincoln's fist came out quickly and socked me so hard in the side of the face that the force of it threw me backwards into the cell. The bones in my jaw cracked and a garbled moan escaped me as I fought for consciousness, stars dancing across my vision.

I'd landed on my hands and knees, two feet from Tessa and Fugly. I worked to stay semi-upright, panting in pain.

Fugly laughed and it reverberated across the entire cell.

Half of me thought Lincoln had really enjoyed that hit because one of his men died trying to free my vampire bestie, but the other half recognized that he was a genius – he'd just unobtrusively gotten me within grappling range of Fugly. Here's hoping the ashpire healing kicked in really fast this time.

Fugly wasn't focused on me. "Oh, I enjoyed that immensely – thank you," he said to Lincoln. Before he could turn his attention back to me or realize that I was regaining my strength, I dug my heels into the cold packed earth and leapt up, swift and silent.

I was pretty sure this could go badly – with me and Tessa both torched like steaks on a grill. As I crashed into the Quorum leader I was relieved to see I had taken him completely by surprise. He tumbled backward a few steps and I heard the clank of the torch hitting the ground. As we started to grapple, I tried my best not to trample Tessa, but at one point I was definitely standing on her leg.

I couldn't worry about that though, there were far more pressing dangers to her body. My palm came up fast, smashing Fugly's nose up as hard as I could. As my hand connected I was rewarded with a crack and a gush of blood onto my palm. The impact sent a shock of pain along my jaw; it was not healed yet – adrenalin was keeping me going. It would take a few hours to fully heal, hours I didn't have.

Fugly recovered quickly, and before I could register what was happening, both of his hands were around my throat, cutting off my air supply.

I heard scuffling behind me, then Lincoln's voice filled the cell: "Don't shoot, you could hit her."

Fugly was using me as a shield. My jaw was killing me and now black spots were dancing across my vision. Before my thoughts completely turned to mush, I had to think: What would Ryder do? But it wasn't Ryder that came to mind. It was Jayden. My hands were on Fugly's forearms, trying to pry them off me, but thinking of my BAFF and what he would do, I let go, and in two quick moves jammed both of my thumbs into the vampire's eyes. I followed this with a knee into his groin.

The satisfying and surprisingly feminine scream that tore from Fugly's mouth was short-lived. In seconds, something grabbed me around the waist and I was tossed to the side. I flipped around in time to see a streak of black crashing into Fugly. Ryder. He was already straddling him, pinning his arms down and pummeling his face with his fists.

"For Marc Delaney." Ryder's fists crashed into him and I wasn't sure if I was hearing Fugly's bones crack or Ryder's knuckles. Maybe both.

"And Jason Scout."

Ryder kept repeating his men's names. One by one.

From the corner of my eye I could see tattoo chick next to Tessa, checking her out.

Another thud had me focusing again on the beatdown. Shit.

"Ryder!" My voice was firm, but he never looked away from Fugly.

I knew my man, and this wasn't him. He wasn't this dark. I needed to save him from doing something that would haunt his dreams. We didn't torture people. Kill them, yes. Torture them by slowly beating them to death, no.

"RYDER!" I shouted, and something in my tone must have caught his attention He stilled and looked up at me.

Fugly looked to be suffocating in his own blood. Droplets were spluttering from his mouth as he tried to suck in air.

"Enough," I said, my eyes pleading with him not to lose himself to this darkness. His chest was heaving as he stared at me, fists still clenched, blood dripping in small plops on the floor. Finally, he blinked, and some black bled back into the silver of his eyes. He nodded and took one last look down at Fugly, before cracking his neck.

I retrieved the torch then, which was still lit, making my way back and handing it to Ryder. He brought it down onto Fugly's comatose body, lighting his hair and clothes. This fucker was clearly going to die, but this way he'd be unconscious right up until the fire finished him off. Like I said, we were civilized murderers.

There were small vents above each cell, and I assumed since the cell was made of stone and earth it wouldn't burn down the entire Hive, but if it did, then so be it.

Zero fucks given at this point.

Ryder slipped an arm around me and we followed the tattooed girl and Tessa out of the cell, closing the door behind us. I raced to Tessa's side and she collapsed against me. She was so thin, her hair lank and dull. They'd been starving her for some time, it was very clear.

"You better start talking," Lincoln ordered me.

I gritted my teeth, jaw aching, and fought the urge to sock Lincoln in the throat. Fucker had punched me out of nowhere. Whether he had grounds to do that or not, it still pissed me off.

Tessa's head flopped back, and I could see her eyes were pulsing, despite the fact she looked half dead. Her face was listless, and it didn't seem as if she recognized me yet.

"We were going to tell you, Linc—"

Before I could finish, Tessa lunged forward with more strength than I thought she had and sunk her teeth into my upper arm, the one that was injured and bleeding.

"Christ, Tessa!" I shouted; the pain was sharp and instant. Gritting my teeth, I fought against the urge to pull her off. The wheels were turning in my mind. Let her drink. Then she'd be human and would be safe from this fucked up world. Badass chick raised her gun, her eyes dark as she watched us closely. I shook my head, stopping her.

"Allistair wasn't lying to you. My blood is the cure. When she's done drinking from me she'll begin the change back to human." I stared down at my bestie. She was calming now as the blood entered her system. By the time I looked up again, Lincoln and the remaining members of his crew looked stunned.

"Why wasn't this the first thing you said to us?" Lincoln asked.

Ryder stepped in front of me and faced off with Blue Eyes. "Because this is a secret that has placed a huge target on Charlie's back. She's been hunted, and will continue to be hunted, until we can end the vampires. We have a plan. It's going to go into action in a few days. I was going to tell you tomorrow, giving you just enough notice to rally the troops. You have to be aware that a lot of the higher-up officials are in the vampires' pockets, paid off or blackmailed. We had to keep this one secret for as long as possible. The enforcers are retrieving some blackmail files right now that might help you control the release of information."

I'd forgotten about that. Lincoln would know who to tell, and how to use those files in the best way. Of course, right now he was in a puddle of disbelief.

"I'm going to have to give a briefing ... I have to report this. You were right to keep this quiet though. Corruption is nothing new, and the human world is rife with it. I'll have to be careful about who I inform. This information will have to be classified above top secret." He was sort of talking to us and murmuring to himself. Finally, he straightened and faced Ryder. "Yes, give me the files. I have a few that I trust, and for the others ... we'll work something out."

Ryder nodded.

Lincoln turned to me then. "I'm sorry for hitting you, Charlie. You took me by surprise. I thought my people had been killed trying to save a vampire, and that's unacceptable to me. Still, I mostly wanted to get you in the room with him without raising suspicion."

Ryder turned on Lincoln then, and I was praying a fight didn't break out in these close quarters. "You punched Charlie?" His voice was low and deadly. Somehow he made it seem even worse when he didn't yell. Like he was beyond that emotion altogether.

"I fucked up," Lincoln shot back. "But you weren't here. Allistair was going to burn her friend. It was very clear. I did what I could to get her into the room. The vamp expected me to react like that. He knew I would be pissed at her, so he never saw the deception."

That was very true. Ryder didn't seem to care though; he advanced on Blue Eyes. I needed to defuse the situation, now.

"His actions probably saved Tessa's life. It was pretty genius."

Although a small part of me was plotting revenge, my jaw would heal and Lincoln had saved Tessa from being charred bacon.

Ryder growled long and low then; the sound echoed around the cavern. Hair rose on my arms at the pure menace, the animalistic nature of his response. Lincoln took a step backwards, and it was the first time I'd ever seen the composed SWAT leader look concerned. Before Ryder could react though, my groan distracted him.

I was feeling faint now. "Help," I murmured, because I wasn't sure I could pry Tessa off myself.

Ryder, his eyes still flaming silver, moved like a swift wind. Leaning down, he covered Tessa's nose and palmed the back of her head to dislodge her from my arm. She only fought for a second before slumping toward me. Ryder reached out and supported us both.

Tessa lifted her head to stare at me, and I could see the way her eyes flared to life with swirls of silver. "Shit, Charlie. I'm…"

The rest of her words were incoherent as she started bawling. I reached out to comfort her.

Lucas cleared his throat. I'd sort of forgotten he was even there. "With Allistair dead, I can take control of the Quorum again. No one liked him, but he had too many secrets on us."

Ryder nodded.

Lucas leaned forward, dropping his voice. "Let me know the day the plan goes into action. I'll do everything I can to make sure this Hive is ready."

I patted the still sobbing Tessa on the back, before handing her off to Ryder and standing to meet Lucas head on. "My promise to you holds. Thank you, friend. I appreciate everything you've done and sacrificed for me." Lucas was one of the rare vampires who didn't lose oxytocin. There was no other explanation for his kindness.

The smile he gave me then was like nothing I had ever seen on him before. I realized then that he loved me, in some weird small way. The way his eyes roamed tenderly over my broken jaw to my lips. I quickly looked at Ryder and the look on his face said that he saw it too. It didn't matter; I would never be with Lucas, I would always belong to Ryder. We would bring the vampires down and I would make sure Lucas had his cure, had his human life back.

We all made our way back to the golden elevator, climbing over broken-necked vampires. The SWAT member we had lost was gone now too. Someone must have retrieved him already.

Once we got to the elevator I turned to Lucas. "Are you sure they'll take you back?" I asked uneasily, eyeing the bodies behind him. Surely they would wake up and talk, right? I couldn't bear it if Lucas died because of me.

Lucas gave me a sly grin, holding up the torch. "I'll have to burn a bit more evidence, but yes, they will. Most of the vampires are under lockdown, they'll have no idea what actually went down tonight."

Okay then. It was hard to believe that Fugly was gone. That bastard had made my life hell, all of our lives hell. Good riddance.

"Thank you," I said, squeezing his hand. He nodded and squeezed back. After stepping into the elevator, we selected the ground floor.

"Kyle?" I asked Ryder.

"Fine," he said.

Tessa had been quiet this whole time, but was managing to walk on her own. I turned to face her. "You're coming with us. By tomorrow you should be human."

She surprised me by bursting into tears again. "Blake," she said.

Fuck Blake. "He can't come," I ground out. That bastard wasn't down in the pit with Lucas trying to help us, so I didn't care about him anymore.

She nodded. "I know ... he's dead. Allistair got to him."

Oh fuck. I was totally kidding before when I said he'd better be dead. Dammit. That explained a lot. That's probably what got her thrown in the pit. A story for another time. I wouldn't ask her about it now in front of everyone.

I just held her as the elevator doors opened. Kyle was waiting on the other side, and the sight of him made my heart soar. My family was okay. We could get through this. We could get through anything.

An hour later we were all back at Lincoln's house. Sanctum had bailed right after the fight, but we'd see them again pretty soon. They already had a lot of their members stationed in the hospitals and blood stations. The others were heading off to join them.

The clock had started now, and we were on a three to four day countdown.

At the moment, Ryder, Kyle, and I were being interrogated as Tessa slept off her vampire hangover in the guest room. Tattooed chick's name was Sasha and she was officially my woman crush Wednesday. She had already stitched up her own thigh wound and was now eye screwing Kyle every second she got.

It was definitely clear she had these boys by the balls. In the last fifteen minutes she had gone around to collect blood samples from all the SWAT team. I guess it was protocol after a bloody fight with the vampires to get checked and make sure no one was infected. She had some type of handheld machine, and she came over to Lincoln, who was mid-sentence.

"...I have about thirty minutes before I have to report everything that went down tonight. We lost a man—"

Sasha grabbed his finger and poked it, letting a few drops fall onto the wand before sticking it into the meter. Then she walked away as Lincoln sucked his finger, and I became very aware that I was thirsty as hell; we hadn't had blood in a while.

Ryder shifted his stance. "Our plan all along was to have the help of the human government. We have no idea what will happen in the few hours after the plan goes into effect. The cure is not instant, and vampires can do a lot of damage in a short time. But it's imperative they don't find out before the plan goes into action, otherwise we're all screwed."

Lincoln seemed to consider me, staring at my forehead like it would unlock something.

"You really think you can cure them all? All of them?" He really stressed the last few words.

I sighed. "Well, obviously not every single one. But the vampires live in controlled little societies. The Hives. And they live on one thing, blood, so I'm pretty damn sure we will get 95% of them."

He seemed pleased with that answer. "A vaccine you say?"

I nodded. "My blood is the cure. Once Tessa wakes up you'll see."

"Boss..." Sasha entered the room with the machine, and for the first time she looked out of control. Her hands even looked to be shaking. "You've been infected."

Lincoln swayed on his feet, and now that she had said it, I noticed he was looking ashen, fine beads of sweat on his face. Shit.

"You know protocol. Call it in," he stated, his expression calming as he managed to hide his shock.

Sasha reached for her phone, but before she could dial I threw both of my hands in her direction, waving like a crazy person. "Calm down, everyone. Let's talk this through." Sasha stalled, holding her phone. "You call this in and they will drop him off at the local Hive. The Hive he just helped slaughter."

Sasha shook her head. "No, it's standard procedure in our specialized units. We don't go down the bloodsucker route. We sign waivers and documents stating this much. He'll be..." She didn't finish, but I heard her loud and clear.

My mouth popped open. "They KILL you?"

Lincoln nodded. "It's what I want. I don't want to be a bloodsucker. No offense."

Been there. Got the shirt. And vamp was so much worse than ash.

"Then let me help you. I'm the cure, remember?"

Lincoln seemed to consider it. "You still have yet to prove that." He gestured to the room where Tessa was recovering.

I levelled a glare on him. "Option one: you think I'm a liar and call this in and get yourself killed. Option two: you trust me, inject some of my blood in your arm, and have the rest of your life as a human. What do you have to lose by trusting me?"

He still hesitated, and I wanted to roll my eyes. Men. Seriously. Idiots.

I crossed my arms and looked at Sasha. This woman had power; she needed to use it. She met my steely gaze and gave me a curt nod before getting in her boss's face.

"Do it. If it doesn't work by morning, I'll kill you myself," she said bluntly. They stared at each other for a painfully long amount of time. Finally, he nodded.

"Do it!" He outstretched his arm and I could see the beads of sweat on his brow were increasing. The fine veins in his eyes were already bloodshot.

The virus was brutal. No wonder more humans died than were turned. Sasha took my blood and transferred it into Lincoln's arm. Here's hoping the human part of him didn't react to the different blood-type before the cure part got going on the virus. I'd never cured someone who wasn't fully turned yet.

I guess we'd find out tomorrow. Not to mention that tomorrow was the day we'd meet up with the rest of the sexy six and kick our plan into action. The next few days would either be the final for us, or the vampires. I know who I had my money on. All five dollars of it.

CHAPTER 10

Morning came around way too fast. It felt like by the time I did multiple checks on Tessa and Lincoln, the sun was already starting to rise. Sasha eventually kicked me out of the "sick room," and barely conscious I showered off the debris from the last twenty-four hours and crawled into bed. Ryder's warm body slid in beside me soon after.

I slept like the dead for a few hours, no dreams, just pure unconsciousness. Ryder's alarm roused us around 9 A.M. We needed to get moving this morning, no time to sleep the day away. Of course, that didn't mean we had no time at all for some activities to increase the pleasure of waking up. I found myself caged under Ryder as he held himself above me. His dark hair was tousled, tawny skin bare to my roving eyes. The silver in his eyes was light but swirling. Some of the agony and guilt over the death of his men had abated. He felt like my Ryder again.

We still had a lot to talk about, him taking off like that and everything that had happened yesterday, but right now I needed some us time. The last few weeks had been crap. I was taking this happiness while it was possible.

Lowering himself onto his left elbow, our bodies were now deliciously aligned, naked skin pressing together everywhere. I swear my eyes pretty much rolled back in my head. Could anything feel better than this? Doubtful. Ryder reached out and gently cupped my face before leaning down and pressing soft kisses to the line of my jaw "All healed," he said between caresses. "Still thinking about killing Lincoln."

I chuckled, starting to squirm beneath him. My body was on fire. I needed him to hurry this up, because as perfect as those kisses were, I needed more. I needed him. Lifting my legs up, I wrapped them around him and pulled him down into me. The movement shifted his face, and as his lips met mine I let out low groan. The kiss started soft but quickly turned into a blazing fire. His lips moved against mine, gently but also firm, his tongue sweeping into my mouth and caressing mine.

This was worth every second of being hunted as an ashpire. Ryder was worth everything that had happened. This one moment of being loved by him was worth more than a million as a human with someone else, and as he continued to touch me I banished all other thoughts from my mind. Right now was time for loving. The rest could wait for later.

Later arrived way too soon. Ryder and I showered together, which might have involved some more hot kisses, but eventually we had to face reality. Thankfully, reality was an awake bestie with familiar hazel eyes.

I ran to her room, skidding to a halt inside the door. She was propped up on some pillows, still thin and pale, but looking much better than yesterday. She'd brushed her hair and everything.

"Charlie!" she shrieked, flinging her arms wide.

I didn't hesitate, diving onto her and pretty much crushing her spine as I hugged her tightly.

"I told you so," I said into her hair, and there was a split second of silence before she cracked up laughing. It burst from her in a torrent as her body shook against mine.

"You've been waiting to say that since the day I turned vamp, haven't you?"

I pulled back and met her laughing eyes. "Yes, you stupid biatch. I could kick your ass so badly, but you have no idea how happy I am to see you alive and human."

She sobered up then, and something dark flittered across her eyes. Her weeks in the Hive had not been a happy time, and I knew it would be a long while before she was okay with what had happened.

"I'm sorry about Blake," I said gently. "I'm so sorry."

Her face crumpled; her hands clutched at my shirt and I could see by how white her knuckles were that she was holding on with everything she had. "I miss him. My heart literally aches just knowing I'll never see him again ... that he'll never touch me again ... that I won't wake next to him one more time. I'm not ready to give him up."

She broke my heart; I felt every single word. If something happened to Ryder I would ... lose my mind. I had no platitudes for her. Sometimes in these deep moments of grief, people wasted words, saying "Everything's going to be okay," and "You're so strong, blah blah." I wouldn't do that to Tessa, I wouldn't cheapen her pain. I knew what she needed and that was for me to listen. So I did.

I nodded and stroked her back and she cried and talked about Blake, and finally when she quieted I realized she had fallen back asleep. Kissing her forehead, I slipped out of the door to find out what had happened to Lincoln. Did he turn? Had Sasha killed him yet? Did my blood do something whack to him? Turn him into a zombie? As I turned the corner and made my way out into the living room, I was relieved to see him alive, drinking orange juice and giving Sasha his finger for her to prick and do another test.

She looked up when she heard me enter and graced me with a huge smile.

"He's being annoying. It's his third test in three hours. All clear!"

I grinned and stepped closer to Lincoln, meeting his gaze. Why not say it twice in one morning?

"I told you so."

He chuckled. "Yes, you did."

Before I could reply, Kyle came running inside from the backyard. He was holding a smart phone, one of Lincoln's guys right on his tail.

"Turn on the TV, boss," Lincoln's boy said.

Kyle met my gaze and just shook his head. Oh fuck. What now? Did the Hive burn to the ground? Lucas dead? The rest of the ash dead too?

The TV blared to life and the emergency warning was going off, that high pitched blaring that the government reserved for times of nuclear war and shit. Then a newscaster came on. Her blond hair was pulled tight into a bun and she looked frazzled, but was smiling holding some papers in her shaking hands.

"The associated press received some startling information this morning." My picture popped up on screen in the upper right hand corner, a place reserved for terrorist and murders. "There's a cure for vampirism, a twenty-one-year-old Portland, Oregon, native, Charlene Bennett. We have confirmed blood results. We are asking for your help in finding this girl so we can work toward a cure for everyone."

"Fuck!" Ryder's loud curse scared me from my stupor. He never said fuck, that was my word. This was bad on a whole other level.

By the time I took a step toward him, Ryder had already hauled Lincoln up out of his chair and had him against the wall. Without missing a beat, Sasha pulled her gun, pointing it at the back of Ryder's head.

"Stop it!" I yelled. "It wasn't Lincoln. Think about it. Anyone could have spilled this information. Fugly might have organized for someone inside the Hive to send my blood results to the humans if he died, or if the Tessa plan didn't work. Come on, this stinks of vampire. They want the humans' help in finding me, and then they'll take me out before anyone even realizes."

Ryder took a steadying breath and set Lincoln down as Sasha removed the gun from his head. Yeah, we all had some trust issues to work on. Lincoln didn't seem fazed though, he just started barking orders at his men, and Sasha came in closer to my side.

"We need to disguise you and you need to run."

She was right. Lincoln would have to report to his superiors again soon. If I wasn't still with him, it would be easier for him to skirt the truth of my whereabouts. Not to mention they'd be hitting every surveillance and CCTV footage in Portland trying to find me. The picture they'd showed on TV was from college, with my long hair, but I was still easily recognizable. The eyes were a dead giveaway.

Sasha pulled my hand and led me into the bathroom. She then retrieved a black makeup case with a skull on it, and after rummaging through she pulled out a small hoop earring the size of a dime.

I busted out laughing. "An earring? That's your disguise? Might as well walk around naked in downtown Portland." I hadn't known her long, but I knew I could joke with her; she had that type of personality.

"Sometimes the best way to stay hidden is to stick out." She messed with the earring and then slipped it between my nose like a septum ring. I sneezed as it scraped my skin, and then turned to look at the mirror. "I'm going goth?" I asked in disbelief. Jayden would shit himself. But if I was honest, this ring was kinda hot.

She smiled and nodded. "You're going goth."

The next fifteen minutes were spent giving me thick black eyeliner and dark purple lipstick, so dark it looked black in certain angles. Then she braided three small cornrows on one side of my hair and spiked up the back with gel.

I turned to look at myself in the mirror and gasped. Holy shit, I didn't recognize myself! "You're good," I said, turning left and right to get the full view.

"We learned this in training." She quickly changed topics. "So I wanted to ask you something … your friend Kyle…"

I gave her a half-grin. "Totally single, and he'd be so into taking you on a date," I assured her.

"Really?" She seemed pleased with my answer.

Seemed even hottie badass chicks had moments of doubt. She had nothing to worry about. I'd seen the way Kyle looked at her.

She was lost in thought; her face went solemn. "We're not allowed to date ash."

I shrugged. "You don't seem like the type to follow the rules."

She chuckled. "You know me so well already."

"Besides, I think rules will be changing once the vampires are gone," I said. Her face brightened, and then we were busy finishing my new look.

After cutting the feet off of black tube socks and making them into arm warmers, Sasha put me in a miniskirt, black fishnets, a red corset, and black boots.

"You just have this shit lying around?" I asked her

She smirked. "We all carry disguises. Comes with the job. And since I'm the only chick, it seems I'm always playing 'the hooker' or 'hot distraction.' Men, they're pigs, but I love their dumb asses."

Right there with you, sister.

Finally Sasha and I exited the bathroom and I crossed back into the living room, where everyone slowly noticed my presence and stopped talking. Ryder was staring at me with his jaw half open, eyes a blaze of silver and lust, that made me think he wanted round two, STAT.

I cleared my throat and they all went back to what they were doing. Sasha slipped outside to get something and Kyle and Ryder walked over to me.

"You're fulfilling a fantasy for me," Ryder said.

I laughed. "Really, gothic?"

He just nodded, eyeing my dark lipstick, no doubt imagining it staining his body.

Kyle meanwhile was staring out the door Sasha had just exited through. I lowered my voice so no one would hear: "If you ask her out, she'll say yes."

He jerked his head back round to face me. "What ... who?"

I gave him a look, one which called him on his bullshit. His eyes flicked back to the door but he didn't say anything. He was intrigued, I could tell.

Ryder put a hand on Kyle's shoulder, clearly seeing the same thing I had. "Great news, buddy. News which you can act on after we take out an entire race of vampires. Right now we need to focus on keeping my girlfriend alive for the next couple of days."

Kyle was attentive again. "Right."

The bromance was back on track. I was so happy to see these two had worked out their differences. Kyle had been pretty mad at Ryder when we first showed up here, but clearly a few life and death situations had smoothed that all over.

Lincoln joined us then. "I'm receiving intelligence that the vampires are leaking all information they have on you. Including the fact that you were working with us last night. People are going to start sniffing around soon, looking for you. You're welcome to stay here, but…"

Ryder clapped Lincoln on the back. "You've been more than enough help. We need to rendezvous with the rest of our group to execute the plan. Just be ready to help when we call."

Lincoln nodded and then looked at me. "Thank you, Charlie. I owe you one."

I didn't take that lightly. I knew he meant it, and that it must have been hard to say.

"We can't take Tessa with us. She's human now and—"

Lincoln cut me off: "I'll keep her safe. Protect her as though she were my own."

A fifty-pound weight lifted off my shoulders. Thank God I wouldn't have to worry about her while trying to save my own ass from the legion of greedy humans that were about to go Charlie hunting.

I ducked back into her room, and Tessa, who was laid out on her bed reading a magazine, let out an almighty shriek. "Holy shit, Charlie. You're goth … hot as heck goth, but still … you have on black lipstick. If I hadn't known your cute ass my entire life I doubt I'd have recognized you."

I laughed. "That's the entire point. The humans are gunning for me now. They know I'm the cure. I need to stay incognito for at least another couple of days, until the plan goes into place."

Tessa swung her legs off the side of the bed and slumped forward. She looked pale, frail, and worn out, almost like her skin was a few layers lighter than it used to be.

"I'm guessing this little visit means you're taking off again and leaving me behind."

I took another step and dropped down beside her, my arm sliding across her shoulders. "Yep, but hopefully this time it's only going to be for a short while, and then the world will be a different place."

I felt some strength come back into her body as she finally straightened and turned toward me. "Stay safe, best friend. I'll do everything I can to help out here and make sure we get the house with the joined backyards. I'll be waiting for you, so you better come back to me alive and minus the bull ring in your nose."

I snorted. "Who has a tramp stamp now, bitch?"

She went even paler. "Fucking Valarie! That bitch is the worst influence ever."

We both laughed, and in that moment everything was okay with us. One last hug, both of us unsuccessfully fighting tears, and then it was time to go. Turning back at the doorway

I blew a kiss to my oldest friend and she returned the gesture. She looked different now, the sunlight pouring in around her. Older. More grown up.

I had been waiting a long time to see the strength of Tessa shine through. For too long she'd let her poor little rich girl life dictate who she was, but finally now, after everything that had happened, she had actually grown up. And while I hoped the fun, frivolous side of her wasn't completely gone, it was nice to see some personal growth. Damn, was I becoming an adult? Ugh. Totally overrated.

Stepping back into the living room, Ryder and Kyle were waiting with our bags at their feet. Both of the guys were dressed very casually, none of their usual badass enforcer gear in sight. All of us were undercover now, and it looked like it was time to jet.

"I have arranged for a car," Lincoln announced as he stepped in from the back entrance. "It's not going to be your usual luxury model, so prepare yourself. You're going incognito."

I wasn't sure what to expect as we followed him out into the huge back garage again. Some old clunker with spray paint on the side maybe.

When the body of our transport finally came into view, I heard the low groan from Kyle and Ryder. Neither of them very happy with our wheels. "At least Markus isn't here," I said with a laugh. "He'd flat out refuse to get in that car."

The Scottish lad loved his stuff shiny and fast, and we were about to go traveling in the retirement special.

The sedan was beige, like for real the color of bleh. Square and boxy, the exact sort of car that early-retired couples used. Of course, this did make better sense than the old painted clunker. This would blend in. No one would even look twice at this POS.

Ryder opened the back door for me, and even the inside was beige. Everything was the exact same color, and I wondered if I was going to get carsick. Oh well, vomit would blend right into that carpet. No problem.

"The back windows are heavily tinted, which will afford Charlie some privacy. It's filled with gas, and I've left a bunch of cash in the center console just in case you don't have access to funds." Lincoln was still talking and it was clear he'd done everything he could to help us with this. Off the books.

We had ways of getting money undetected. Sam was our boy after all. But it was good to know we were set for some time. The next few days were going to rely big-time on stealth. Ryder and Kyle settled into the front seats, and I spread myself out in all the beige luxuriousness of the back. The engine was surprisingly smooth, very silent compared to our usual ride, and it was with great middle-aged speed we exited the garage, Lincoln and a few of his men waving us off.

"So what's the plan now?" I leaned forward. For some reason my nerves settled down whenever we went over the plan. Like I could just take one step at a time and we'd eventually get there.

Ryder lifted his head and our eyes met in rearview mirror. He looked tired, and worried. "Right now we're heading for Idaho. We have to get out of Portland straight away. The guys contacted us last night. Cure is in the bottles and trucks are ready to go. The warehouse is in Idaho, so we'll meet them there and pick up our truck."

Great to know that Sanctum was on board so far.

Ryder continued: "International shipments have already gone out and will be arriving to the Sanctum spies soon. Cali and Texas are going to be a little more difficult. They don't take postal shipments, it's all hand delivered. Plus, I agree with you about overseeing as much as we can, so we'll split up and drop the cure-filled bottles off in person to those locations."

I nodded a few times. I was glad the Cellway base was in Idaho because everyone would expect to find me in my home town. It was good to get out of Portland.

"Okay, so the international stuff is covered." Hopefully. We were putting a lot of faith in Sanctum and whatever delivery service they were using. "And we'll be posing as delivery people and dropping off the cure bottles to the hospitals. Sanctum will add the blood and make sure they're distributed to the Hives?"

Kyle nodded, shifting around to see me better. "Yep, Sam got on the secure line last night when you were asleep. He ran through everything with me. Now we're just waiting to hear from Sanctum's international ash that the cure is in place."

I dropped back against the seat. So many things could go wrong with this plan. So many. It was widespread, and had people all over the place involved. Just one slip-up and everything would fall to shit. Unease began to gnaw at my belly. Maybe we had done this ass backwards. The humans were key to our plan. Maybe we should have told them first? Now they were gunning for me in hopes of getting the cure, but completely ignorant to the fact that we were already working on it. I ran my hand through my freshly shorn hair. Fuck, I really hoped I survived this. Ryder's eyes met mine in the rearview mirror as if he'd heard that thought. They burned with intensity and I knew that if I died, Ryder would die too, because he wasn't going to let anything happen to me while he was still breathing and on this Earth. That thought should have comforted me, but it only served to make me sink deeper into depression.

It was roughly a six-and-a-half-hour drive to Boise, Idaho, but we had to stop a few times to stash me in the trunk because there were border checks that were uncharacteristic to this part of the country. Thankfully, they weren't at a level yet to actually open trunks or look inside of luggage, but even the fact they were stopping vehicles was a little scary. Once we finally passed through the last check, Ryder pulled over and let me out.

"I don't like it. They're looking for you everywhere already," he said, as he ushered me into the back seat and then took his place at the wheel.

Even with my gothic getup, we weren't risking it with cops. Better just to have two guys in the car; they were clearly on the lookout for a woman. It was lucky, too, that the boys had their contacts in and glasses on. All ash were going to be treated as suspicious.

Kyle was frowning. "Let's turn on the radio. Maybe something has changed."

He fiddled with a few knobs. After finding a news station, we sat with rapt attention as Ryder crept back out onto the road. A nasally male voice came through the speaker mid-sentence: "—bring families back together. This could change the way we live our lives forever. If there's a cure, there's no fear of getting the virus. There would be a way to bring back our family members that have been affected. But we need that girl. Tests need to be done. It's going to take time to figure out exactly how to replicate the curative components of her blood. We also need to meet with the leaders of the Hives to talk about how to administer the cures."

I snorted. "HAH! They're delusional. The humans actually think the vampires will voluntarily take the cure?"

The radio announcer continued with his nasally speech: "Multiple ash equality and rights groups have sprung up, arguing that the girl should be able to choose if she wants to offer the cure willingly."

"Thank you!" I said loudly from the backseat.

"But even more privately funded groups have come forward offering millions, and in one case, over a billion dollars, for the girl's capture—"

The announcer's voice cut off as Ryder smashed the power button, leaving us all to sit in an uncomfortable silence. Fuck. A billion dollars for my "capture." I shrank into the seat, staring at the open road ahead of us. This was an epic Charlie screw up. Now I was running from a billion-dollar manhunt. People go crazy and kill for fifty bucks nowadays. I couldn't imagine what they were going to do for that sort of paycheck.

I stretched myself out onto the back seat so that I was lying fully prone. Depression settled into my bones as I realized I most likely wouldn't make it out of this alive. That was the last thought I had before I dozed off.

I awoke to muffled talking; the back window was rolled down a few inches and my heart lifted at the sound of my Australian enforcer's deep baritones.

"Is Charlie in the trunk? Who's the hooker?" I tilted my head back to see Jared gesturing to me sprawled out in the back seat. My skirt had lifted, showing my fishnet covered ass. I popped my head up and glared at him.

"Who you calling a hooker, jackass?" I shot back, and Jared looked shocked.

"Holy shit, Charlie. I didn't recognize you."

I just grinned, flinging the door open and flying into his outstretched arms. Sam, Markus, and Oliver were all here too. I gave them each a big, long hug. We were together again; we were going to finish this. I hadn't forgotten my last morose realization of my impending death, but for some reason, back with my boys I was confident again.

I saw now that the car had been pulled out into a thick cornfield and we were completely hidden from view. My eyes lingered on each of the enforcers, their familiar faces so precious to me. I couldn't believe it had only been a couple months that I had known these guys. We had been through hell and back together, and now we were going to end this. Sam was giving me a look I couldn't interpret. The man with a thousand plans, the man who was always calculating, always planning the next step.

"The disguise is good, but not good enough," he finally commented.

Ryder clapped him on the back. "I know what you're thinking, brother, but she deserves to see this through."

My eyes narrowed at Sam. "I don't know what he's thinking! Tell me, Sam, what are you thinking?"

He pulled a syringe out of his pocket. "AT20 you and stash you with a friend until this is over."

I stiffened. Fucking Sam. Always trying to knock me out and hide me! The only reason I wasn't pulling my gun out now and shooting him in the knee was that I knew he suggested it because he loved me; he wanted to make sure he saw my face next week. I approached him.

"Sam..." I placed both of my hands on his shoulders and met his gaze. "I used to jog the streets of Portland, go to Starbucks, and laugh with Tessa on the campus lawn. My only problem was what to wear to the club that night." My face hardened. "They took that from me. They forever changed who I am. They made me a murderer. They forced me to kill, to fight for my life when I could have just been left to live out my days in peace with my mother and Tessa. Ash aren't contagious. The vampires have designed this entire Hive world to benefit them, with ash as their slaves! Well, enough is enough! We've suffered enough."

He surprised me with a hug. "Okay, Charlie." He stashed the AT20 back in his pocket.

I turned to see Ryder looking at me with blazing silver eyes. "Ready?" he asked, and reached out to hold my hand.

I nodded. "Ready."

We were split into three groups. Ryder, Kyle and I. Sam with Markus. Oliver with Jared. California was the bigger of the blood distributors, so two trucks were going there. I followed the boys through the cornfields and out onto a two lane highway. Three huge semi-trucks with hazards on were pulled off the side of the road. They all bore the same red, yellow, and blue logo that I recognized from visiting my mother at the hospital. The Cellway distributors. Ryder, Kyle, and I got in the red truck. Sam gave Ryder the keys, with a few instructions on how to handle the rig. Apparently they'd all learned to drive trucks many years ago, but Ryder was a little rusty.

"You guys head on over to the Texas blood receiving station." Sam said finally. "It's on the outskirts of Dallas. They ship out to the east coast and it will be less likely that anyone will recognize Charlie. We'll head to Cali and drop our shipments there. If all goes well, meet back up in Portland at the lake house. If shit hits the fan, hide."

Ryder nodded and they bro-hugged and that was it. We were in a massive rig packed full of hundreds of thousands of specialty bottles, all filled with the cure for vampirism. Now we just needed to get it to the Sanctum dudes already in place in the hospitals, then it was done. Easy-peasy, right? What could go wrong?

This rig was of the super deluxe variety. I had always wondered what the inside of one of these looked like, and this one did not disappoint. It was like a motel on steroids.

Ryder was in the captain's chair, expertly controlling the massive semi and wearing his Cellway blood lab group vest. Kyle and I were behind him, playing cards on a table set up in the mini five foot living room. Yes, a freakin' living room! Also in here were two couches that faced each other and a tiny kitchenette equipped with all the mod cons, including sink and the cutest tiny microwave you ever saw.

It was well over a day's drive to Dallas, so we decided to take shifts sleeping and driving and just go all the way through. We were stopped a few times during Ryder's shift, when we needed to weigh our load, but luckily no one looked too closely at me.

When Kyle switched with Ryder, I found myself snuggled in my boyfriend's arms. Both of us squished on the little twin-size couch. I knew he was exhausted from driving, but he still tucked me into his body, facing him, and played with my hair.

His silvery eyes locked onto mine, staring at me in that way he had, where I knew I was the only thing he saw. I didn't say anything, cherishing this time we had together. It might be the last snuggle before hell broke loose.

"Charlie…" His voice was gruff.

"Yes?" I said, resting my hand against his face.

"Have you ever been to Hawaii?" His eyelids were drooping, but my laugh had them snapping open again.

"No. Random. I have not been to Hawaii." Hello, I grew up with a single mom. I had barely ever left Portland unless Tessa was paying.

He graced me with one of his insanely sexy smiles. "There's this little cove. It's a secret only locals know about. It's full of turtles. I want to take you snorkeling there when this is all over."

A huge smile broke out onto my face at the thought of walking hand in hand on the white sand beaches of Hawaii with Ryder. The sun high in the sky. Not a care in the world. Yes, I wanted that. His eyes were closing again and I knew he was seconds from sleep.

"I'd like that." I kissed his chin and let his rhythmic breathing lull me to sleep.

Chapter 11

Kyle's deep voice awoke me from what had been a surprisingly restful sleep. "Wake up, kids! It's almost show time."

I peeled my eyes open to see Ryder staring at me. Had he been awake watching me? Creepy or cute? Hmm ... little bit of both. I sat up, pretty sure that my gothic makeup had officially dripped all over my face and I now looked like a half dead zombie.

Ryder sat up as well. "How far out until the hospital drop?" he asked as I fiddled in my bag for my toothbrush.

"About three miles out. I got a text from Sanctum. They're in place."

And just like that my stomach scrunched with nerves. Brushing my teeth quickly in the tiny sink, I decided it was best not to try and find a mirror. Adjusting my nose ring, and running my hands through my hair would have to count as "getting ready."

After Ryder brushed his teeth, he opened the small fridge and passed around some bottles of blood. "Drink up. We need to look as normal as possible if this is going to go down."

I guzzled the blood and then we all made sure our contacts were in. Kyle and Ryder still looked way too gorgeous to be normal humans, but hopefully they would pass for really hot models that happened to have side jobs truck driving.

It could happen.

As Kyle maneuvered through the streets, which was easy with the huge lanes here, we all kept an eye out for University Medical Centre, which was the hospital in this region that handled blood for the Hives. The moment the distinctive building came into view, I shrugged on my Cellway vest and settled myself in near the back of our rig. No need to draw attention to the clown makeup goth girl. I'd let the boys handle any security.

Part one of our plan went off without a hitch. Sam had detailed maps explaining the back entrance and how we get to the loading docks. Besides two rent-a-cops on the entrance gate, we had no one stop us and soon we were pulling up to the large, industrial space. Kyle swung himself out of the rig and took some time to chat with whomever worked these docks. Ryder let him go, waiting for the signal to start unloading.

Kyle's blond head popped in through the now open back door. "All set, let's unload the bottles." Ryder got out straight away, but I knew I was to remain hidden, although I might have snuck over to peer out the window. My eyes were immediately drawn to the five men standing on the edge of the dock. They were wearing white lab coats, and three of them had glasses. They looked very much like Becca in her science lab glory, but I recognized at least four of them as Sanctum people. Not that there was anything immediately obvious, but I knew some of their faces, and I also recognized the way they moved. Ash did not move in the same way as humans, they were more like jungle cats. Not to mention they were all gorgeous.

They prowled. Took control. Sat at the top of their jungle abode and disdainfully stared down at everything rushing past them. It was also how I knew at least one of those five was a human, an actual lab person who would probably, unknowingly, help to add this cure to all Hive blood.

I could hear them chatting through the window. "All the humans are here, in the back area," a Sanctum male said. "We'll give them the flu shot and then the bus ships them out in four hours."

The humans were going to be injected with a version of the cure – under the pretense of a vaccine to keep them healthy – which would reproduce in their blood, and as long as they were fed on within the next month or so, the vampire would get a full dose. The bottled blood was going to be the time-consuming part. The donated blood was stored in bags in the refrigerators. Each of those bags was used to fill the UV bottles, which were then delivered to the Hives. Apparently it took a full day for them to distribute the blood into the bottles with special machinery. The bottles were then sealed, a process which mixed the cure and blood cells together, before going into the refrigerated containers and onto private jets which dispatched to all the Hives.

It was a huge job. But there was no other option.

Ryder and Kyle were offloading the wooden pallets from the back of the rig. There were hundreds of pallet crates, and within each was a thousand cure-laced bottles.

The human was right there in the midst, unknowingly helping us take down the vamps. Sanctum wore game faces, but they were excited, I could tell. They wanted us to take out the vampires.

A few hours later the last box was dropped onto the back dock area and we were done with our part of this plan. Ryder opened the door and got back into the captain's chair.

"Everything is in place," he said, starting the rig. "Sanctum have full control of the blood bank area. They've been here for a few days learning the ropes. They won't make any mistakes. The cure will be reaching the Hives within the next day or two."

I nodded, my breath catching in my chest. I was already sick of this cloak and dagger, hide Charlie in the back of the van bullshit. I wanted my life back.

Kyle got in and shut the door firmly. "They're going to text when it's all done. They have six more members in the labs, and will work through the night to get the blood into every single bottle."

"Did the other guys run into any trouble?" I asked, wishing I had a phone to get updates and stuff on. Sort of felt naked without technology in my hands.

Ryder shook his head. "Nah, they're all good. Few checkpoints, but each looking for you. Sanctum was in place, as promised, at the Californian hospital."

The rig was on the road again, back in downtown Dallas. "So now we just lay low and wait for the shit to hit the fan, right?"

Somehow it all seemed too easy, like we should be fighting and stabbing vampires in the neck with cure-filled syringes.

Ryder laughed. "Yes, we now have to wait. We'll head back to Portland and prepare ourselves for war."

He dialed a number then and put it on speaker. It rang a few times before a familiar voice answered.

"Talk to me, Ryder," Lincoln said, voice hard.

"Plan is in place. E.T.A forty-eight hours. You?"

"Files in action. Cities around the globe on standby, everything looking rosy on our end. Will inform you if anything new arises. Waiting on bottle delivery now."

They weren't exactly speaking in code. I understood exactly what was being said. The army was already heading to the Hive towns. They were going to be on standby for the possible fallout of the cure.

Lincoln continued: "All members have darts filled with liquid from a Dr. Leander. None will escape."

The boys exchanged a few more words before ending the secure call.

Ryder looked pleased. "Everything is in place. Lincoln has used the files to ensure silence from men with power. They have multiple teams in all cities and are loaded down with cure. Becca made sure to send them all her extra. We are as ready as we'll ever be."

Okay. Wow. He got a lot more than me from that conversation. But it was all good news. Settling in to the couch, preparing for a long drive home, I sent out as many positive thoughts as I could. This had to work.

The next two days went by agonizingly slow. Everything was in place. The UV resistant bottles were on their way to the Hives; human donors had arrived already at most places. Everything was perfect. A little too perfect.

"So there has been no chatter on the network?" I asked Sam for the hundredth time. "Nothing to indicate that the vampires know about our plan?"

He glared, before running a hand through his dark hair. It was getting long; he needed a cut. "No, there's still nothing. Normal chatter. Nothing in code. So far we're good."

The seven of us were camped out in another safe house. Not in Portland. There were still mass searches going on for me there, but in the nearby Salem area, about an hour's drive away. We'd been spending our time playing cards and obsessively checking the online updates.

"Blood just hit Canada," Markus called, leaning back and stretching out his long body. He'd been in that chair all day. "And Florida has theirs now."

Sanctum were updating us via the untraceable cells. So far eighty percent of shipments had arrived today.

Sam sat a little straighter in his chair then, his fingers flying across the keyboard.

"What's happening?" I leaned forward, unable to stop myself from asking.

"Vampire celebrations underway in Chicago. Ash enforcers there said the blood and donors are out in force, and that vampires are indulging themselves."

I exchanged a smile with Kyle. Awesome, this was exactly what we hoped would happen. New blood days were almost always a celebration. The blood was the freshest, and they had new donors to ravage. The old blood was distributed to ash and the freshest was for vampires.

Fuckers.

Becca had assured me that the cure didn't hurt ash, because they were born and not made. She'd tested it on donated blood from the boys, which meant all the ash in the compounds were going to be okay. They just had to wait it out.

"Blood hit Mexico twenty minutes ago," Jared said. "Their celebrations are underway too."

I had to get to my feet and start pacing. This was too much for me to handle. It was happening. Shit. This was actually happening. What would go down when the first vampire began to turn human? Would they figure it out right away or think he was a fluke? Oh God. I was going to be sick with nerves.

A knock at the door had all of us on high alert. Our location was completely secret. Sam had set the safe house up, and so far we'd done all our communicating via secure cell phones. Our internet signal was pinged and directed all around the world so that no one could trace it. Well, no one below Sam's level of hacking.

So who the hell was knocking on the door? Ryder didn't hesitate. Weapon locked and loaded, expression hard, he strode to the entrance. There was a peephole, which he used for a few seconds, before raising his brows to me and opening the door.

A Viking stepped through, and I was already running. My dad, mom, Becca, and Jayden were standing in the doorway. I crashed into the open arms of my father. We had never hugged, not like this. He might have only been my sire on paper, but in my heart he was my real dad. I squeezed him even tighter, thankful to him for keeping my mom safe this whole time. His scent was not familiar to me, but I felt comforted by the citrus and fresh autumn aroma that covered me now. Every girl needed a dad, whether he was blood or not. I had already chosen him as my father.

We had to get to know each other more, but hopefully there would be time for that. Stepping back, I was crushed into a hug between my mom and Jayden. Tears pricked my eyes. A part of me had wondered if I'd ever see them again.

They let me go and I turned to Becca. "Come here, girl." I opened my arms and she smiled shyly before jumping into them.

I gave her a quick hug and then Sam was there. She threw her arms around him, and his face softened as they hugged.

"I told you to stay put," he growled as he pulled back.

She smirked. "Nice to see you too."

He scowled before ushering everyone inside.

Carter gave Ryder a nod. "I went back to Alaska looking for you. I found some signs of fresh tracks around the safe house these kids were in. Didn't like it. So I brought them with me."

Sam and I shared a look. Would the humans have known I was in Alaska? WTF. They must have people on the inside looking into my trail. CIA maybe. Shit, this was bad. This is why we were so cautious about spreading the word of the "cure takedown vamp plan" with humans. They had big mouths.

"It's probably nothing," Ryder assured me.

Before I could answer, I had a muscular, fine-ass BAFF in my face. "Bitch, I've been here five minutes and you haven't said a word. How about, 'Damn, Jayden your fingernails look busted. Why? Oh that's right, you've been up for forty-eight hours packaging the cure.'" He crossed his arms and Oliver and I began slowly walking toward him.

Jayden was a sensitive flower and needed to be tended too. "Awww." I picked up his hands and inspected the chipped nails and blisters. "Poor baby. Manicure, on me, when this shit dies down," I said, and was rewarded with a broad smile.

Oliver stepped forward then and I was completely forgotten. That enforcer was very good at distracting him. My mom looked me up and down. I had ditched the gothic getup, but my hair was still short. "You've grown up, Charlie bear."

Why do parents feel the need to call you by your childhood name in front of your boyfriend? And grown up? Hah. The understatement of my life. She had no idea what I had been through and I would never tell her. So I simply nodded, my smile weak but genuine.

"I'm so glad you're okay," I said, pulling her close for another hug.

"Shit!" Kyle's curse echoed around the room. He looked up from the computer perched on his lap and my gut dropped when I saw his face. Something very, very bad had happened.

Ryder and I practically crashed into Sam, all of us fighting to get over to Kyle.

"What is it?" Ryder demanded.

"Those motherfuckers." Kyle was still swearing, and I was about to crack him over the head when he spun the laptop in our direction. It took me about five minutes to wrap my head around what I was seeing. I recognized the images, but my brain was having trouble processing.

Holy shit! We had been expecting some backlash. Lives did hang in the balance when it was anything to do with vampires ... but this, this was so much worse.

The video footage was image after image of vampires spilling out onto the streets as the sun was setting in New York. They were attacking humans. Killing them, turning them, drinking from them, destroying homes and buildings, causing damage for the sake of causing damage. Shit! What was happening? Had some started to turn to human already, and the rest went crazy? Were they going to take out as many as they could before the cure kicked in?

Ryder's jaw was clenched. "Three hours."

"Huh?" My brain was still processing the video.

Ryder turned to everyone in the room. "The sun goes down in Portland in three hours."

Well ... fuck. Maybe I wasn't getting out of this alive. Because you bet your ass if the vampires were coming for the people of Portland, I was going to be there to stop them.

"It's a one-hour drive, so we have two hours to suit up and make a plan."

Jayden offered up an idea. "Let's burn that damn place to the ground."

Personally, I'd love to see the Hive burn, but Carter shook his head. "No. They'll be on high alert. Snipers in every window. We won't get close enough to the Hive. The vampires may not be trained like ash, but they are strong and have an arsenal that would put the Marines to shame. You won't get within five hundred feet without losing your head. Not now. They're expecting it."

Fuck. Not to mention our ash buddies were still inside.

I met his gaze. "Then what?"

He started to pace. "I'm guessing eighty percent of them were in the celebration of new blood and feeders. They will be cured, eventually. The other twenty percent won't go down without major bloodshed. Lock down the humans, martial law, curfew, the whole bit. Then we go in and fight them old-school. Like the culling, give them everything we got."

Kyle spoke up again, his eyes trained to a second laptop he had open. "Vampires have warnings going out to all the Hives now. Looks like this bitch is gonna get ugly."

I swallowed roughly. "Did any of them get cured?" Please tell me that my father was right, that at least eighty percent were knocked out. Vampire numbers were nothing on humans, so we'd have a chance if a good lot ingested the cure.

Kyle typed a few times, and finally glanced my way. "I've interrupted the alerts for now. They think they're sending it out into the world, but it's just staying on their particular server." He paused, seeming to be choosing his words. "Sanctum is updating me; they believe that a good percentage of the vampires, in all Hives, have partaken of the cure blood. In some places the change to human is already kicking in. Thankfully, by the time they've fully changed back to human, the majority will have taken the cure."

He flicked his head across to Becca, standing in Sam's shadow, who had barely stepped two foot from her. "Whatever you put in the cure serum to speed up the process is really working. In fact, it's much faster than we anticipated, which is why New York is already going crazy. Their celebrations started a few hours ago, and already vampires are showing signs of humanity."

Becca paled, stepping around Sam to see the footage better. "Crap! I'm sorry. I thought it would be better to get the cure acting straight away on them all. I thought I'd calculated the right amount of time so that no one would notice until all had time to drink."

She looked devastated, her eyes running across the footage again and again. Stepping over, I took her hand. "This is not your fault. This is war, girl, and there are always casualties in war. We're trying our best to free humans from the control of these assholes. We have to stay strong now, and go and do our best to save them all."

Ryder's cell rang then, and all of us fell silent as he answered it on speaker.

"Ryder here. Talk to me."

Blue Eye's voice came through loud and clear. "Red alert, Ryder. The cure is working, but as we suspected the small numbers who did not drink, or noticed early, are out on the streets trying to turn humans. Build their numbers back up." He sounded harried, but not crazy pissed or anything.

"We saw the New York footage," Ryder said. "We're about to suit up and hit Portland Hive before they can get to the humans."

"I'm on my way there too. I already have men stationed there, on standby. The other Hive cities are quiet so far, and I have people in place to handle any that get out of control. The international ones have required me to call on their local law enforcement. All have been more than willing to help. Hopefully when the dust settles, the Hives will no longer be there. I'll check in with you over the next few hours, but for now, things are as good as we could expect. Head to Portland if you feel you must. I'll see you there."

He hung up before any of us could say another word, but a small sliver of hope flickered in my belly. It had worked, sort of. Most of the vampires were being cured right now, and the Special Forces were going to try and contain and cure the others.

"He's right," Kyle said. I could see the New York footage had changed again. There were SWAT and Special Forces all over the streets, their fatigue and camo gear distinctive. Shouts and fighting. Vampires were still trying to rip the humans to pieces, but the moment they stopped to feed, they were shot up with AT20 and the cure.

Carter was already striding toward the door. I dashed across and stopped him. "You can't come with us, Dad. You're a vampire. No one will tell the difference now between good and bad vamps. You'll be targeted."

Silver eyes swirled crazily, and I had to look away. Too easy to fall into those mesmerizing depths and I needed a clear head for this argument. "Charlie, sweetheart, I want to be cured. I want a human lifetime with your mother … and you. I want us to be a family. I'm not afraid of the cure, and if you think I'm letting you go out there without me, you're sadly mistaken."

Well, shit, when he put it like that...

"No, you stay here and keep Mom, Jayden, and Becca safe."

He narrowed his eyes on me and I returned the gesture. I knew we looked similar, and I wondered how much of his virus blood had actually shaped me during my development in the womb. Like he was actually my blood father in some ways, after all.

"Sweetheart," my mom said, interrupting our epic stare-off. "I would feel much better if Carter was there to keep an eye on you. We'll be safe here. There are no vampires in this area, and there's no reason for them to leave Portland. They're trying to take their city back."

I huffed, crossing my arms over my chest. "Fine, you can come, I guess."

Markus snorted then, and that set off a chain reaction of chuckles from the rest of the enforcers. Even Carter cracked a smile, before hugging me again.

"Thank you for the permission, daughter."

"Uh, and I'll be coming too, BAFF, unless you want to throw down ash style right now." Jayden had untangled himself from Oliver long enough to hear about him staying behind. "You and Oliver are my family. Not to mention the rest of these meatheads. I'll be there keeping your backs safe. Don't even try to stop me."

I sighed again. "Can't keep you assholes safe, nope. No one listens to Charlie."

Jayden gave me the perfect single raised eyebrow. He was an expert at the WTF expression. "How about you stay here, girlfriend. I'd like to know you're safe for once, instead of gallivanting around like you're bulletproof and shit."

That shut me right up, until I saw Ryder open his mouth and I swung around to him. "Don't even think about it. I'm going! This is my fight. I'm the cure for a reason."

"Well, in that case …." Becca stepped forward, but before she could say more, everyone in the room let out a resounding, "NO!"

She dropped back onto the couch. "Fair enough," she said, scowling at all of us. Which honestly looked so adorable on her bespectacled face.

There was no more arguing. It looked like everyone besides my mom and Becca were hitting the city. I had a brief thought for Tessa, and hoped Lincoln had stashed her somewhere really safe. Preferably not in any Hive cities.

Ryder was all business now. "Okay then, time to suit up. We need full gear, plus the cure weapons and extra darts." He was already in his black enforcer gear, weapons practically dripping off him.

So freakin' hot. Give me a man with a big gun any day. Actually, just give me Ryder. He was way more than I could handle, and would keep me on my toes forever.

When I reached his side, he captured my hand and I lifted my head so he could press his lips to mine. The moment I tasted him my legs went weak and my heart started fluttering. He caught me around the waist, and for so many moments I was lost in everything that was Ryder. The strength, goodness, and warrior personality was one part; the other was the way he treated me, how he stared into my eyes like I was the only one in the world. The intensity he loved me with was breathtaking, and I would never be ready to give it up.

"We'll have our forever, Ryder," I said, pulling back slightly, our faces so close I could see every facet of silver and black in his eyes. "I love you."

With a low growl he pressed his lips to mine and we were kissing again, and it was only when more than one throat cleared that I realized the rest of our group was standing around us, geared up and ready to go. I didn't even blush when we pulled away from each other. No regrets. Hope they enjoyed the show, because there would be many more in the future.

It took me about five minutes to gather my shit, hug my mom and Becca goodbye, and then we were out the door and into two vehicles. Not as horrible as beige POS, but still plain, non-descript sedans. It was late afternoon and we were in a race to beat the sun.

"Do we have extra cure in the trunk?" I asked Ryder. I was in the passenger seat, no need to worry about rambunctious cure hunting humans today. The radio had informed us that all humans, unless those specifically trained to handle this type of situation, were on lockdown. Homes and offices were being barricaded, and armed forces were gathering in the streets. Curfew was in effect, no one was allowed outside during night hours.

During our drive the boys all got lots of updates. Kyle was still blocking off alerts from other Hives, and Lincoln continued to confirm that the cure was working. In some Hives we had a 95% cure rate. New York had been one of the lowest at 70%.

"We should be good here, right? I mean Lucas is sort of in charge, and we already wiped out so many of their numbers in the last battle," I said into the silent car. "Right?"

Carter leaned forward; he was in the seat behind Ryder. "Don't underestimate Portland. Have you heard from Lucas?"

I had to shake my head. Despite repeated attempts to contact him, no messages seemed to be going through.

Carter didn't say any more, but we all knew what he was thinking. Portland vampires hated me and the enforcers, and they had most likely killed Lucas and brought in reinforcements to their Hive. They would have been ready for war, even before the cure started making the rounds. Great. As if we weren't in enough danger, we were heading for the town filled with vampires who had nothing but vengeance on their minds.

Chapter 12

The sun was sinking into the western sky, the last rays of safety brushing across Portland. We were camped out about two miles from the Hive compound. So far we hadn't run into any special forces even though Lincoln said they were stationed somewhere nearby. They must be in hiding, waiting for some signal. The streets were empty enough that we wouldn't have missed them. So far all we'd seen was a police van driving the streets blaring a message for the citizens of the city: "You are under martial law. Do not leave your homes, vampires are attacking the city. We will let you know when you can come out. Stay inside. Report any activity to 9-1-1."

Ryder's phone buzzed between us. He glanced down before bringing it to his ear.

"Lincoln," he said quietly.

He was silent for many minutes, listening as the SWAT leader barked information at him. When he hung up, he swiveled around slightly so everyone could hear him. "The Army has been ambushed in the northeast part of the city. Some vampires got them on the road, and here's the odd part. They emerged from inside a building which had been empty not five minutes earlier."

WTF? How did they get in there with the sun still out? It just went down.

"Lincoln says more armed forces are on the way, but for now we're all that stands between Portland and the Hive. Red alerts are going out across all news outlets, social media, and even text alerts are being sent. Lincoln said some humans from smaller towns in Oregon have come out to help fight. Which is a pain more than anything because they don't have a chance in hell against vampires. All they're going to be giving them is blood and targets to turn. So we not only have to keep the Hive contained until the Army manages to get through, but we also need to keep an eye out for any human heroes."

Wicked. So it was eight of us versus hundreds. I had to ask him: "How the hell were they coming from inside the buildings? The sun just dropped."

Ryder shrugged. "I don't know, but Lincoln seemed livid. That area had been cleared already, so no one expected an ambush. They must have somehow preplanned this, hid inside buildings for a few days."

Possibly, but it didn't quite seem right. Someone would have noticed them surely. But if they weren't already hiding in the buildings, how were they moving without going into the sun? And without being seen? As far as I knew, none of their ten houses' superpowers included turning invisible. It was almost as if they were…

My stomach dropped when the realization hit me. My hands were shaking as I brought them up to brush my short hair off my face. "Oh fuck of all fucks."

My dad raised an eyebrow at that one. "You know what's up, Charlie?"

Without acknowledging anyone, I snatched the phone from Ryder and speed-dialed Lincoln. We didn't have a second to waste. The moment I heard Blue Eyes' voice, I said the two words that any Portland native would know.

"Shanghai tunnels." I then hung up. I had no time to chat with the SWAT dude any longer.

The moment I mentioned the tunnels, color drained from the faces around me, and the entire sexy six burst into action with a collective "Fuck!"

I swallowed, hoping to hell I was wrong, but my gut was saying I was right. My mom took me on the tour of the underground tunnels when I was twelve. In the 1850s to about 1940, these tunnels were built under all of the bars and hotels in Portland. A drunk bar patron would be sitting in his stool one minute and the next minute a trapdoor would open and the man would be sucked down into the tunnels to be robbed and sold as a slave on a ship and taken out to sea.

Not the proudest Portland history, but these tunnels existed all over the city, and I would bet my life the vampires had connected the Hive to them. They were smart enough to ensure they had a way to stay out of the sun and still get around. Fuckers were probably in every one of the older building in Portland right now, waiting until the darkness hit to burst out and fuck up the city. Well, darkness had just hit and we were so screwed.

Even my father looked concerned. He stated the obvious: "We're on the wrong side of the river." The Hive and the airport were on the East side of the Willamette. The majority of the tunnels were on the West Side. We needed to cross the Willamette now. Holy shit, there must be over twenty spots where the tunnels came up into bars and businesses. Where would we even begin?

Sam halted us before we could burst into action. "They expect us to steer clear of the Hive. We should go in, find the tunnel they used, and surprise them from behind."

My mouth dropped open. "I'm not a fan of suicide, Sam, but thanks." That was a really bad idea when there was no way to know for sure the tunnel thing was right. I wouldn't bet all of our lives on it. Carter had already told us that if we got within five hundred feet of the Hive and they were waiting for us, we'd all be dead.

Of course, now he'd changed his mind. With a nod he joined in: "You're right. They wouldn't expect us to figure out the tunnels until it was too late. If we can infiltrate the Hive and come up at their backs, we'll have the element of surprise."

When did the world stop rotating around the sun? Was I now the cautious one? The adult in this situation? I knew nothing about adulting; it was scary and outside my wheelhouse. But I couldn't lose any of my boys, so I needed to step up here.

"It's too risky! We'll get our heads blown off if you're both wrong," I said, trying to put as much command in my voice as possible. It just came out full of anger. Anger was my response to impending doom.

My father strode over to me and cupped my chin. "I love you, Charlie. You've grown into a beautiful young woman."

Before I could respond to his emotional display, he crouched and pushed off the ground, sailing into the air and flying fifty feet above our heads.

"No! Get back here!" I ran after him, but I wasn't fast enough. My father was an Original and holy shit he was full-on flying in a huge arc across the sky, headed right for the Portland Hive.

"Why would he do that?" I shouted, turning to scramble with the rest of the enforcers into the cars.

Ryder just squeezed my hand as we flew into the back seat and Kyle gunned the car. "He's going to make sure it's safe for us to go in."

Fuck! I wanted to get to know him, have him in my life before he decided to go off as a hero and get killed. I fought back the tears, searching for some inner positivity, some hope. I couldn't write him off yet. He was an Original. He would be okay.

Kyle spun the wheel and took a hard turn. We had been a mile or so out, so it only took us a few minutes to see the gated compound. It looked deserted, but that didn't mean anything. The front gate was closed, repaired from the last time we'd smashed through it. One of the guys jumped out and managed to pulverize the locks and cut the chains tying it all together. We weren't in reinforced SUVs now, so smashing through was a bad idea.

There were no ash or vampires on the front gate. And none in any of the security huts which littered the grounds. I'd never seen those buildings empty. Maybe the boys were right, maybe all of this Hive had gone into the tunnels. Kyle drove like a maniac, the tires squealing the entire way before we slammed to a halt at the front door of the compound. He didn't bother with the underground parking, we'd been ambushed there by vampires too many times.

Sam paused for a second before opening his door, and looked up in the sky. The others all followed suit and I knew they were scoping for snipers.

"Sam, maybe—"

I didn't get a chance to finish before he was out of the car. Not one to be left behind, I followed the boys and was relieved when my head didn't get blown off. The front door was secured, but Sam overrode that pretty easily. The Hive wasn't in lockdown mode, so the extra securities were not initiated. Bad move on their part. Unless of course this was all a big trap. Then the bad move was ours.

I couldn't see Carter anywhere in the front entrance, but he most likely went in through the roof or something. Dude was a superhero and could leap sixty stories no problem. No noise or anything trickled through the Hive; it was eerily quiet, but we remained on high alert, creeping through, weapons up and ready to use.

"Remember, the cure darts will not stop them coming for us, we need to inject and then knock them out." Ryder's voice was low, but in this noiseless tomb very easy to hear.

"Or just kill them if your life is in danger," he said, stating the obvious.

On and on we crept, up the stairs to the floors above. There was not a single soul here. Completely deserted. On the fifth floor a scuffing noise had all eight of us spinning around. Jayden was shoved back by Oliver; he ended up next to me. I saw the flash of pissed off on his face as he growled at his fiancé's back. None of us moved, waiting ever so patiently for the noise maker to emerge, and only released our tight hold on the guns as Carter popped into view.

"Dad!" I hiss yelled. "We could have shot you."

He grinned, all confident and shit. Damn Viking Original vampire. "You don't have to whisper. This place is deserted. At least in the upper levels."

Where the hell was Lucas? Damn, I hope they hadn't killed him. He'd done so much to help us. I wanted him to get that normal life he'd been dreaming of forever.

"We need to head into the lower levels," Sam said. He was carrying around a tiny tablet laptop looking thing. Some weird hybrid computer, and as always was typing away one handed at a million miles a minute. "I pulled up some old underground plans from the water and sewer department. They keep the most updated information. There are definitely tunnels underneath the Hive. I think these are fairly new ones, but I can see half a dozen places where they might connect into the old Shanghai Tunnels."

Holy shit. Did that mean I'd been right? Vampires were hiding under the city everywhere, and the humans had no idea.

Kyle quickly darted over to the elevators and hit the button. With a ding the doors slid across. "Much faster this way," he said.

None of us wasted another second, filling the metal box. Sam reached out and hit the button for one of the sublevels. This Hive was filled with secrets. Here's hoping this doorway into the tunnels was revealed easier than many of the others.

When the doors slid silently across, Ryder and Markus stepped out first, guns raised. I recognized this space as soon as I walked from the elevator. The smooth rock walls with the fire lanterns up high, their flickering lights making everything look Medieval. This was the level I'd come to back when I was in the culling, with the nasty redhead vampire. She'd brought me here to see my mom, Lucas' gift to me.

Just like that time, we went straight to the large, ornate double doors, the one with the engraved emblem, unrecognizable words, and a secret pattern thing to get inside.

Carter was all business, slamming his huge hands down on the emblem and getting it open. It was useful having an ancient, all knowing vampire on our team. Inside looked the same still: huge table, fireplace which was not lit this time, and ornate wall adornments.

"The entrance is here somewhere?" Sam said. "Do you know where, Carter?"

Clearly I wasn't the only one who'd noticed how at home my father seemed here. He'd obviously spent much time in Portland over the years. Had a man on the inside or some shit.

My father took his time observing the room, and if I wasn't mistaken he looked to be counting stones along the far side of the circular space. Eventually he strode over and ran his fingers lightly across the wall.

"He needs to hurry up," Jared said, Australian accent strong. "It's been dark for at least ten minutes now. The humans are going to be sitting ducks."

Jayden snorted. "Dude, I'm so not telling that hot-ass warrior to hurry up. He'll crucify you, and ain't no one gonna stop him."

"Dude!" I mimicked him. "That's my dad you're talking about. Please, no more hot-ass stuff."

Jayden winked at me and Oliver swung around to narrow his eyes at him. I was getting the vibe that they were in a silent lover's tiff right now. Too much stress could kill the strongest of relationships. But I knew they were solid. I was already planning what to wear as Jayden's best man. A wedding was something to look forward to. Something to fight for. A happy ending for all of us.

Further conversation was cut off by the sound of stone moving on stone, a weird grating screech. Carter lifted the tapestry closest to him, and sure enough, there was an open doorway leading to some narrow stone stairs.

For the record, I hated being underground like this. And taking those creepy stairs which led into old haunted tunnels was also not my idea of an entertaining day. This shit was fun when you were twelve years old and with your mom. Not so much as an adult with a fear of being crushed in a tunnel collapse. Damn vampires. Would have been much better if they were friendly, got along with all the kids in the playground. But no, they had to be nasty little assholes who like to kill and maim.

It was dark down here. The boys flicked on their Maglites, which gave us just enough light to see a few feet ahead. As we descended, a damp scent and heavy feeling filtered through the tunnel. The stairs ended in a narrow walkway, the sound of water all around us.

"This area is part of the underground water treatment." Markus pointed across to the far wall with his light so we could all see the huge pipe running there.

"Stay close," Sam added. "And watch your step. There are lots of grates and divots in the ground."

The water grew louder as we marched along. I knew Sam was leading us according to his underground schematics. Here's hoping the vampires had not adjusted them too much. We could be lost under here for weeks.

Nothing much happened for the next few minutes of fast walk-running, hauling ass knowing time was against us and that we were a few miles from where the main tunnels in northwest Portland were, but just as the sound of water died off, something else came into view. There was illumination ahead, and the space seemed to be quite large. There was no hesitation. We dashed toward it, preparing to fight.

"Holy vampire babies in hell," Jayden shouted as we skidded to a halt on the edge of the lit-up room. His dark eyes flashed across to me. "It's like we stumbled into a scene from the exorcist."

He wasn't kidding. The tunnels had opened up into a large, caged space. Twenty feet wide, it was like a small apartment, and not what you would expect for underground living, with low ceilings and lots of artificial light. It was still stone, and damp, but some attempt at home comforts had been made. There were hospital beds, cushions, medical equipment, and a small kitchen area installed, which was just great, because the hundreds of humans down here would have needed something to keep themselves alive.

Faces turned in our direction. Well, all the ones who weren't dead, because quite clearly there were plenty who hadn't made it through the vampire's little experiments.

"What are you doing here?" a female said, stepping forward. She wore a simple white shift dress, bare feet, hair all matted. "Ash aren't allowed in our breeding den."

I'm sorry ... their what? Jayden and I exchanged another wide-eyed look. Not only had the vampires clearly tried to change a bunch of humans to get their numbers up, but they were also illegally breeding with humans? Why the heck? They hated ash? Why would they want more? Nausea made my stomach roll as I imagined the "breeding" down here.

I must have spoken some of my questions out loud, because she answered. "They knew you would come for them, and they wanted to make sure their seed lived on. Ash are better than humans anyway. We were paid quite handsomely for this gift. Don't you worry yourselves about us." She held her chin high with an air of snobbery, but I could see the humans were caged behind bars. A few of the women looked like they may have originally signed up for the deal but were now regretting it.

Kyle snorted. "And should we not worry ourselves about the dead humans all over the place?"

She shrugged again, and I caught sight of the scars on her neck. She was a damn feeder. Clearly they'd taken their female feeders and impregnated them, and the males were turned to vampires. Well, some of them.

"Only the worthy survive," she said. "We burn the dead when they start to smell, and the ones who survive the virus go into the special holding area. Besides, if you die, they compensate your family. You'll find no victims here. The vampires took the newly changed just before they went through the tunnels."

Her face shuttered then, and I knew she had not meant to let that slip. But at least we knew we were on the right track.

"Vampire rule is over," Ryder said to them, his deep voice vibrating with anger. "War is going down tonight. We'll come back for you because tomorrow a new world will start and the ash will be in charge of you."

If we survived, was the unspoken sentiment. Many stares followed us as we turned, leaving the light, to continue along the path. Motherfucking vampires. I didn't even want to cure them now. I wanted to kill them. Every single freakin' one. And where the hell was Lucas in all of this? I was torn between mourning him, fearing for his life, and worrying he'd been playing us all along. He did so many wonderful things for me, risked his life for mine more than once. Surely that had not all been a ploy. Maybe he was playing along with them now to try and keep a man on the inside until we arrived. Or maybe I was a naïve moron. Either way, my heart hardened a little then. A thin frosty shell covered it as I unholstered my gun and clicked off the safety. Fuck the cure darts. The vampires clearly were not going to surrender. I was out for blood now, to avenge those rotting humans back there in the cell and the ones knocked up with ash babies.

We reached a swampy patch of ground. Water seeped through a few of the divots in the stone.

"We're under the Willamette," Sam announced, and I shuddered. An entire river was over my head. Oh God, get me the hell out of here!

"The Shanghai Tunnels led to the river but never under it. They led right up to the boat dock so the people could be taken on ships," Ryder said

Who the fuck cares? I couldn't breathe. But my father seemed to get what he was blabbing about.

"Yes, they've clearly been planning this a while. Must have taken months to build. Probably when Charlie first showed up to the Hive. Or maybe even before," he said.

My stomach dropped. Fugly. He knew. He had a hunch from day one about what I was and he'd probably had this backup plan in place ever since. Asshole. Even dead he was still messing with my life.

Screw it. No time to worry about it now. We were out of the swampy mess and into the tunnels I recognized. These were the Shanghai Tunnels I had toured as a child. Surprisingly large and open, and above all, creepy.

Sam stopped and put his fist into the air. We all froze, holding our breath.

Sounds ripped through the silence. "Let's go! It's dark out!" a man roared. A voice I didn't recognize.

Lucas' voice made the hair on my arms stand up: "Waiting a few more moments won't hurt the plan. No one knows we're here. Give the humans time to scramble and run about in fear."

No. No. No. He couldn't be in on it. He couldn't.

The other voice seemed perturbed. "The others have already begun to fight. You're making me question your loyalty, Lucas."

Lucas let out a nervous laugh and then I heard skin hitting skin, that sound of crunching bone, and a body hitting the cold floor.

"Lucas!" I screamed, running forward, feeling awful for doubting him. He was clearly stalling so he could mess up their plans.

There were gas lamp torches lighting up the walls, and as I strode into view I saw about twenty hulking vampires staring at me. Lucas was standing over another vampire's body.

"Down!" I shouted at him, and he hit the deck as bullets sprayed from my gun.

Dear God, please don't let one of these ricochet and hit my head. That would be a very uncool way to die.

Air whooshed past me as my father sailed over me and slammed into the oncoming wall of angry bleeding vampires. I halted my firing, not going to risk hitting him for a second.

My eyes widened as the Viking started to move. My father was an efficient neck breaking machine. He literally severed a dozen spinal cords within moments. Ryder and the boys took care of the rest. Once they were unconscious, we shot them with cure darts. I gave my father the stank eye for interrupting my gunfire, but he ignored it. Running to Lucas, I helped him up.

"I knew you would figure it out," he said, his voice cracking. "You're a smart girl."

Did Ryder just growl?

I shook my head, ignoring it. "What the hell happened, Lucas? Vampires in the Shanghai Tunnels and a breeding program with humans."

Lucas looked sick. "I didn't know until today. Allistair made these plans after kicking me out of the Quorum and I had no idea. Charlie, once he found out there was a cure, just before you killed him, he told the Hive to be suspicious of the new blood shipment."

My stomach dropped. "No ... no, don't tell me."

Lucas nodded. "When the new shipment came, it was put into storage per his orders before he died. Portland Hive did not partake in the celebrations. He said to wait and watch around the world. If in a few days no one was cured, then we could drink. Until then we were to feast on old refrigerated bottled blood, and in worst case steal humans through the Shanghai Tunnels and feed from them.

"Dammit!" I clenched my fists tightly, trying to control my anger. How bad could it be? We'd wiped out a lot of Portland in the last battle, and had just taken down another twenty. How many more were loose on the city?

Lucas gave me a devilish smile. "Of course, I wasn't going to let Allistair win from the grave. We luckily got our shipments earlier than a lot of the Hives, so I've been peeling the dates off of the new shipment and replacing it with the old blood dates. I haven't slept for days."

Relief exploded into my chest and I crashed into him, giving him a huge hug. "Lucas! You're brilliant."

He smiled as I stepped back. "Don't get too excited. It was just me. I only got about forty to fifty percent of those bottles to the vampires. So half the Hive." His smile went huge, all white teeth and excitement. I couldn't help but return that smile.

"So if fifty percent got the cure-blood … that leaves us with…?"

My father answered: "About five hundred vampires."

I stifled a groan. "So some of the vampires are already turned to human? Where are they? And the ash?"

Lucas smoothed a hand over his hair. "Yep, most of them turned quite fast, and that's when the rest of the vampires decided to declare war on the city and headed for the tunnels. All ash and humans are stashed in the pit. The vampires plan to kill them when they return. They had no time with the sun setting, and they didn't want to waste the blood."

We could not let that happen.

"So there are still five hundred uncured vampires, and they've just hit the city?" I wanted confirmation of the numbers.

Lucas nodded. "But it won't last long. I knew I hadn't gotten to enough bottles done in time, so as a last ditch effort

I spiked all of my remaining bottles of blood wine with the cure laced blood. And when Thomas called for a toast before battle just an hour ago, we all drank. Me included. I can feel the change starting already. The others won't be far behind me."

That got a grin from all of us.

"Lucas, you might have just saved everyone. If we can hold them off until the cure sets in."

He nodded and even though it was subtle, I was starting to notice some color coming back into his face; his eyes glowed a little less silver.

Carter placed a hand on Lucas' shoulder "Thank you. Now, let's get up there. A lot of lives can be lost in a few hours."

Way to rain on my parade, but he was right. I saw a ladder to my right. "Where are we? What's the plan?"

"We're on Third Street, beneath Hog's Head tavern. Plan is to go out shooting and … well, stay alive."

Okay, so not exactly a plan, but good enough. Lucas stepped onto the ladder, ready to climb up, but I grabbed his arm.

"You've done enough. Go back to the Hive and wait for us there," I said.

He looked back at me, his face filled with all these softer emotions, and I swear his gaze was locked on my lips. Awkward.

"I'll be okay, Charlie. I need to see this through," he said as he started climbing again.

I didn't have time to argue so I just began climbing after him. Once we had all made it into the room, a wine cellar, I immediately heard screaming and gunshots. Sam jumped on his cell.

"Lincoln, we're about to come out of Hog's Head tavern. Don't shoot us," he ordered. After a few minutes he nodded and hung up.

"What's going on out there?" Ryder asked.

Sam's voice was tense. "Lincoln said that some vampires got into a nearby apartment building, killing humans left and right."

No! Shit. "Let's go!" I said. No one argued, they all just swung into action behind me.

This was it. This was the battle I had been planning for. This could very well be the last day of my life. A smart girl would jump back down that ladder and run like a little bitch back to the Hive and wait. But that wasn't me. I was as loyal as they come, and I wasn't leaving my boys to fight alone. I wasn't letting the humans or Portland be attacked because of me. These vampires were reacting because of my cure.

Sam, Lucas, Carter, Jayden and the others left the wine cellar, then it was just me and Ryder. We both seemed to know that this could be goodbye. I didn't want to say anything, didn't want to hear it. I just crashed into him as his arms came around me and our mouths found each other, tongues exploring for one last time. All the deliciousness that was Ryder. The scent, his touch, the way he treated me like shit for the first month and then loved me so hard I could barely breathe. This man was my soulmate. After one intense kiss he just pulled away and pinned me with blazing eyes.

"Hawaii," he whispered, and I smiled.

"Hawaii."

With that we walked hand in hand out into the vampire war.

CHAPTER 13

The second we hit the streets, it was clear all hell had broken loose. The streetlights cast an eerie glow and I could see the muzzle of guns lighting up a nearby apartment building. Screams and the smell of smoke assaulted me. Every window around us was smashed, trash and debris scattered everywhere, as if looting as well as murder was going on.

"Psst!" a familiar voice sounded behind me. Turning, I saw Sasha in full SWAT gear with Lincoln and his team behind her. They ran quickly to our location and we all took cover in the entrance of a nearby building.

Lincoln wasted no time: "Over thirty vampires stormed the building. We should split up and attack from all four sides. Crash into windows, kick down doors. Do whatever you have to and get in there. Protect the women and children first."

We nodded, but I felt a little bad for the men who we were protecting only second. Before we could move out, Carter jumped and leapt up, landing on the apartment roof and taking out a vampire sniper.

"Jesus H Christ, is he with us?" Lincoln asked, sounding slightly concerned.

I nodded. "Yep, he's one of the good ones, so please try not to shoot him."

We were on the move. I instinctively stuck to Ryder's side, knowing it made both of us feel better. We split up then into four groups. Sasha and Lucas were with us as we stormed the front entrance. What I saw had fresh hot rage igniting inside of me. Women were being dragged out of apartments by the hair, vampires feeding off of their necks. Female vampires were making the men drink their blood, exposing them to the virus.

"Party's over, fuckers!" Sasha yelled, and tossed a flashbang grenade. She waited a second before dive rolling straight into the center of the chaos. I grinned. I'd forgotten how much I loved this chick. She was totally my spirit animal.

Despite my desire to stay close to Ryder, we were soon separated in the absolute chaos. I had my gun held tightly as I ran straight into the fray, shooting to kill as many vampires as I could. The humans' lives depended on us moving quickly; a lot of them were close to death as it was.

For the infected humans I used my other gun, the one with the cure darts. Cure in my right hand, kill gun in my left. These humans would hopefully survive, but with the massive blood loss it was always a worry.

"Are the hospitals full?" I shouted to Lincoln, who was close by wrestling a vampire. For a human, he was holding his own.

Too impatient to wait for him to finish to answer, I swapped hands and used my "kill" gun, shooting the vampire right in the forehead. Lincoln jumped to his feet, his hands automatically going to wipe away the blood he'd just had spatter all over him.

"Fuck, Charlie. You could have hit me."

I waved him off. "Nah, I'm an excellent shot. Besides, I owed you that for the broken jaw."

He didn't argue with me again. I might have even seen a small smile.

"So, hospitals? Should we be trying to get these humans there? Or is it a complete waste?"

Sasha dashed past us, chasing down a female vamp, and it looked like she had the upper hand. "Ten-hour backlog in hospitals already, no point taking them. We just need to do the best we can in the field."

Dammit. That's what I was worried about. Blue Eyes lifted a small comm device then and barked some orders. Within a minute three or four field medics burst into the building. I moved closer to them, determined to keep them safe from any vampires. This floor was relatively clear now, but I couldn't see any of my boys. Even Jayden was gone, and he'd been close by too.

"Get the humans stabilized. Make sure all of them get a shot of the cure, no matter what." Lincoln was off again, shouting and killing as he went. Once it looked like this floor was secure, I went into action, dragging the humans across the street to the medic building. They worked fast, already having set up a triage zone. It was soon filled with human casualties.

"All need to go to triage first," a tall, thin male was shouting. "More urgent to the west end, and the least to the east."

Dude, seriously! If you want me to follow directions, please never include the words west or east. Thankfully I figured it out; it was clear which were in the worst condition. One near the end had pretty much had her throat torn out, and two Army people were working to stabilize it.

"Charlie, help!"

The faint call caught my attention. I quickly deposited my human somewhere in the middle of the triage line. She was conscious but had lost a lot of blood. Following that call from outside, I holstered my cure gun and kept the kill one out. The streets were no better than before. In fact there looked to be a lot more humans and vampires out.

Come on. The cure had to start working soon. In this case, Becca couldn't have made the change fast enough. As I darted across the road, searching for the one who'd called my name, I sent out a brief hope that other cities weren't hit as hard as Portland. New York seemed to be under control fast; it had to be the same in other places. I would never be able to live with myself if by curing the vampires I killed off 10% of the human population.

"Charlie!" I knew that voice better than any other. Tessa. She was in trouble.

Full on sprinting through the streets, I tapped into the heat at my center and levitated across the road, landing right before a dark, creepy alley. Of course. Why not? I stepped with very little hesitation, even as the darkness engulfed me. Most of the streetlights were busted, and power seemed to have been cut to lots of buildings. I had ashpire vision but it was still damn dark.

"Tess?" I said, barely more than a whisper. What the fuck was Tessa doing out in the middle of downtown Portland during the war?

The only reply was a low whimper. My heart was pounding heavily, my breathing doing something weird. I couldn't seem to get enough oxygen. This alley was long and narrow. Multiple doorways led off it, and even a few other small alleys. I was about halfway along when I heard her cry out and realized she was to the left, down a side access. I took off, gun still held firmly.

It was stupid of me to come here alone. I knew that the moment I entered the alley. But there was no time to turn back. Tessa needed me. My boots slammed against the pavement, and as the end of the alley came into sight, the rapid pulsing of my heart increased.

WTAF? Tessa was pinned up against the wall by a vampire. A vampire I thought was long dead.

"Hello, Charlene, so nice of you to join us." Blake had the full creepy stare going on, and I was sure he'd been feeding from my bestie. I could see the blood on his chin and on her throat.

Think, Charlie, you need to defuse this situation right now.

"What are you doing, Blake? You love Tessa. You promised me you'd never hurt her."

He threw back his head and laughed, this stupid chuckle which was irritating enough that my finger flexed on the trigger. He must have noticed, shaking his head twice at me.

"I wouldn't do that, Charlie. I have a knife right at the base of Tess's neck. Even if your bullet hits me, I'll have enough time to insert the blade."

Tessa whimpered again, and I could see the flash of blade that Blake was talking about.

"What do you want then?" I said, my tone hard as I took a step closer, about ten feet from them.

Blake's silver eyes were dead, flat of color and life. The silver actually looked really faded ... almost like he'd been...

"Have you been injected with the cure?" I asked him.

The smile fell, and he was less like a blond Cabbage Patch Doll now and more like a psycho serial killer. "Your best friend here forgot to tell me the cure stays in a human's system for days, and that she was dosed to her eyeballs."

Tessa's eyes narrowed; some of her fear fled as dark anger crossed her face. It was definitely only the knife in her spine keeping her from smacking him in the face. "I thought you were dead, you stupid motherfucker. You broke into my safe house and fed from me without my permission. You've gotten everything you deserve."

Blake tightened the grip he had in her hair, his knife-wielding hand sliding closer, and I knew the blade was starting to cut Tessa. I could see her pain, smell the blood.

"I was Allistair's favorite. He knew he could trust me right from the start, that you would be a weakness he could utilize against Charlie." His eyes flicked up to me. "He suspected you would be all of our downfall, and he had so many plans in place to make sure you didn't succeed, but then somehow you always had someone powerful on your side keeping you safe. In the culling it was Lucas and Ryder. They manipulated everything to make sure you would get through. After that you were so deeply involved with the enforcers it was impossible to touch you. So Allistair figured Tessa was our next bet. I was sent in to cultivate her love of vampires. To put her in a position to be used against you."

Tessa was crying now, and I could see guilt clear across her beautiful features. While Blake was monologuing, I was creeping closer, in the smallest of increments, but there was only about six feet between us now. I could almost reach out and touch my oldest friend.

"You tried to grab my mom too, didn't you?" Everything was starting to make sense now. The way Blake had come out of nowhere and "loved" Tessa so much. The council allowed her change so easily.

The curly-headed asswipe nodded. "Yep, more than once, actually. Then she disappeared, and so did you, just when things were getting interesting."

I noticed movement then, on the side of the building above his head. Was someone up there?

Hoping they were friend and not another vampire douche, I started talking to keep Blake's focus on me.

"I'm here now, and I'll do whatever you want if you let Tessa go. She's human now. She had nothing to do with any of this."

Blake growled, but his fangs looked quite small now, almost like regular human incisors. The flat gray was fading to blue in his eyes. The cure was starting to work. I wondered if the human version of him was fast enough to stab her before I shot him. Clearly the oxytocin wasn't pumping out yet, or it never would. Some people were just born dicks.

"Do whatever I want? I want you dead!" he seethed, "I want my old life back, before there was a cure."

His arm shifted, the one which had been wrapped in Tessa's hair. He pulled a gun, sliding his arm around Tessa, and pointed it right at me. Fuck. One shot to the head and I was gone. He must have seen the fear in my eyes because he flexed his fingers on the trigger, his creepy grin kicking up a few notches.

The next sixty seconds happened so fast, there was no time for me to do anything but shout his name. Blake's finger squeezed the trigger as a streak of white dropped from the dark alley, landing right in front of me. Multiple shots sounded, the deafening noise echoing off the brick walls.

"No!" I screamed as the person in front of me took three bullets.

Tessa spurred into action while Blake was distracted. She managed to spin in a whirl of grace and knee him right in the balls.

He dropped the knife and went limp, hunching forward. I heard his curses, my heart freezing as he recovered enough to raise his gun hand. Before I could shout out a warning to Tessa, she wrapped her hand around the gun. They wrestled with it for a moment, but Tessa had surprise on her side.

Her eyes were wild as she twisted it back into his body, and no hesitation squeezed the trigger, nailing him right in the chest. The bang was deafening, and blood splattered on Tessa's white hair. Blake's body dropped to the ground at an odd angle.

Knowing my friend was safe now, I could finally turn toward the body on the ground, the man who had saved me. I'd known the second I saw the white coat, but even as I dived across the rocky ground toward him, my mind refused to believe it was Lucas.

A whimper left my throat as I crashed to his side, the rough ground tearing through my pants. Lucas was bleeding from his stomach and chest. I ripped off my jacket, trying not to panic at the way his breaths were coming out in short, labored bursts. I pressed my jacket to his wounds, focusing on the one over his chest.

"Medic!" I shouted, as hot tears ran down my face. This couldn't be happening, not to Lucas. He'd sacrificed so much and had been this close to a normal life. My head spun around, trying to see if anyone was coming to help. "Help!" I screamed again.

Tessa stood there frozen, shaking from shock. She just killed her fiancé. I couldn't blame her for not running to get help.

"Shh," Lucas told me, and coughed as blood dripped and spluttered out his mouth.

I moved my face closer to his, keeping the pressure firm on his chest, but also needing to hug my friend.

Our gazes locked, and already his dark blue eyes looked glassy. Shit, he had blue eyes. I never knew that. He attempted to smile, but it was weak. "No, no, no," I cried, hugging myself even closer. "This wasn't supposed to happen. You were supposed to have a happy ending."

Those big blue eyes disappeared for a second. He blinked, and it took a long time for his eyes to open again. He was fading away. Dammit! He was human. A vampire would survive these wounds. In a way, it was my cure that killed him.

Lucas reached out and stroked my cheek. "I saved you ... I'm going to be ... with my wife and kids now." His breathing was raspy as he struggled for words. "I got to be human ... that's happy enough for me."

I couldn't hold back the sob that hit me. You know how there are moments when you're supposed to try to be strong for those around you? This was one of those and I couldn't do it. I couldn't keep myself from ugly crying all over him.

"Shhh," he said again, and that was his last word. Life left his eyes. I clutched him closer to me, even though I knew he was gone. His body was still warm, but the essence which had always followed Lucas around was no more. He was no more.

Eventually cold hard anger replaced my sorrow. Lucas had saved me so many times. From my first day in the Hive up until now, he had been my angel. And now he was dead in an alley. He deserved better.

"Fuck!" I shouted, wiping my tears and pulling out both of my guns, replacing the cure cartridge with bullets. Fuck the cure. Any vampire left now was a dead one. They'd chosen to fight, to follow Allistair and his minion Blake. Now they would face the consequences.

Tessa looked afraid. "Charlie?"

I must have looked like a maniac, covered in Lucas' blood, holding two guns, streams of tears still coating my cheeks.

"Humans are dying. I gotta help and you're not safe alone. You know how to use a gun?" She sure as hell had handled Blake like an expert. I held one of my kill guns out to her and she took it, stepping even closer. Her eyes were sad as she knelt beside Lucas. She made the sign of the cross over his chest and closed his eyes. "Lucas taught me to protect myself," she said, standing again.

Of course he did. I told him to look after my bestie in the Hive, and he did, like a fucking gentleman. The world had lost a good man.

"Stick to my ass, and if you see any vampires, shoot to kill." I wanted these assholes to die. I wanted revenge. Blake's death wasn't enough. Lucas had been human, and he'd drunk the blood wine at the same time as everyone else, which had to mean most were or would soon be human. I needed to take out as many vampires as I could before they were human too.

A shout cut through my red murderous haze. As if the universe thought I hadn't been through enough tonight, Oliver's bellow rang through the night. "JAYDEN!"

"Oh fuck!" I shouted, and took off running like I was in the goddamn Olympics. "Oliver!" I shouted, trying to pinpoint where I'd heard the scream.

"Charlie!" Oliver screamed and when I burst out of the alley. I took a right, heading toward his voice. I kept close to the walls but bullets snapped at my feet. Shit. Sniper. I was pleased to hear Tessa's footsteps pounding behind me. Bitch hated running, and at this speed she would probably collapse and die when we got there. But I couldn't think about anything other than Jayden. Oliver was a badass mother, and nothing short of death would make him scream like that.

"Charlie!" Oliver shouted, and I burst into the open building. The door had been blown off. Holy shit, this was my favorite coffee shop. Oliver was crouching over Jayden's lifeless body. Oh my God, so much blood. Jayden was lying in a pool of blood as big as an elephant. Oliver was holding his leg, which was spurting in tiny little streams.

A dead vampire lay on the ground next to them.

I turned to see Tessa wheezing, trying to catch her breath. She wouldn't be able to run and get help. Oliver was holding Jayden's leg together.

"I'm getting a medic," I said to Oliver, and he nodded. His face was drained of color, tears streaming down his cheeks.

Turning to Tessa, I gave her a serious look. "Guard them with your fucking life." Tessa was born into privilege, never went through the culling, and before Blake had never killed anyone. But I needed her to be a badass right now.

Tessa nodded, clenching her jaw, and tightened the grip on her gun, standing in front of the café door like a sentinel.

I didn't wait. I took off running.

I was the fastest runner I knew, other than Ryder. I WOULD get to a medic. I WOULD get some fucking blood and I WOULD save Jayden's life. He'd bled a lot during the culling and he'd survived, I told myself. He could survive this.

Fuck! I forgot about the sniper. Bullets snapped all around me as I ran in a zigzag back to the place where the medical triage had been set up. In the end I tapped into my center, letting the heat take me over as I soared close to the medic building.

"Charlie!" Ryder's voice came to my left, as a bullet nicked my shoulder and I tripped over my legs. Tucking down my left shoulder, I braced for the fall, rolling with it, before quickly popping up to find Ryder at my side, shooting the shit out of the guy on the roof.

"Jayden is dying! Needs blood," I shouted to him, and took off running again. He kept pace with me easily, guns out, firing at anyone who got in our way. We dashed into the building. I ran right up to the first person I saw.

"I need to do a blood transfusion STAT!" I all but shouted in her face.

She was in the middle of bandaging someone's neck, so she motioned over to a cooler. "Blood pouches in there. IV lines on the on table. Help yourself."

Okay. I could do a blood transfusion. How hard could it be? My mom was a nurse. I threw open the top of the cooler and grabbed three bags labeled AB-negative. I grabbed two IV lines and took off running again. Ryder was right with me the whole time; he was my muscle, shooting any remaining vamps down.

Once I had time to think, I'd realize how damn happy I was to have Ryder close to me again. As a team we kinda rocked. Plus, knowing he was alive was everything. Couldn't focus on that though, I had a BAFF to save. I'd already lost one friend tonight, and I would not lose another.

I was back at the café in record time and nearly got my head blown off by a trigger-happy Tessa. She pulled her hand away at the last second and shot the ground.

"Jesus, Charlie. Announce yourself!" she barked.

"Sorry!" Damn, she took the protector role seriously. Good girl.

Oliver was shaking; there was too much damn blood, pouring everywhere, coating the floor around them. How was it possible to lose that much blood and not be dead? Jayden had better not be dead.

I sat in the blood, getting as close as I could to my BAFF.

My hands shook as I ripped open the IV lines and attached the blood bag. I felt Ryder's hulking mass behind me, and when I brought a shaking hand down to my best friend's arm, Ryder placed his hand over mine to steady it. I took in a deep breath, and then with more focus I placed the line with Ryder's help. He'd had to do this a few times in the field with his men, so he was actually a massive help.

Jayden's veins were nearly nonexistent with the blood loss, but we got one. Standing, I held the blood high so it could drip down into his body. Ryder must have grabbed a med kit at the triage center, because he was ripping open packages, his hand steady as he began suturing Jayden's leg wound.

I tried not to think too hard. My mind already felt stretched so thin it was barely lucid. I held Jayden's hand; Oliver had the other, and we waited. The longest goddamn wait of my life. My eyes were trained on the very shallow and minuscule rise and fall of Jayden's chest. If he stopped breathing, I would die. I would literally give up on life. Jayden was someone I couldn't live without. Thank God he was an ash; a human would have been dead long ago.

We must have stood there in silence forever. But after the gunshots died down, we heard a van drive by, loudspeakers blasting a message: "Vampires have surrendered. It's safe to leave your homes. Get your wounded to a local triage center."

"Did you hear that? Get my ass to a triage center." Jayden's weak voice filled the silent room and I broke down in tears. I didn't realize it until now but my arm holding up the blood bag was completely asleep. I let it drop, leaning forward to gently hug Jayden.

Oliver was openly crying, and even Ryder's eyes looked a bit damp.

"That didn't exactly go as planned," Sam said from the doorway, and we turned to see him with Jared, Markus, and Kyle. Kyle's shoulder was bleeding, but he looked okay. I was just opening my mouth to ask about Carter when he walked in after them, looking like he'd just been to a day spa. Despite his efforts, which most certainly had saved a lot of lives, he had not a hair out of place. I blew my father a kiss, and then all the enforcers.

They were alive. Thank you, God, Jesus, and all the saints. They were alive. My family was alive, and with a bit of luck the cure was working around the world. Vampires' numbers were decimated.

I couldn't contain my joy, laughter spilling from me as my eyes continued running across my family. There was a small part of my heart that mourned for Lucas; the fact that he didn't make it would haunt me forever, but I was determined to remember that everyone else was alive and I would count my blessings.

Chapter 14

One month later.

The sunset was absolutely spectacular as I made my way toward the pink carpet stretching out across the sand of the private beach in Turtle Cove. The background noise consisted of a small trio playing local music, and the crashing of waves against the warm, golden sand. My bouquet of flowers was fragrant enough for even humans to scent.

As I reached the edge of the aisle, the music changed slightly, signaling that it was time for me to walk the final steps to the end. My eyes were locked on Ryder, standing beside his best friends. The six of them were decked out in white, which they didn't usually wear, but really should more often. Ryder looked absolutely spectacular, his shirt open at the collar, pants fitted to his delectable body.

His grin had me stumbling my way down, but I managed to recover before completely face-planting it. He was going to be the death of me. Taking a few deep breaths, I did spare a glance for Oliver; he was the man of the hour, but there was no way I could keep my eyes from Ryder for long.

I had to keep it together. The guests' attention was on me. I was Jayden's best man after all. He'd decked me out in a beachy dress, all flowy and sunset colors. I even had gems adorning my bare feet, and cuffs around my ankles. My hair had grown out a little and was softly curled around my face. Jayden had overseen every single aspect of my appearance, and then gave his stamp of approval before kicking me out the door to walk in the bridal party. A party that consisted of me, Becca, and Tessa, who were dressed the same as me, walking a few yards behind.

Sam looked more than a little gobsmacked by the sight of our Becca all dressed up. She'd even ditched her glasses for the day, although I preferred her with them. They suited her so well. My heart soared at having all of our friends and family here. My mom and dad were in the crowd, along with plenty of others we knew from our life in the Hive, and before.

I couldn't believe Jayden had pulled this all together in a few weeks. After the battle in Portland, where I'd almost lost my BAFF, Oliver refused to wait any longer to marry him. Ryder and I had been talking of a trip to Hawaii, and as soon as Jayden heard he ran with it, and started planning the wedding of the century. Something nice to look forward to in the midst of rebuilding our world. The vampires had destroyed much on that night, but in the end, at least ninety percent had been cured or were dead. The Hives were being demolished, and the small number of vampires who'd survived were in hiding, and for now were staying there. Lincoln and his team now headed up a newly formed government division: VAT. Vampire Acquisition Taskforce. They kept us updated with news. Carter worked for them too. He'd taken the cure and was no longer vampire. But he had been one of the Originals and held a plethora of information on vampire hideouts around the world.

He and my mom were in love. Like so in love. If I still lived at home, I'd have to get soundproofing around my room just to stay there. Seeing them together made me happy. I now understood why my mom had been single for so much of her life. I'd be the same with Ryder. When you love someone like that, there is no replacing them.

Ever.

Ryder's eyes were practically silver as they remained locked on me. That gaze reminded me of the many hours we'd spent wrapped around each other in the past month. Yeah, my mom wasn't the only one getting some action.

Okay, gross, no more thoughts of mom action.

Ryder and I were determined to make up for every second we'd been apart. Or had almost died. I was kinda getting addicted to him. His touch. The way he loved me up so fully that sometimes I couldn't even remember my own name.

As I took my place beside the officiant, Ryder winked at me and I saw so many promises in his expression. Damn, I could not wait for the honeymoon. And it wasn't even my wedding.

Tessa and Becca joined me then too, and suddenly Jayden was at the end of the aisle. He looked breathtaking. I expected him to wear something pink and glittery, but instead he was in all white, like his soon-to-be husband. Okay, so there were some glittery pieces, and he had jewels across his feet, but mostly he looked like my beautiful best friend. His ash colored eyes looked a bit misty as he started his walk, and to be honest, I'm not sure there was a dry eye in the entire place as we watched the way Oliver and Jayden stared at each other.

When Jayden was about halfway down the aisle, Oliver moved, striding across and meeting him there. I raised a hand to my mouth, to cover up the small sob which wanted to escape. That was so beautiful; he literally couldn't even wait for him to walk down the aisle to have him at his side. That's how these two would do everything from now on, as a team.

The officiant started the ceremony, but I don't think Oliver or Jayden heard a word. They were enthralled with each other, and had to be prompted twice to repeat after him. A cheer went out when the wedding was complete. "I now pronounce you partners for life, husbands, lovers, and friends," said the officiant. Oliver and Jayden kissed then, before he could get to that part.

No one was surprised.

"Woohoo!" Tessa shouted next to me, and I found myself enthusiastically wrapped in her arms. It was nice to see her happy; those hazel eyes had been dull and lifeless for many weeks. Not only did she have to mourn Blake twice, but she'd had to come to terms with the fact that she shot him, and that he had betrayed us all in the worst way. At Lucas's funeral she'd had a complete breakdown and had to be sedated. I think my pain was too much for her, and the guilt that she was partly to blame for his death.

I sat by her bedside for days, but eventually she came back to me, and the healing had begun for us both. The road to recovery was long, but we were all taking the first steps.

Becca was next to be wrapped up in our group hug. Tears were streaming down her cheeks as she sobbed. "It was just so beautiful, so beautiful. Jayden and Oliver are so lucky."

The rest was incoherent, but I was starting to see our science girl was a romantic softy deep down. The wedding had touched her heart and she was all a mess of emotion. Arms wrapped around me from behind, and I sank back into the familiar embrace.

"You look beautiful, Charlie." Ryder's deep voice washed over me and I closed my eyes to savor the moment. The crashing of the waves, the warmth of Hawaii, the soft music on the warm breezes. This was kinda my version of heaven.

I had to spin in his arms, and our mouths met in a searching kiss. It was soft, and hot, and tongue and ... coherent thought was gone.

Eventually we stopped the PDA and followed everyone else down the aisle and across the beach to the huge marquee which had been set up earlier by the very talented wedding coordinators here. Jayden of course had to give his final approval, but anyone could see this was totally his style. It was just sunset now, so the countless candles were set off beautifully, not to mention multiple chandeliers casting light across the black and white decorated space, with a few bright splashes of color mixed amongst for dramatic effect. Oliver always liked to say that Jayden was the splash of color in his world, and this was a tribute to that.

I couldn't wait. This was going to be a party to remember, right down to the drunken karaoke that was scheduled in the next few hours. Jayden had decided to forgo all speeches or any structure in regards to food and drinks. Everything was already laid out on banquet tables across the room; people would help themselves whenever they wanted. And the bar was fully stocked, even with the good stuff. Ash everywhere were getting drunk tonight.

We hit the bar first and I found myself slamming back a shot with Tessa and Becca. Blood wine for Becca and I, tequila for Tessa. Our poor science girl didn't know it, but there was a plan tonight. I was getting her hammered and she was going to have another shot at Sam. This unrequited star-crossed lovers thing they had going on drove me nuts. I was going to be interfering-Charlie for one more night, and if that didn't work I was out.

"Gah, it's really not appealing. I hate to think of the damage to my body with this poison," Becca said, huffing in and out after her shot.

I snorted. "You're an ashpire, girlfriend. Ain't nothing damaging our liver."

She shook her head at me. "You know what I mean. Anything that tastes like burning cannot be good for you."

"Sam!" I yelled, noticing him across the room. He didn't look uncomfortable – Sam was hardly ever out of his element – but he did kind of look like he wished he was anywhere else but here.

When he didn't cross to me immediately, I stalked over and dragged him to the bar. "Do a shot with us," I said, turning my most pleading expression on him.

He glanced over my head, and I knew the poor dude was exchanging a glance with Ryder. No doubt they both knew what I was up to. Brains and beauty that was my boys.

"I really need to keep a clear head. I have a lead on Sanctum, and it's in our best interest to closely monitor that group."

Jayden came upon us then. "Hells no," he said to Sam. "No working at this awesome wedding. Sanctum are not going anywhere, and so far their ploy for world domination has resulted in nothing. They don't have the numbers or support anymore. Too many humans. Too much still going on. You can take this one night off."

Sam sucked in a deep breath, let it out, and surprisingly enough some tension left his shoulders and handsome face. "One shot," he said, his eyes resting on Becca.

She nervously adjusted her blond curls, but didn't protest when a whole row of shots were dropped in front of us and everyone grabbed one. I noticed Tessa and Jared out of the corner of my eye then. The pair were standing very close together, deep in conversation on the edge of our group. They turned to do a shot with us, and I swear stepped even closer together.

Whoa! They looked so hot together, all blond beach babes. And my bestie was smiling, a true and happy smile.

Maybe we would all get our happy ever after. Even Tessa.

As the party raged on, we sang, we danced, we loved. Jayden got so drunk that he and I declared our undying love for each other and promised to get a best friend tattoo in the morning. I was mildly tipsy, but trying to keep my head on so I could make sure operation Sam and Becca was going to happen. When I saw them sitting next to each other but not really engaging, I decided it was time to play hardball.

Stalking across the room, I found Jason. He was hot as hell, like all ash, and he was someone I sort of knew from the Portland Hive.

"Jason, I need a favor," I said to him, only the slightest of slurs in my voice. I was nailing this sober thing. He nodded, a huge grin spreading across his face, although he also looked to be nervously checking over my shoulder. Was he looking for Ryder?

Gee. He wasn't that scary.

"Anything," he finally said, getting his fears under control.

"Go ask that blonde sitting with Sam to dance."

Jason's eyes bugged out. "Sam has already claimed her. Rules are not to go near her."

That angered me even more. How dare Sam set that rule and then not go for Becca.

"Yeah, well, the rules have changed, and trust me, he'll thank you later. I'll make sure he doesn't kill you," I added.

Jason seemed to consider it. Finally, he nodded. "Okay, but you're going to owe me one."

"Yep, fine," I said, pushing him in their direction.

I stayed close, because I couldn't actually be sure that Sam wasn't going to try and kill him. Walking five paces behind him, I casually acted like I was looking for a waiter. When Jason got two feet from Becca, both her and Sam looked up.

Jason cleared his throat and I knelt, pretended to be adjusting my dress.

"Would you like to dance with me?" he asked, extending his hand in Becca's direction.

She looked utterly shocked, her eyes so huge without glasses hiding them. Sam's head shot around, his gaze absolutely feral, and it wasn't aimed at Jason. He locked eyes directly with me.

Ah fuck. Abort mission.

"Oh ... um ... sure," Becca said, distracting everyone when she took Jason's hand.

Oh shit. Sam shot up lightning fast and stepped between Jason and Becca.

"I was just going to ask her. Why don't you go get yourself a drink?" His voice was very quickly developing into the growl register.

Jason swallowed hard and nodded. Sam's gaze bore into me with a fire that said he would be plotting my death soon. Then he spun on Becca.

"Here's the thing, Becca. I know you don't want to ruin our friendship, but I can't stand by and watch you date other men. So ... will you please dance with me?"

Becca swallowed hard, eyeing Sam's outstretched hand, then a blaze of silver lit up her eyes and she placed her hand into his. He pulled her so hard into his body that I could tell he'd knocked the wind out of her a bit. They remained molded like that, and then started gently swaying to the music. It was a slow romantic song, and dammit I was tearing up again.

On the dance floor, close to them was Tessa and Jared. Definitely something going on with those two. And was that ... well, I'll be damned. Looked like Kyle was going full steam ahead with his Sasha plan. Although, knowing that kickass chick, she'd been the one with the plan all along. Sasha had been the only SWAT human to accept the wedding invitation, but I was still going with my theory that she wasn't actually human. Too much awesome in there for her not be something a little more.

"Can you take a break from all of your evil plotting?" Ryder came out of nowhere and I turned, smiling.

"What did you have in mind?" I raised an eyebrow. It was very dark out now, with only candles and the moon to light the night.

He leaned in close and whispered in my ear. "I've always wanted to have sex on the beach."

I grinned. "What a coincidence. So have I."

Jayden caught my eye as we were leaving and blew me a kiss. I winked and blew him one back.

Okay, so sex on the beach was a loose term. I wasn't really that keen on sand in my ass. Thankfully, Ryder had already thought of that, and we had rented an exclusive cabana house on stilts that was literally out in the ocean.

We didn't really speak; there was no need for words as Ryder slowly undressed me, his mouth caressing every part of my bare skin. The warm breezes embraced us though the open windows, white sheer curtains flowing in the wind as Ryder made love to me. He kissed me at least a thousand times over every inch of my body, touching each spot reverently.

This was it.

This was my happy.

I didn't need marriage or kids with Ryder. Just being together, like this, forever. That's all I wanted. No labels required.

Afterwards, when I was barely coherent, and my body still trembled from the sensations, Ryder held me tightly, stroking softly up the side of my neck. After a while he sat up, the sheet falling to reveal all of his glorious naked body. He pulled out his cell phone.

"I want to show you something," he said, flicking through his phone quickly before handing it to me.

It was a house. The front of a beautiful, modest, Craftsman. The address said Portland. I couldn't help the grin that spread across my face.

"What's this?"

"Our new home," he said. "If you want," he added quickly.

OMFG, he'd bought us a house. "I want!" I shouted, and threw myself on him, kissing him.

He smiled. "Good, because it closes next week and Oliver bought Jayden the house down the street."

Jayden and I were going to be neighbors? Oh the shenanigans we would get up to. If I had it my way, then Tessa and Jared wouldn't be far behind us. Then Sam and

Becca. I was grinning like an idiot and Ryder was looking at me with a serious gaze.

"What?"

He chuckled. "When I saw you all those months ago at the club, I knew you would be special, but I never thought you were capable of this. You changed everything, Charlie. You changed the way the world lives. But most importantly, you changed me. I was a shell of an ash and man. I never even knew what I was missing." He kissed my lips softly. "I love you."

I was lost in his kiss, before pulling back to express my absolute adoration and love for him. I'd never imagined a few months ago, when I turned ash and I thought my whole world was falling apart, that I would end up here. I had found my family. Or added to it at least. I had so much more now than I ever imagined.

"You know it wasn't just me that changed the world," I said, kissing him softly. "We did it together. I love you more than anything. You are my greatest reward." The rest of my words were lost in our kisses. I never wanted to stop kissing him. He was the best thing that ever happened to me. They all were.

THE END

Loving books from team Jaymin & Leia? Keep your eyes peeled for Queen Heir, Book One in the NYC Mecca Series, their new fantasy paranormal romance crossover coming early 2017.

Acknowledgements

Leia Stone: As always I am so thankful to my amazing best friend and writing partner Jaymin Eve. She took a chance on me when I said I had a fun idea but didn't know what to do with it and asked her if she wanted to co-write something with me. Now we have created this amazing world with these amazing characters that I will always love. You have made this process so fun and I can't wait for our next series together. A big thank you to Steven Smithen for the big rig consult =) We really appreciate it. Also to all of my readers and especially the Ash Enforcers, we love you guys so much! I'm so grateful to my supportive husband for taking time off of his career to support mine and help with our kids. Love you to the moon and back babe~!

Jaymin Eve: The end of an era. Okay, not really an era, but it has felt like an epic nine months of being in the Hive world. First, and always, I love Leia Stone. She is the best friend an author, human or other could ask for. We talk a lot about fate bringing us together, and I have never been more sure of that. Written in the stars. BAFFs for life. Next I want to thank Andi for being a truly supportive friend. She beta reads all of my books (usually more than once) and is always there for support and reassurance. When I fall into a heap of author mess, she picks me up, dusts me off, kicks my butt, and sets me on my way again. She's a keeper. Huge thanks to my release team. I'd love to mention you all by name, because I feel like we're a family, but just know I love and appreciate every single one of you. Also to my Nerd Herd and Ash Enforcers. You guys rock!! I love spending time with you all. Your support means everything. Thank you to Lee for your awesome editing, as always, you took our words and made them so pretty. And to Tamara, our cover artist. You're awesome! We love every single thing you do for us, you bring our worlds to life. To my family. Thank you so much for all your support and love. I couldn't do what I do without you, and I never forget that. I love you more than words. And I'm an author with a lot of words. Lastly to our fans. We love you. You have no idea how blessed we feel to be able to do this as a job, to be able to create worlds, and fall in love with these amazing characters. And we can do that because of you. All of our books are for you. xxx

Books from Leia Stone

Matefinder Trilogy (Optioned for film)
Matefinder: Book 1
Devi: Book 2
Balance: Book 3

Matefinder Next Generation
Keeper: Book 1

Hive Trilogy
Ash: Book 1
Anarchy: Book 2
Annihilate: Book 3

Stay in touch with Leia: www.facebook.com/leia.stone/
Mailing list: http://goo.gl/0EX98P

Books from Jaymin Eve

A Walker Saga - YA Paranormal Romance series (complete)
First World - #1
Spurn - #2
Crais - #3
Regali - #4
Nephilius - #5
Dronish - #6
Earth - #7

Supernatural Prison Trilogy - NA Urban Fantasy series
Dragon Marked - #1
Dragon Mystics - #2
Dragon Mated - #3

Supernatural Prison Stories
Broken Compass - #1

Sinclair Stories
Songbird - Standalone Contemporary Romance
Hive Trilogy
Ash - #1
Anarchy - #2
Annihilate: #3

Stay in touch with Jaymin:
www.facebook.com/JayminEve.Author
Website: www.jaymineve.com
Mailing list: http://eepurl.com/bQw8Kf

Printed in Great Britain
by Amazon